Faith

BRIDES ⸱OF⸱THE WEST

Faith

LORI COPELAND

TYNDALE HOUSE PUBLISHERS, INC.
CAROL STREAM, ILLINOIS

Visit Tyndale's exciting Web site at www.tyndale.com

TYNDALE and Tyndale's quill logo are registered trademarks of Tyndale House Publishers, Inc.

Faith

Cover designed by Beth Sparkman.

Interior designed by Catherine Bergstrom.

Edited by Diane Eble.

Scripture quotations are taken from the *Holy Bible,* King James Version.

Library of Congress Cataloging-in-Publication Data

Copeland, Lori.
    Faith / Lori Copeland.
        p.   cm. — (Brides of the West 1872)
    ISBN 0-8423-0267-0 (sc)
    I. Title.   II. Series.
PS3553.06336F35   1998
813'.54—dc21   98-23844

ISBN-13: 978-1-4143-1534-8
ISBN-10: 1-4143-1534-1

Printed in the United States of America

13   12   11   10   09   08   07
 7   6   5   4   3   2   1

In loving memory
of Tonya Sue Garnsey
and Myrt Petersen.
Your memory lives on
in our hearts.

Prologue

"You're what?" The tip of Thalia Grayson's cane hit the floor with a whack. Riveting blue eyes pinned Faith Marie Kallahan to the carpet like a sinner on Judgment Day.

Faith swallowed, took a deep breath, and confronted her auntie's wrath with steeled determination. "I'm sorry, Aunt Thalia, but it's done. We took a vote; we're going to be mail-order brides. There's nothing you can say to change our minds."

Thalia's eyes pivoted to Faith's sisters, Hope and June. "Don't tell me you go along with this nonsense."

June nervously twisted a handkerchief around her forefinger. "We've prayed diligently about it."

"Well, I never!" Thalia blustered. The pint-sized figure could turn into thunder and lightning when agitated. Faith didn't relish the coming storm.

A cold wind banged shutters and rattled dead branches of weathered oaks outside the window. Snow lay in dirty patches along leaning fence posts. March wasn't a pretty sight in Michigan.

Faith took a tentative step toward her aunt, hoping to temper her wrath. She knew the news came as a shock, but Aunt Thalia was old, and she couldn't bear the financial burden of three extra mouths to feed. "Aunt Thalia, I know the news is unsettling, but it's the only solution."

Thalia's hand came up to cover her heart. "Marry complete strangers? Thomas's children—mail-order brides? Have you lost your minds? Faith, your papa always said you were rowdier than any two boys put together! Mail-order brides." Thalia shuddered. "How can you break your auntie's heart like this?"

"Faith. The size of a mustard seed. We are embarking upon this journey with faith that God answers his children's needs." Faith hugged her auntie's stooped frame. "Isn't it wonderful!"

"No, it's not wonderful! It's a terrible idea!"

Faith sighed. Yes, Papa had said she made Belle Starr, the lady outlaw, look like a choir girl, but her tomboyish ways had never hurt anyone. She might favor bib overalls rather than dresses, but the last thing on earth she wanted was to worry or upset anybody—especially Aunt Thalia.

Hope rose from the settee and moved to the hall mirror, fussing with her hair. "Aunt Thalia, it isn't so bad, really. We chose our mates carefully."

"Answering ads like common—" Thalia fanned herself with a hanky. "And just how did you decide who would get what man?"

Hope smiled. "By age, Auntie. Faith answered the first promising response. Then I took the next, then June."

"We've prayed about it, Auntie. Really we did," Faith said.

Opening the magazine in her lap, June read aloud from

the classified section they'd answered: *Wanted: Women with religious upbringing, high morals, and a strong sense of adventure, willing to marry decent, God-fearing men. Applicants may apply by mail. Must allow at least two months for an answer.*

Smiling, she closed the publication. "Shortly after Papa's death we decided to answer the ad."

Thalia turned toward the window and made a sound like a horse blowing air between its lips. "Father, have mercy on us all. Thomas would roll over in his grave if he knew what you're planning."

More proud than ashamed for solving what once seemed an impossible situation, Faith calmly met her sisters' expectant gazes. They had agreed. Becoming mail-order brides was the only reasonable way to handle their circumstances. Aunt Thalia was approaching seventy. Although her health was stable, her financial condition wasn't. Her meager funds were needed for her own welfare.

Papa's untimely death had shocked the small community. Thomas Kallahan had pastored the Cold Water Community Church for twenty-six years. While in the midst of a blistering "hellfire and damnation" sermon one Sunday morning three months earlier, Thomas had keeled over dead.

The impassioned minister dead, at the age of forty-two. The community could scarcely believe it.

Mary Kallahan had died giving birth to June sixteen years earlier. With Thomas gone, Hope, Faith, and June—the youngest, so named because Thomas had felt anything but charitable toward the baby at birth—had no one but Aunt Thalia.

Aside from his deep, consistent faith, Thomas had left his daughters with nothing.

Faith had taught school in the small community while Hope and June had taken in sewing and accepted odd jobs. Each had a small nest egg they had earned, but their combined funds could not support a household on a continual basis. For now, they lived with Thomas's elderly sister, Thalia, aware that the arrangement was temporary. Faith had reasoned that they were grown women; they should be starting their own families.

At nineteen, Faith was the oldest. Hope was seventeen; June, sixteen. It was high time the girls found suitable husbands, an unenviable task for any woman in a small community where men were either married, too young, or too senile to be considered matrimonial prospects.

Kneeling beside Thalia's chair, Faith tried to calm her. "We'll be fine, Aunt Thalia. Why—" she glanced at Hope for support—"God truly must be smiling down upon us, for all three of us found a husband within a month."

Hope brightened. "Three fine gentlemen have asked for our hands in marriage."

"Rubbish." Thalia sat up straighter, adjusting her spectacles. "You've agreed to go off with three strangers! Three men you know nothing about! What has Thomas raised? A gaggle of hooligans?"

"They're not complete strangers," June pointed out. "All three gentlemen have sent letters of introduction."

"Hrummph. Self introductions? I hardly think they would write and introduce themselves as thieves and misfits. There's no telling what you're getting into." Her weathered features firmed. "I cannot permit this to happen. As long as there's a breath left in me, I will see to my brother's children. Families bear the responsibility to care for one another. The Lord says those who won't care for their own relatives are worse than unbelievers."

Stroking her aunt's veined hand, Faith smiled. "We know you would care for us, Aunt Thalia, truly. And it would be ideal if there were three young gentlemen in Cold Water in need of wives, but you know there isn't an eligible man within fifty miles." The good Lord knew Papa had tried hard enough to get his daughters married.

Thalia's lips thinned to a narrow line. Her blue eyes burned with conviction. "Edsel Martin lost his wife a few months back. Edsel's a good man. Hardworking. Deacon in the church."

"Sixty years old," June muttered under her breath.

"Merely a pup," Thalia scoffed. "Lots of good years left in Edsel."

Edsel made Faith's skin crawl. She'd never seen him wear anything other than faded overalls and a soiled shirt to cover his enormous belly. His pea-soup-colored eyes cut right through a person. She shuddered. The corners of his mouth were always stained with tobacco spittle. Edsel was looking for a wife all right, and she only needed to be breathing to meet his criteria.

Faith was plain worn out avoiding Edsel's invitations. The past two Sunday mornings, he'd been insistent that she accompany him home for dinner. She knew full well she'd end up cooking it, but she went, cooked, cleaned his kitchen, then hung his wash, even though it was the Sabbath. And Edsel a deacon! It wasn't the kind of "courting" she'd expected.

Edsel might be a "good man," but Faith wanted a young, strong husband to work beside. She could chop wood, plow a field, or build a fence as well as any man. What she didn't do well were womanly things: cooking, cleaning, tending house. She'd attracted a fair share of criticism because of it, but she was a tomboy at heart and just once she'd like to find a man who valued her help—her ability to seed a field or shoe a horse as good or better than any man.

A gust of wind rattled the three-story house, sending a shower of sparks spiraling up the chimney. Faith shivered, rubbing warmth into her arms. Aunt Thalia's parlor was always cold. Bare tree branches rapped the windowpane; frigid air seeped through the cracks.

Hope left the mirror to kneel beside Faith at Thalia's feet. Arranging the old woman's shawl more securely around her shoulders, Faith said softly, "When I get settled, I'll send for you, Aunt Thalia. You can come live with me."

"Hrummph." Thalia looked away. "Best not be making such promises until you know how your new husband feels about that."

"Oh, I can tell by his letter he is most kind." Frosty shadows lengthened into icy, gray twilight as Faith shared her future husband's promises of a good life and a bright future when they married. "He said he would always look after me, I would want for nothing, and he promised to be a wonderful papa to our children."

Hoarfrost covered the windowpanes as darkness enveloped the drafty old Victorian house. Patches of ice formed on the wooden steps. A pewter-colored sky promised heavy snow by dawn as the women knelt and held hands, praying for their future—a future none could accurately predict.

"Father," Faith prayed, "be with each of us as we embark upon our journeys. Stay our paths and keep us from harm. We pray that we will be obedient wives and loving mothers. Thank you for answering our prayers in a time when we were most needy of your wisdom and guidance. Watch over Aunt Thalia, guard her health, and be with her in her times of loneliness. May we always be mindful that thy will be done, not ours." With bowed heads and reverent hearts, they continued to pray, silently.

Finally, June rose and lit the lantern. Mellow light filtered from the coal-oil lamp, forming a warm, symmetrical pattern on the frozen ground outside the parlor window.

Tonight was Faith's turn to fix supper. She disappeared into the kitchen while June and Hope kept Thalia company in the parlor.

Pumping water into the porcelain coffeepot, Faith listened to Hope's infectious laughter as she thumbed through the family album, regaling Thalia with stories of happier times.

Beautiful Hope.

Faith the tomboy.

June the caregiver.

Frowning, Faith measured coffee into the pot and thought

about the decision to marry and leave Cold Water. She ignored the tight knot curled in the pit of her stomach. Weeks of prayer and thought had gone into her decision. She had prayed for God's wisdom, and he had sent her an answer. Nicholas Shepherd's letter gave her hope. Nicholas needed a wife, and she needed a husband. She hoped the union would develop into one of loving devotion, but she would settle for a home with a godly man. During prayer she had felt God's guidance for her to embark upon this marriage.

The idea of leaving Cold Water saddened her. Aunt Thalia wouldn't enjoy good health forever. Who would care for Thalia when she was gone? And who was this man she was about to marry—this Nicholas Shepherd? She really knew nothing about him other than that he lived with his mother in Deliverance, Texas, a small community outside San Antonio, and that he penned a neat, concise letter.

Sighing, she pushed a stray lock of hair off her cheek. Not much to base a future on. Through correspondence she'd learned Nicholas was in his midthirties and a hard worker. She was nineteen, but the difference in their ages didn't bother her; she found older men more interesting. And she was a hard worker. She smiled, warming to the idea of a husband who would always treat her well, who would not allow her to want for anything, and who promised to be a wonderful papa to her children. What more could a woman ask?

She would work hard to be an obedient wife to Nicholas Shepherd. The Lord instructed wives to obey their husbands, and that she would. It bothered her not a whit that Nicholas's mother would share their home. Mother Shepherd could see to household duties, duties Faith abhorred, while Faith worked beside her husband in the fields. The smell of sunshine and new clover was far more enticing than the stench of cooking cabbage and a tub full of dirty laundry.

Laying slices of ham in a cold skillet, Faith sobered, realizing how very much she would miss her sisters. Hope would travel to Kentucky, June to Seattle. She herself would reside in Texas.

Worlds apart.

The thought of June, the youngest sibling, brought a smile to her face. June was impulsive, awkward at times, but with a heart as big as a ten-gallon bucket. Unlike Hope, June wasn't blessed with beauty; she was plain, a wallflower, some said, but with patience a saint would envy. June possessed a sweet, inner light superior to her sisters'. June was the caretaker, the maternal one. Faith prayed daily that June's husband would be a man who would value June's heart of gold and would never break her spirit.

Faith asked the Lord for patience for Hope's soon-to-be husband. He would need plenty of it. The family beauty was shamelessly spoiled. Hope assumed the world revolved around her wants and wishes. Hope's husband would need to be blessed with a wagonload of fortitude to contend with his new bride.

Nicholas Shepherd would need a hefty dose of patience himself. Those who knew Faith said she could be cheerful to a fault, but she knew she had to work hard at times to accept God's will. It wasn't always what she expected, and she didn't always understand it.

The sisters would exchange newsy letters and Christmas cards, but Faith didn't want to think about how long it would be before they saw each other again.

Sighing, she realized the new lives they each faced were fraught with trials and tribulations, but God had always fulfilled his promise to watch over them. He had upheld them though Mama's death, overseen June's raising, and filled times of uncertainty with hope of a brighter tomorrow. When Papa died, they'd felt God's all-caring presence. He was there to hear their cries of anguish and see them through the ordeal of burial. Faith had no less faith that he would continue to care for them now.

Faith.

Papa had always said that faith would see them through whatever trials they encountered.

Besides—she shuddered as she turned a slice of ham—anything the future held had to be more appealing than Edsel Martin.

Chapter One

Deliverance, Texas
Late 1800s

S HE'S late." Liza Shepherd slipped a pinch of snuff into the corner of her mouth, then fanned herself with a scented hanky.

Nicholas checked his pocket watch a fourth time, flipping it closed. Mother was right. His bride-to-be was late. Any other day the stage would be on time. He poked a finger into his perspiration-soaked collar, silently cursing the heat. He'd wasted half a day's work on Miss Kallahan, time he could ill afford. Fence was down in the north forty, and ninety acres of hay lay waiting to fall beneath the scythe before rain fell. He glanced toward the bend in the road, his brows drawn in a deep frown. Where *was* she?

Calm down, Nicholas. Work does not come before family obligations. Why did he constantly have to remind himself of that?

A hot Texas sun scorched the top of his Stetson. Fire ants

scurried across the parched soil as the town band unpacked their instruments. Tubas and drums sounded in disjointed harmony. He wished the town wouldn't make such a fuss over Miss Kallahan. You'd think he was the first man ever to send for a mail-order bride—which he wasn't. Layman Snow sent for one a year ago, and everything between the newlyweds was working out fine.

Horses tied at hitching posts lazily swatted flies from their broad, sweaty rumps as the hullabaloo heightened.

High noon, and Deliverance was teeming with people.

Men and women gathered on the porch of Oren Stokes's general store. The men craned their necks while womenfolk gossiped among themselves. A few loners discussed weather and crops, but all ears were tuned for the stage's arrival.

Nicholas ignored the curious looks sent his direction. Interest was normal. A man his age about to take a wife fifteen years his junior? Who wouldn't gawk? Running a finger inside the rim of his perspiration-soaked collar, he craned to see above the crowd. What was keeping that stage? It would be dark before he finished chores. He stiffened when he heard Molly Anderson's anxious whispers to Etta Larkin.

"What is Nicholas thinking—taking a wife now?"

"Why, I can't imagine. He owns everything in sight and has enough money to burn a wet mule. What does he want with a wife?"

"I hear he wants another woman in the house to keep Liza company."

"With the mood Liza's in lately, she'll run the poor girl off before sunset."

"Such a pity—the Shepherds got no one to leave all that money to."

"No, nary a kin left."

Nicholas turned a deaf ear to the town gossips. What he did, or thought, was his business, and he intended to keep it that way.

A smile played at the corners of his mouth when he thought about what he'd done. Placing an ad for a mail-order bride wasn't something he'd ordinarily consider. But these were not ordinary times. In the past two years since his father had died, he and Mama had been at loose ends.

Eighteen years ago he'd thought love was necessary to marry. Now the mere thought of romance at his age made him laugh. He'd lost his chance at love when he failed to marry Rachel.

Looking back, he realized Rachel had been his one chance at marital happiness. But at the time, he wasn't sure he was in love with her. What was love supposed to feel like? He'd certainly been fond of her, and she'd gotten along well with Mama—something not many could claim, especially these days. Rachel was a gentle woman, and in hindsight he knew he should have married her. He had come to realize that there was more to a satisfying union than love. Mama and Papa's marriage had taught him that love of God, trust, the ability to get along, mutual respect— those were the important elements in a marriage. Abe Shepherd had loved Liza, but even more, he had respected her. Nicholas knew he could have built that kind of relationship with Rachel if he had acted before it was too late.

Well, water over the dam. Rachel had married Joe Lanner, and Nicholas had finally faced up to the knowledge that love had passed him by. He would turn thirty-five in January, and he had no heir. There was no blood kin to carry on the Shepherd name. No one to leave Shepherd land and resources to.

Mama thought he'd lost his mind when he sent for a mail-order bride, and maybe he had.

He smiled as he recalled her tirade when he told her what he'd done—"Why on God's green earth would you want to complicate our lives by marryin' a stranger?"

Why indeed? he thought. God had blessed him mightily. He could stand at the top of Shepherd's Mountain, and for as far as the eye could see there was nothing but Shepherd land.

Shepherd cattle.

Shepherd pastures.

Shepherd outbuildings.

Some even said the moon belonged to Shepherd—Shepherd's Moon, the town called it, because of the way it rose over the tops of his trees, beautiful, noble in God's glory. God had been good to him, better than he deserved. He owned all he wanted and more, yet at times he felt as poor as a pauper.

The emptiness gnawed at him, a misery that no abundance of material possessions could assuage. Where was the love he should have known? Rachel had walked through his life, then walked out of it. Had he been so busy acquiring material wealth that he let the one missing ingredient in his life, the love of a woman, slip past him? The question haunted him because he knew the answer: He had let Rachel walk away and marry a man who, rumor had it, now drank and mistreated her. He should have seen it coming—Joe was not a godly man. But he'd done nothing to stop her, and now he had to watch her suffer for his mistake.

There were other women in the town who would have given anything to marry Nicholas Shepherd, but he had never loved any of them. Then, after his father died and Mama became so unlike herself—so moody, so irritable, so stingy—he didn't think anyone would put up with her. At the same time, he wondered if what she needed more than anything was another woman around to talk with, get her mind off her grief. He began to think that maybe he should marry—not for love, but for other reasons. To have someone to keep Mama company, help her around the house. Mama wouldn't think of hiring help, though they could afford it. But maybe a daughter-in-law would be a different matter.

Then there was the matter of an heir. What good was all his fortune if he had no one to leave it to? Perhaps a daughter-in-law, and eventually grandchildren, would help Mama and make all his hard work mean something. He had amassed a fortune, and it would be a shame if no blood kin were able to enjoy it.

He had been praying over the matter when he'd come across the ad in the journal for a mail-order bride, and the thought intrigued him. The answer to his problem, and his prayers, suddenly seemed crystal clear: He would send for a mail-order bride. Much like ordering a seed catalogue, but with more pleasant results. He would, in essence, purchase a decent, Christian woman to marry with no emotional strings attached.

This marriage between Miss Kallahan and him would not be the covenant of love that his parents had had; this was a compromise. He needed a wife, and according to Miss Kallahan's letters, she was seeking a husband. He had prayed that God would send him a righteous woman to be his help-mate. To fill his lonely hours. Someone who would be a comfortable companion. Love didn't figure into the picture. When Miss Kallahan accepted his proposal, he accepted that God had chosen the proper woman to meet his needs.

Admittedly, he'd grown set in his ways; having a wife underfoot would take some getting used to. He valued peace and quiet. What his new bride did with her time would be up to her; he would make no demands on her other than that she help Mama around the house, if Mama would permit it. And he did like the thought of children— eventually—although he wasn't marrying a brood mare.

Mama didn't seem to care about anything anymore. She still grieved for Papa, though he'd been dead almost two years now. Nicholas's fervent hope was that having another woman in the house, someone Mama could talk and relate to, would improve her disposition, although he wasn't going to kid himself. He couldn't count on Mama's taking to another woman in the house. But as long as Faith understood her role, the two women should make do with the situation.

Removing his hat, he ran his hand through his hair. What was keeping the stage?

"Brother Shepherd!" Nicholas turned to see Reverend Hicks striding toward him. The tall, painfully thin man always looked as if he hadn't eaten a square meal in days. His ruddy complexion and twinkling blue eyes were the only things that saved him from austerity. Vera, a large woman of considerable girth, was trying to keep up with her husband's long-legged strides.

"Mercy, Amos, slow down! You'd think we were going to a fire!"

Reverend paused before Nicholas, his ruddy face breaking into a congenial smile. Turning sixty had failed to dent the pastor's youthfulness. "Stage hasn't gotten here yet?"

"Not yet." Nicholas glanced toward the bend in the road. "Seems to be running late this morning."

The Reverend turned to address Liza. "Good morning, Liza!" He reached for a snowy white handkerchief and mopped his forehead. "Beast of a day, isn't it?"

Liza snorted, fanning herself harder. "No one respects time anymore. You'd think all a body had to do was stand in the heat and wait for a stage whose driver has no concept of time."

Reverend stuffed the handkerchief back in his pocket. "Well, you never know what sort of trouble the stage might have run into."

Vera caught Liza's hand warmly and Nicholas stepped

back. The woman was a town icon, midwife and friend to all. When trouble reared its ugly head, Vera was the first to declare battle.

"We missed you at Bible study this morning. Law, a body could burn up in this heat! Why don't we step out of the sun? I could use a cool drink from the rain barrel."

"No, thank you. Don't need to be filling up on water this close to dinnertime." Liza's hands tightened around her black parasol as she fixed her eyes on the road. "Go ahead— spoil your dinner if you like. And I read my Bible at home, thank you. Don't need to be eatin' any of Lahoma's sugary cakes and drinkin' all that scalding black coffee to study the Word."

"Well, of course not—" The Reverend cleared his throat. "I've been meaning to stop by your place all week, Liza. We haven't received your gift for the new steeple, and I thought perhaps—"

Scornful eyes stopped him straightway. "We've given our tenth, Reverend."

A rosy flush crept up the Reverend's throat, further reddening his healthy complexion. "Now, Liza, the Lord surely does appreciate your obedience, but that old steeple is in bad need of replacement—"

Liza looked away. "No need for you to thank me. The Good Book says a tenth of our earnings." Liza turned back to face the Reverend. "One tenth. That's what we give, Reverend."

Reverend smiled. "And a blessed tenth it is, too. But the

steeple, Liza. The steeple is an added expense, and we sorely need donations—"

"There's nothing *wrong* with the old steeple, Amos! Why do you insist on replacing it?"

"Because it's old, Liza." Pleasantries faded from the Reverend's voice as he lifted his hand to shade his eyes against the sun. His gaze focused on the bell tower. "The tower is rickety. It's no longer safe—one good windstorm and it'll come down."

"Nonsense." Liza dabbed her neck with her handkerchief. "The steeple will stand for another seventy years." Her brows bunched in tight knots. "Money doesn't grow on trees, Reverend. If the Lord wanted a new steeple, he'd provide the means to get it."

The Reverend's eyes sent a mute plea in Nicholas's direction.

"Mama, Reverend Hicks is right; the tower is old. I see no reason—"

"And that's precisely why *I* handle the money in this family," Liza snapped. She glowered toward the general store, then back to Vera. "Perhaps a small sip of water won't taint my appetite." She shot a withering look toward the road. "A body could melt in this sun!"

An expectant buzz went up and the waiting crowd turned to see a donkey round the bend in the road. The animal advanced toward Deliverance at a leisurely gait. Nicholas shaded his eyes, trying to identify the rider.

"Oh, for heaven's sake. It's just that old hermit Jeremiah," Liza muttered. "What's that pest doing here?"

Nicholas watched the approaching animal. Jeremiah Montgomery had arrived in Deliverance some years back, but the old man had kept to himself, living in a small shanty just outside of town. He came for supplies once a month and stayed the day, talking to old-timers who whittled the time away on the side porch of the general store. He appeared to be an educated man, but when asked about his past, he would quietly change the subject. The citizens of Deliverance were not a curious lot. They allowed the hermit his privacy and soon ceased to ask questions. Jeremiah neither incited trouble nor settled it. He appeared to be a peaceful man.

"Who's that he's got with him?" Vera asked, standing on tiptoe.

The animal picked its way slowly down the road, its hooves kicking up limpid puffs of dust as it gradually covered the distance. The crowd edged forward, trying for a better look.

"Why—it looks like a woman," Reverend said.

As the burro drew closer, Nicholas spotted a small form dressed in gingham and wearing a straw bonnet, riding behind Jeremiah. A woman. His heart sank. A *woman*. A woman stranger in Deliverance meant only one thing. His smile receded. His bride-to-be was arriving by *mule*.

Nicholas stepped out, grasping the animal's bridle as it approached. "Whoa, Jenny!" His eyes centered on the childlike waif riding behind the hermit. She was young— much younger than he'd expected. A knot gripped his mid- section. A tomboy to boot. Straddling that mule, wearing men's boots. The young girl met his anxious gaze, smiling. Her perky hat was askew, the pins from the mass of raven hair strung somewhere along the road.

"You must be Nicholas Shepherd."

"Yes, ma'am." His eyes took in the thick layers of dust obliterating her gingham gown. The only thing that saved the girl from being plain was her remarkable violet-colored eyes.

Jeremiah slid off the back of the mule, offering a hand of greeting to Nicholas. Nicholas winced at the stench of wood smoke and donkey sweat. A riotous array of matted salt-and-pepper hair crowned the old man's head. When he smiled, deep dimples appeared in his cheeks. Doe-colored eyes twinkled back at him as Nicholas accepted Jeremiah's hand and shook it. "Seems I have something that belongs to you."

Nicholas traced the hermit's gaze as he turned to smile at his passenger.

Offering a timid smile, she adjusted her hat. "Sorry about my appearance, Mr. Shepherd. The stage encountered a bit of trouble."

"Lost a wheel, it did, and tipped over!" The hermit knocked dust off his battered hat. "Driver suffered a broken leg. Fortunate I came along when I did, or this poor little mite would've scorched in the blistering sun."

Nicholas reached up to lift his bride from the saddle. For a split moment, something stirred inside him, something long dormant. His eyes met hers. His reaction surprised and annoyed him. The hermit cleared his throat, prompting

Nicholas to set the woman lightly on her feet. He finally found his voice. "Where are the other passengers?"

"Sitting alongside the road. Stubborn as old Jenny, they are. I informed them Jenny could carry two more but they told me to be on my way." Jeremiah laughed, knocking dirt off his worn britches. "They'll be waiting a while. The stage sheared an axle."

"I'll send Ben and Doc to help."

"They're going to need more than a blacksmith and a doctor." Jeremiah took a deep breath, batting his chest. Dust flew. "You better send a big wagon to haul them all to town."

The Reverend caught up, followed by a breathless Liza and Vera. "Welcome to Deliverance!" Reverend effusively pumped the young woman's hand, grinning.

Faith smiled and returned the greeting. The band broke into a spirited piece as the crowd gathered round, vying for introductions. The donkey shied, loping to the side to distance itself from the commotion.

"Nicholas, introduce your bride!" someone shouted.

"Yeah, Nicholas! What's her name?" others chorused.

Reaching for the young lady's hand, Nicholas leaned closer, his mind temporarily blank. "Sorry. Your last name is . . . ?"

She leaned closer and he caught a whiff of donkey. "Kallahan."

Clearing his throat, he called for order. "Quiet down, please."

Tubas and drums fell silent as the crowd looked on expectantly.

"Ladies and gentlemen." Nicholas cleared his throat again. He wasn't good at this sort of thing, and the sooner it was over the better. "I'd like you to meet the woman who's consented to be my wife, Miss Faith . . . ?"

"Kallahan."

"Yes . . . Miss Faith Kallahan."

Sporadic clapping broke out. A couple of single, heartbroken young women turned into their mothers' arms for comfort.

Faith nodded above the boisterous clapping. "Thank you—thank you all very much. It is a pleasure to be here!"

"Anything you ever need, you just let me know," Oren Stokes's wife called.

"Same for me, dearie," the mayor's wife seconded as other friendly voices chimed in.

"Quilting bee every Saturday!"

"Bible study at Lahoma Wilson's Thursday mornings!"

Liza stepped forward, openly assessing her new daughter-in-law-to-be. "Well, at least you're not skin and bone." She cupped her hands at Faith's hips and measured for width. "Should be able to deliver a healthy child."

"Yes, ma'am," Faith said, then grinned. "My hips are nice and wide, I'm in excellent health, and I can work like a man."

Women in the crowd tittered as Nicholas frowned. What had God sent? A wife or a hired hand?

"Liza!" Vera stepped up, putting her arm around Faith's shoulder. "You'll scare the poor thing to death with such talk. Let the young couple get to know each other before you start talking children."

Children had fit into the equation, of course, but in an abstract way. Now he was looking at the woman who would be the mother of his children.

"Pshaw." Liza batted Vera's hands aside. "Miss Kallahan knows what's expected from a wife."

When Nicholas saw Faith's cheeks turn scarlet, he said, "Mama, Miss Kallahan is tired from her long trip."

"Yes, I would imagine." Liza frowned at Jeremiah, who was hanging around watching the activity. She shooed him away. "Go along, now. Don't need the likes of you smelling up the place."

Jeremiah tipped his hat, then raised his eyes a fraction to wink at her. Liza whirled and marched toward the Shepherd buggy, nose in the air. "Hurry along, Nicholas. It's an hour past our dinnertime."

The crowd dispersed, and Faith reached out to touch Jeremiah's sleeve. "Thank you for the ride. I would have sweltered if not for your kindness."

The old man smiled. "My honor, Miss Kallahan." Reaching for her hand, he placed a genteel kiss upon the back of it. "Thank *you* for accepting kindness from a rather shaggy Samaritan."

Nicholas put his hand on the small of her back and ushered her toward the waiting buggy.

As he hurried Faith toward the buggy, his mind turned from the personal to business. Twelve-thirty. It would be past dark before chores were done.

Nicholas lifted Faith into the wagon, and she murmured thanks. Ordinarily, she would climb aboard unassisted. She wasn't helpless, and she didn't want Nicholas fawning over her. She hoped he wasn't a fawner. But she was relieved to see her husband-to-be was a pleasant-looking man. Not wildly handsome, but he had a strong chin and a muscular build. He looked quite healthy. As he worked to stow her luggage in the wagon bed, she settled on the wooden bench, her gaze focusing on the way his hair lay in gentle golden waves against his collar.

His letter had said he was of English and Swedish origin, and his features evidenced that. Bold blue eyes, once-fair skin deeply tanned by the sun. Only the faint hint of gray at his temples indicated he was older than she was; otherwise, he had youngish features. He was a man of means; she could see that by the cut of his clothes. Denims crisply ironed, shirt cut from the finest material. His hands were large, his nails clean and clipped short. He was exceptionally neat about himself. When he lifted her from the back of Jeremiah's mule, she detected the faint hint of soap and bay-rum aftershave.

She whirled when she heard a noisy thump! Nicholas was frozen in place, staring at the ground as if a coiled rattler were about to strike.

Scooting to the edge of the bench, Faith peered over the wagon's side, softly gasping when she saw the contents of her valise spilled onto the ground. White unmentionables stood out like new-fallen snow on the parched soil. Her hand flew up to cover her mouth. "Oh, my . . ."

Liza whacked the side of the wagon with the tip of her cane. "Pick them up, Nicholas, and let's be on our way." She climbed aboard and wedged her small frame in the middle of the seat, pushing Faith to the outside. "A body could perish from hunger waiting on the likes of you."

Nicholas gathered the scattered garments and hurriedly stuffed them into the valise. Climbing aboard, he picked up the reins and set the team into motion.

As the wagon wheels hummed along the countryside, Faith drank in the new sights. She'd lived in Michigan her entire life; Texas was a whole new world! She remembered how she'd craned her neck out the stagecoach window so long the other passengers had started to tease her. Gone were the cherry and apple orchards, gently rolling hills, and small clear lakes of Michigan. She still spotted an occasional white birch or maple, and there were pines and oaks, but the scenery had changed.

With each passing day on her trip, the landscape had grown more verdant and lush. The closer they drew to San Antonio, the more the countryside transformed. They passed beautiful Spanish missions with tall bell towers, low adobe dwellings covered with vines of ivy, and bushes of vibrant colored bougainvillea. At night the cicadas sang her to sleep with their harmonious *sczhwee-sczee*. Ticks were plentiful, and roaches grew as big as horseflies!

The elderly gentleman seated across from her had leaned

forward, pointing. "Over there is mesquite and—look there! There's an armadillo!"

Faith shrank back, deciding that was one critter she'd leave alone.

"It's beautiful land," the gentleman said. "You will surely be happy here, young lady."

Faith frowned, keeping an eye on the animal scurrying across the road. She would if those armadillos kept their distance.

Deliverance gradually faded, and the wagon bounced along a rutted, winding trail. Faith suspected her new family wasn't a talkative lot. Liza sat rigidly beside her on the bench, staring straight ahead, occasionally mumbling under her breath that "it was an hour past her dinnertime." The tall, muscular Swede kept silent, his large hands effortlessly controlling the team.

Faith decided it would take time for the Shepherds to warm to her. She hoped they would be friendlier once they got to know her. Still, the silence unnerved her. She and her sisters had chatted endlessly, talking for hours on end about nothing. Generally she was easy to get along with and took to most anyone, but the Shepherds were going to be a test, she could feel it.

Please, Lord, don't allow my tongue to spite my good sense.

She might not be in love with Nicholas Shepherd, but she had her mind made up to make this marriage work. Once she set her mind to something, she wasn't easily swayed. Besides, she *had* to make the marriage work. She couldn't burden Aunt Thalia any longer, and she sure wasn't going to marry Edsel Martin without a hearty fight. She would work to make Nicholas a good wife, to rear his children properly, and be the best helpmate he could ask for.

She glanced at Liza from the corner of her eye. Now *she* would need a bit more time to adjust to.

Her gaze focused on the passing scenery, delighted with the fields of blue flowers bobbing their heads in the bright sunshine. The colorful array of wildflowers nestled against the backdrop of green meadows dazzled the eye.

She sat up, pointing, excited as a child. "What are those?"

Nicholas briefly glanced in the direction she pointed. "Bluebonnets."

"And those?"

"Black-eyed Susans."

"They're so pretty! Do they bloom year round?"

"Not all year."

The wagon rolled through a small creek and up a hill. Rows upon rows of fences and cattle dotted lush, grassy meadows.

"Just look at all those cattle!" Faith slid forward on the bench. She had never seen so many animals in one place at the same time. "There must be thousands!"

"Close to two thousand," Nicholas conceded.

"Two thousand," she silently mouthed, thunderstruck by the opulent display. Why, Papa had owned one old cow—and that was for milking purposes only. She'd never seen such wealth, much less dreamed of being a part of it.

Nicholas glanced at her. "Shepherd cattle roam a good deal of this area. Do you like animals?"

"I love them—except I've never had any for my own. Papa was so busy with his congregation and trying to rear three daughters properly that he said he had all the mouths he cared to feed, thank you. I remember once Mr. Kratchet's old tabby cat had kittens. They were so cute, and I fell head over heels in love with one. It was the runt, and sickly, but I wanted it so badly."

Sighing, she folded her hands on her lap, recalling the traumatic moment. "But Papa said *no,* no use wasting good food on something that wasn't going to live anyway." Tears welled to her eyes. "I cried myself to sleep that night. I vowed when I grew up, I'd have all the sick kittens I wanted. Mama said, 'Be merciful to all things, Faith'—did I tell you Mama died giving birth to my youngest sister, June—did I mention that in my letter? Well, she did. Faith, Hope, and June—"

Liza turned to give her a sour look.

"June," Faith repeated, her smile temporarily wavering. "Papa was kinda mad at June when she was born. He took his anger out on that poor baby because he thought she'd killed Mama, but later he admitted the devil had made him think those crazy thoughts. It certainly wasn't the work of the Lord. Lots of women die in childbirth, and it's not necessarily God's doing—but by the time Papa got over his hurt, it was too late to call the baby Charity, like he'd planned to do in the first place. By then, everybody knew June as 'June' and it didn't feel right to call her anything else. Now Mama always said—" Liza's iron grip on her knee stopped her.

She paused, her eyes frozen on the steel-like grip.

"Do you prattle like this *all* of the time?"

"Do you chew snuff all the time?" Faith blurted without thinking. She had never once seen a woman chew snuff. She was fascinated. Perhaps Liza would teach her how—no, Papa would know. And the good Lord.

"Hold your tongue, young lady!" Liza returned to staring at the road.

Faith blushed. "Sorry." She watched the passing scenery, aware she was starting out on shaky footing with her soon-to-be mother-in-law. She vowed to be silent for the remainder of the trip, but she couldn't help casting an occasional bewildered look in Liza's direction. *Mercy!*

What did it hurt to talk about some poor kitten she hadn't gotten in the first place?

Chapter Two

FAITH shifted in the uncomfortable high-back chair, keeping a close eye on the mantel clock. Minutes ticked slowly by. Two, two-thirty, three o'clock. Nicholas had risen before dawn, eaten a large breakfast, then disappeared to the barn. Liza informed Faith shortly after Nicholas's departure that the marriage ceremony was scheduled to take place in Reverend Hicks's parlor at four o'clock.

Faith glanced at the ticking timepiece, worrying her lower lip between her front teeth. Already 3:12, and her bridegroom had not appeared.

Twisting her mother's handkerchief in her lap, Faith watched the doorway, listening for the sound of Nicholas's footsteps. Was he ever coming?

Her gaze meandered through the Shepherd parlor. The

furnishings were nice, but uncared for. Drab cotton sheets covered most of the upholstery. Everything smelled musty. A rose-colored brocade sofa lined the east wall; two rigid-back chairs in a darker hue sat beside a cold fireplace. The room was devoid of warmth, with nothing to counter the wretched dreariness. Faith wondered what pictures had hung where patched places now spotted the wall. There were no colorful rugs to soften the neglected floor. Heavy drapes blocked a faint breeze that struggled to make itself felt through the open window. Homesickness washed over Faith when she recalled Papa and Mama's cheery home. The Kallahans were as poor as church mice, but their rooms were brightly painted and always smelled of soap and sunshine.

In the brief time she'd been here, one thing was clear: Nicholas and Liza Shepherd were not happy people.

Isolated, nonresponsive to one another, they were so different from the laughing, happy family she'd grown up in. Was Aunt Thalia right when she'd warned her not to pursue this plan? Had she made a mistake by coming here? She glanced at Liza, who hadn't moved in hours. Only the occasional staccato click of knitting needles reminded Faith that she wasn't alone.

Supper last night had been an ordeal. Grace was offered for the food and the hands that prepared it. Then silence settled over the table. Not a word was spoken as they ate a heavy fare of meat, potatoes, gravy, and rich yellow butter spread on biscuits.

Faith winced, still feeling the way the food had lodged in

her throat. She'd been exhausted from the long stagecoach ride, barely able to keep her eyes open, but she had made an attempt at polite conversation. Her efforts were rewarded by Liza's reprimanding scowl. Faith had fallen silent, concentrating on the mound of overcooked beef in the center of her plate.

After supper they had retired in silence to the parlor, where Nicholas conducted the daily devotion from 1 Peter. "Beloved, think it not strange concerning the fiery trial which is to try you, as though some strange thing happened unto you: But rejoice, inasmuch as ye are partakers of Christ's sufferings; that, when his glory shall be revealed, ye may be glad also with exceeding joy." He had looked up, his gaze focusing on her for a moment before turning back to the page.

She'd felt her cheeks burn. Why had he looked up at her? Did he already consider her a "trial" in the short time he'd known her? He hadn't addressed her once since they'd arrived at the Shepherd farmhouse. The rambling two-story house towered between the barn and a few weathered outbuildings. Wealth was certainly not evident in the spartan-like setting with neglected flower beds and the house badly in need of a new coat of paint. There wasn't an ounce of friendliness to welcome visitors. Faith was certain a ranch this size would need hired help, but she'd seen no evidence of a bunkhouse or other lodging.

Nicholas had carried her bags to a small, airless front bedroom, then left without a word. Breakfast this morning had been conducted in the same uncommunicative manner. Fat

wedges of ham, eggs swimming in bubbly grease, gravy . . .
biscuits washed down with scalding, bitter coffee. Neither
Nicholas nor Liza had given any acknowledgment that Faith
was at the table. They'd kept their heads bent to their plates,
their utensils methodically scraping back and forth across the
chipped blue-and-white dishes.

Faith's eyes focused on Liza. The drab calico print she
had donned this morning had seen more than its share of
washings. How old was she? Sixty? Seventy? Faith wasn't a
proper judge of such matters. Once she had guessed Eldora
Farthington's age to be fifty, and the poor woman had
suffered the vapors. Eldora didn't look thirty-five, as she
claimed; still, Papa had instructed Faith to pray for
forgiveness for offending Eldora's delicate nature.

Liza couldn't be too old. She seemed to have all her facul-
ties. Faith's eyes skimmed the older woman's hair. Faded
blonde braids with streaks of silver were stringently pulled
back from her face and secured at the crown with a hairpin.
Though the afternoon heat was brutal, she kept a worn
black shawl fitted tightly around her shoulders.

Faith sighed. Did she truly intend to see her only son
married in that getup?

"Do I have a bird on my head?"

Faith jumped at the sound of Liza's clipped query.

"No, ma'am."

"Then stop staring at me."

Faith blushed, embarrassed she'd been caught gawking.
She pressed her lips tightly together, afraid to speak. Her
gaze dropped to her own gown, a pretty white Irish linen

Aunt Thalia had paid Rose Nelson, Cold Water's only seamstress, to make. For a surprise, June had saved her egg money and purchased a hat the exact same shade from Edmund Watt's mercantile. She'd presented it to Faith with great flourish, and the three sisters agreed Faith would be the most fashionable bride Deliverance had ever seen.

Faith grinned, thinking about June and the laughter they'd shared so easily. The hat and gown made Faith feel like a princess, but in view of Liza's spartan attire she wondered if she weren't overdressed.

She quickly laid her handwork aside when she heard the back door open. Springing to her feet, she absently smoothed the linen into place, then checked her hair, wondering if Nicholas found her comely. She wasn't, of course. She was rather ordinary, and she couldn't hold a candle to Hope's beauty, but she did her best to keep a tidy appearance.

Nicholas walked to the kitchen counter and deposited a pail of milk. She heard the metal clang of the handle as he dumped the contents into a large pitcher. The mantel clock struck the half hour. They would have to hurry to be at the Reverend's by four o'clock.

Nicholas glanced toward the parlor, and she smiled.

Dismissing her with a curt nod, he disappeared into the small bedroom just off the kitchen. Of course, he would want to change clothes.

He reappeared moments later, still dressed in the clothing he'd milked in. "I'll hitch the wagon."

Faith nodded, her smile fading as she assessed her bridegroom's attire. Wasn't he going to change into something

more suitable for his wedding? The old clothes reeked of
barnyard waste.

Liza laid her handwork aside and got up. Pulling the
shawl snugly above her shoulders, she sidestepped Faith on
her way to the kitchen. "Come along. Nicholas can't dally
all day."

Dally! Getting married could hardly be considered dally-
ing! Practically biting her tongue, Faith jerked her white hat
into place and trailed Liza through the kitchen and out the
back door where Nicholas was bringing the horse and
wagon around.

Taking her arm, he helped her aboard. A strong current
passed between them, and she whirled, surprised. The
strength in his hand was like corded steel. His features softened, and he said, "I could hitch the buggy if you would be
more comfortable in it."

"No, the wagon is just fine." Their eyes met. "Thank
you." His concern was touching. Perhaps he wasn't as
formidable as he seemed, just shy.

Liza settled herself in the middle of the bench, staring
straight ahead as Nicholas climbed aboard and set the wagon
into motion.

Faith followed the Shepherds' lead and sat quietly beside
Liza, her eyes trained on the road.

They'd ridden for over ten minutes when Faith finally
squirmed, unable to keep quiet any longer. After all, her
wedding day was somewhat of a celebration. "God has
provided a beautiful day for our marriage!"

Her cheery observation was met with stony silence.

She studied the scenery, determined to retain a sunny outlook. It wasn't every day that she got married. The Shepherds would warm, eventually.

Overhead a cloudless blue sky provided a lovely canopy. Lush meadow grass waved at her, and bubbling streams glistened in the hot sun. Meadowlarks flitted overhead, and bees drank their fill from the heads of bobbing buttercups. She wondered if she would ever get used to the sight of so many cattle. Nicholas must own every one in the county!

The wagon rolled past field after field of cows that Nicholas called Shorthorns. The animals were strong framed and looked to be of hearty constitutions. They were big cows, with short, sharp horns and a coat of red with white splotches. She stifled a laugh as she watched the playful antics of baby calves leaving their mothers' side to romp through open fields.

As they rounded a bend in the road, Faith heard a loud bellow. The sound was filled with abject misery. Grabbing the side of the buckboard, Faith held on as Nicholas abruptly brought the wagon to a halt in the middle of the road. "There's a cow in trouble."

Faith stood up as he bounded out of the wagon, her attention centered on a cow that was down on its side in the pasture. It was apparent the animal was in labor. Without thinking, Faith hitched up her skirt and climbed down.

Liza slid to the edge of the seat, her face suffused with color. "Young lady! You get back in this wagon! Nicholas will see to the problem!" Liza whipped out her handkerchief, fanning herself, her face glowing beet red.

"Can't! Nicholas needs help!" Faith darted up the embankment and quickly slipped between the wooden fence posts.

The cow, which had been down a minute ago, was now on its feet, pacing in a circle, sniffing the ground. Her tail stood straight out in back of her. Releasing a pitiful bawl, she dropped to her knees and lay down again.

"Tell me what to do." Faith knelt beside Nicholas, her eyes focused on the animal.

"Go back to the buggy. You're disturbing the mother." Nicholas's hands slid along the animal's heaving sides. He frowned. Faith noticed his touch was infinitely gentle.

"I want to help—will she be all right?"

"I don't know; she could be in trouble. The calf is in the birth canal. It'll suffocate if she can't deliver it soon."

Faith remained at Nicholas's side, listening to the mother's rapid breathing. Her sides rapidly rose and fell. Each pitiful bawl brought a gripping pain in Faith's midsection.

Five minutes passed, and Nicholas was getting edgy. "It's not going fast enough." He moved Faith to the front of the cow for safety. "Stay here, and keep out of the way."

Faith obliged, relieved he wasn't going to make her go back to the wagon. She'd witnessed live births before; each one a wondrous new experience.

Ten minutes passed and the cow, though actively straining, was making no progress. Faith continued to edge toward the back for a closer look. Nicholas was pulling on the calf's leg that was farthest back in the cow. The leg would progress a little, and he would switch legs, working slowly, gradually increasing the traction as he pulled with the mother's contractions.

Faith's gaze riveted on his strong arms as, little by little, he advanced the calf out of the canal a little way, then worked on the other leg. Back and forth, back and forth. Nicholas relaxed when the mother relaxed. When the cow quit pushing, it appeared Nicholas was losing ground, but he'd regain it with the next contraction. By now, Faith was on her knees in the dirt beside him, holding the mother's tail out of the way. Occasionally, Nicholas pushed the calf back a little into the mother to correct a position while the mother was resting. Finally, Nicholas got to his feet and motioned for Faith to grasp the calf's left leg. Using both their strengths, they pulled the newborn safely from the birth canal.

Exhausted, Faith dropped to her knees, reeling with exhilaration. Tears ran down her cheeks as she looked at the messy newborn lying on the ground, worn out from its entry into the world. "Praise be to God," she whispered, then waited until the mother prodded the calf to its feet.

Nicholas stepped beside her, and they watched the baby struggle to get to its feet, trying over and over again to gain footing. When it finally did, they clapped, cheering it on.

When the excitement died away, Nicholas checked the mother to be sure she was experiencing a normal birthing process. "She's fine and healthy."

He stepped back, hands on his hips, and surveyed Faith. She could swear she saw a hint of respect lurking in the depths of his blue eyes. "We best get you home. You'll want to clean up."

Faith realized there would be no wedding today. She looked down at her blood-spattered white Irish linen, thinking how appalled Rose Nelson would be if she could see it right now. But dresses were only material, and material didn't matter. With a good scrubbing, she could have the dress presentable in no time. What did matter was that she had felt a bond with Nicholas Shepherd. Albeit a small one, and certainly a precarious one, but they'd managed to make a brief, personal connection. She could hardly ask for anything more this soon. Praise be to God! Nicholas's inclination toward silence had started to worry her.

Chapter Three

THE day she'd most dreaded had arrived.

Lord, I know I should surrender Nicholas gracefully. I just can't.

Liza bent over the stove, suffused with heat. Merciful heavens, the kitchen was a blast furnace this morning! Her back ached, and she felt as if she were coming down with ague. Frustration overwhelmed her. She wasn't supposed to come to the end of her days alone, lonely.

There was no one left to care about her. That was the plain truth. Nicholas respected her, but he didn't need her anymore. He was a grown man, soon to be married.

Married.

The final separation of mother and son.

Oh, Nicholas was an honorable man like his father. She was his mother; he would dutifully look after her until the end, but marriage would bind him to a wife.

Vigorously stirring the bubbling pot, Liza blinked back scalding tears. Faith thought she was old and cranky. She could see it in her accusing looks. Well, she *was* cranky, and getting worse every day. She didn't like who she'd become, but she couldn't seem to do a thing about it. Her chin rose a notch. Giving up a child fell to all mothers one day. It would fall to young, dewy-eyed Miss Kallahan, too. Was a mother expected to give her son, her life blood, to another woman with a kiss and a smile?

Well, she couldn't. God forgive her, she couldn't.

What did it matter that Nicholas didn't love Faith Kallahan? He would eventually. Siring a child would create an unbreakable bond. And though she knew Nicholas would honor God's teaching to honor his mother, it didn't make her pain any more bearable.

His heart would belong to another woman.

Faith, this stranger—this "mail-order bride"—was about to take the last remaining thing that held any meaning in her life. Without Nicholas, Liza would be completely alone. Abe taken, now Nicholas. The thought rose like bitter gall in her throat.

Pitching the spoon aside, she turned from the stove, stripping off her apron. Why was she feeling so insecure? She had never felt possessive toward Nicholas before. She wanted him to marry and find the happiness she had shared with Abe; it was God's plan. *Forgive me, Father. I don't know what's wrong with me!* Reaching for the small brown vial she kept hidden behind the sugar bowl, she uncapped the bottle and took a sip.

"Desperation, Liza," she muttered. Replacing the cap on the bottle, she held it before her, squinting to read the label: "Lydia E. Pinkham's Vegetable Compound." In smaller letters it read "Restores to vigorous health the lives of those previously sorely distressed." Well, she was "sorely distressed" all right. Oren Stokes had recommended the silly compound, saying it had helped other women to restore vitality. Uncapping the bottle, she took another tiny sip. She didn't need any women's "compound" to see her through her troubles—besides, the tonic only made her feel good temporarily.

Shoving the bottle behind the sugar bowl, she absently checked her hair. Enough of feeling sorry for herself. She had better things to do than sip some useless tonic and blubber all day. Maybe she'd attend the quilting bee. Hadn't been in weeks, and folks were beginning to think she was shutting herself away in the house.

Straightening her dress, she took a deep breath and reached for her bonnet.

"Mama?" Nicholas pushed opened the screen door leading to the back porch.

Liza had excused herself during supper and left the table. He was worried about her. This past year she'd gone from being a woman trying to cope with the loss of her husband to being a moody, unhappy shrew. Her moods were getting worse every day, and he didn't know how to help her.

Nothing made her happy. He'd caught her in the kitchen

last week crying again. He'd insisted—no, ordered her—to see Doc. So far she had resisted all efforts to get to the bottom of her problem. Was her behavior a sign of a serious illness? Her hand favored her heart a lot lately . . . was that the problem?

One thing he knew for certain: If her strange behavior kept up, he was going to take the matter into his own hands. He was taking Mama to the doctor himself. Maybe then he'd get some peace.

Tonight Liza was sitting on the porch, fanning herself, staring at the moon. Just staring at the moon while Faith cleared the supper dishes. Letting the screen close behind him, he joined her. "Mama, are you ill?"

"I'm healthy as a horse. What a thing to ask."

Her tone didn't indicate it. *Mean* as a horse, he'd concede. Lately she snapped at him like a fishwife. At times he was tempted to snap back, but he held his tongue. For the sake of peace and quiet, it was better to just let her have her say and get it out of her system.

Sitting down on the first step, Nicholas glanced toward the barn. Lantern light spilled from the windows. That meant a ranch hand was late getting through with his chores. Mama didn't like the help in the barn after dark. Once she had been a fearless woman—a wildcat couldn't intimidate her; lately she was scared of her own shadow. A year ago she'd insisted the bunkhouse be relocated to the back of the property in order to keep the help at a safe distance. The move had been costly and a considerable headache, but he had complied with her wishes in hopes it would assuage her uneasiness.

It hadn't.

"Glad to see you attended the quilting bee this afternoon."

"Didn't enjoy it."

They sat in silence for a few moments.

"What do you think of Miss Kallahan?" He kept his tone casual, aware he was wading into quicksand.

"Appears to be a hooligan to me. Wallowing around in that muck like a man."

Nicholas let the subject drop. Faith had been a help to him yesterday. Most women would have avoided the problem. "Nice night."

"It's hotter than a smokehouse." She fanned harder, wiping drops of perspiration off her forehead.

It wasn't that hot. An earlier shower had blown through and cooled the air. "Windows are all open. Should cool down real nice tonight."

Liza dabbed the hanky along her jawbone. "Suppose you'll be inviting Miss Kallahan to services with us in the morning."

"Mama. I am about to marry Miss Kallahan. I can hardly leave her sitting in the front parlor Sunday mornings."

Liza sniffed, reaching for a can of snuff. "Shouldn't have sent for her in the first place. I told you she'd be a peck of trouble—trouble we don't need."

Nicholas eyed the snuff. "I wish you wouldn't do that." His tone was sharper than intended. When Liza had taken up chewing a few months back, he had strongly reprimanded her. Papa would have rolled over in his grave, Nicholas said, but she paid him no mind. Lately, she just seemed bent on being ornery.

Liza shoved the box of snuff aside and promptly burst into tears. Burying her face in her handkerchief, she sobbed, great weeping howls that rendered him defenseless.

Nicholas muttered under his breath. "Mama! Have you seen the doctor about these . . . spells?" He tried to be understanding, but the good Lord knew he was at the end of his rope! He didn't know what to do with her when she got like this!

She looked up from her hanky. "You watch your tongue, young man. You're still not too big for me to take a switch to your behind." Bolting from the chair, she stormed past him, rapping him on the top of his head with her knuckles, then jerked the screen door open and let it slam shut behind her.

Dropping his head back against the post, Nicholas stared at the overhead canopy of stars. Thirty-four years old, and Mama was still thumping him on top of the head. He'd hold his tongue if it killed him—which it likely would if he didn't get to the bottom of her strange moods, and soon.

The sound of rattling dishes drifted from the kitchen and he briefly wondered if Miss Kallahan shared the same disposition for meanness. Was Mama's affliction peculiar to all women? His head pulsed at the thought of two women under one roof—his roof—each afflicted with the same madness.

What did Miss Kallahan think of his letting Mama run roughshod over him? He mentally groaned. Not much, he

conceded. B   sn't Mama—hadn't been for a long
time now.   grieving for Papa, and the Reverend
said only   heal her wounds. Well, almost two
years ha   d she was getting worse.

Quit   didn't matter what others thought. He
had c   d himself to answer to, and he would
hon   er—however weak and indecisive he
ap   aith Kallahan, or anyone else for that matter.

morning Faith snuggled deeper beneath the sheet,
g to the sound of rain dripping off the eaves. During
ght, thunder and lightning had shaken the old house
n the same fury that must have rocked old Noah's ark
hen the flood came. Toward dawn, heavy downpours
had given way to gentle showers. The smell of damp earth
drifted through the open window, and she could hear
someone moving around downstairs. The fragrant aroma
of perking coffee teased her nose.

Stretching, she wiggled her toes, trying to wake up. It was
the Lord's Day. It was the first time she would attend services with her new husband. She frowned, remembering
the mother cow. Her *soon-to-be* husband, she amended.

Her gaze focused on the white dress hanging on a hook
beside the beveled mirror. Ugly blood splotches and grass
stain soiled the front of the Irish linen. It would take some
time to clean the dress, and even then the gown might be
ruined. Sighing, she rolled to her back, grateful Rose Nelson wasn't there to witness the sad sight.

What *would* she wear for her wedding? And when would they attempt to marry again? She owned few garments— a blue-and-white gingham, a paisley green print, a yellow-sprigged cotton, a serviceable dark blue calico, a black wool, two pairs of bib overalls, and a plaid shirt.

She rolled to her side. Maybe the yellow cotton, with a little new lace tacked around the front. . . .

The rooster crowed daylight as she rolled from the bed and descended the stairway for breakfast thirty minutes later. Liza was at the cookstove, turning thick slices of bacon in a cast-iron skillet. She didn't look up when Faith walked into the kitchen.

Summoning her cheeriest tone, Faith said, "Good morning!"

Liza opened the oven door and took out a pan of biscuits. "Make yourself useful. Get the cream and butter from the springhouse."

"Yes, ma'am." Faith glanced out the open back door, smiling when she saw two of the most beautiful horses she'd ever seen standing in the corral. The small dark blotches on a white coat, and striped hooves, took her breath. She knew a ranch this size must have many horses that would be used to pull steel plows, harrows, cultivators, hay rakes and reapers. But the two splendid Appaloosas drinking from the water trough were undoubtedly Nicholas's private stock.

For a moment she forgot all about cream and butter in her desire to take the animals a cube of sugar, touch their cold noses, smell their warm, shiny coats. But one look at Liza's dark countenance made her beat a path hurriedly to the springhouse.

"Shall I tell Nicholas breakfast is ready?" she asked as she returned, setting the tub of butter and pitcher of cream on the table.

"He doesn't need to be told when it's time to eat."

"Yes, ma'am." Faith dropped into a chair and waited for Nicholas to come in from the barn. Would he let her pet the horses if she slipped out the back and—

She glanced out the window and saw him striding toward the house. She wouldn't be petting any horses this morning.

Breakfast was eaten in silence. Except for an occasional "pass me this" or "pass me that" Nicholas and Liza didn't address each other. Afterward Faith helped Liza wash dishes as Nicholas dressed for church.

Around nine they set off for the church. A gray drizzle peppered the top of the buggy as it rolled into the church-yard. Reverend Hicks, Bible neatly tucked beneath his arm, stood at the door, greeting arrivals.

"Nicholas, Liza, Miss Kallahan." Reverend's pleasant smile lit the dreary morning. "So sorry about the unfortu-nate turn of events. Is the cow all right?"

"She's in good health," Nicholas said. Liza steered Faith ahead of her as the two men shook hands. Two more wag-ons rattled into the yard. A crying infant shattered the morning serenity.

"Oh my." Reverend Hicks clucked. "I don't know how Dan Walters does it."

Faith turned to see a stocky, redheaded man climbing out

of the wagon, trying to shield a squirmy infant beneath his rain slicker. The man looked harried—and very young; Faith guessed him to be no more than twenty-two. The baby, screaming at the top of its lungs, looked to be only a few months old. A redheaded girl toddler with friendly green eyes was uselessly trying to plug up the noise by wedging a sugar tit between the baby's gums. A dark-haired boy, no more than five, valiantly wrestled to the ground a thick bag crammed with bottles and diapers. It sounded to Faith as if the circus had come to town.

Reverend Hicks cupped his hands to his mouth. "Need any help, Dan?"

Dan glanced up, grinning. One of the baby's shoes was missing. "Thanks, Reverend. I've got it under control!"

Heads turned as the rowdy ensemble entered the church and marched down the aisle, the baby kicking and bucking in protest as Dan settled his noisy brood in the pew.

The Shepherds filed into the church to take their seats as the Reverend closed the double doors. Perched at the pump organ wearing a bright pumpkin-colored dress and hat, Vera awaited the Reverend's signal to begin the services.

Faith leaned closer to Nicholas and whispered, "Who is that young man?"

"Dan Walters and his brood."

She frowned. "Where is Mrs. Walters?"

As the organ music swelled, Nicholas reached for the pew hymnal, whispering, "She died giving birth to the baby."

Faith's eyes returned to the young father who was trying to extricate a strand of hair from the baby's hand. The baby had the head of the poor woman sitting in front of them drawn back like a bow. *Poor man,* she thought.

The opening stanza of "Onward, Christian Soldiers" shook the rafters, and the congregation got to their feet. Faith stood beside Nicholas and in a clear, sweet alto sang her Papa's favorite hymn. Closing her eyes, she imagined his booming baritone energetically bolting out verse after verse as if indeed "marching oonn to waaar." She sang with him, matching his tempo, rejoicing in song. When she felt eyes fixed on her, she opened her eyes to see Nicholas staring at her. She smiled, pointing to the hymnal. "Papa's favorite song."

The singing died away, and the congregation sat down. Reverend Hicks approached the podium, Bible tucked beneath his arm, armed for battle. Baby Walters's muffled frets were the only sound in the room.

Reverend placed the Bible on the podium, then fixed his eyes upon the congregation.

"Brethren, this morning I prayed long and hard about today's message. My first inclination was to bring a message on the joys of giving, and then God reminded me not everyone considers it a joy to give." Relaxing, the Reverend smiled. "Many are unduly upset when the subject of money is broached, but we all know and understand that God doesn't want money; he wants obedience. Better that I preach a message of hope and encouragement to my flock, but the subject of a new steeple weighs heavily upon my mind—"

"Oh, good grief," Faith heard Liza moan under her breath.

"Here now! There'll be no moaning out loud, Liza Shepherd! This is just a friendly discussion before I preach the Word. As unpleasant as the subject is to all of us, we need a new steeple."

"Nothin' wrong with the one we got!" Clarence Watts bellowed. Faith jumped at the outburst. During Papa's services no one ever dreamed of talking back.

A farmer dressed in overalls stood up. "It's gonna fall down round our heads, Clarence, that's what's wrong!"

"It *is* a mite worn," another man conceded before his wife jerked him back to his seat.

"Hush up, Elmer. We cain't afford no new steeple!"

"People." The Reverend attempted to hush the sudden uprising. "The old steeple has served the church well for seventy years, but it's worn out. One good windstorm, and it'll come down, and woe to the unsuspecting soul who is unfortunate enough to be standing beneath it."

He fixed his eyes on Liza.

Faith's eyes pivoted to Liza. If Liza felt the Reverend was speaking directly to her, she showed no sign of backing down.

Whipping out a hanky, she fanned her reddened face as if there weren't a stiff breeze coming through the open windows. She plucked at the top buttons of her blouse, her hand favoring her heart.

Reverend's features softened. "Now I know you don't like to talk about money—none of us do. But there comes a time—"

Liza spoke up. "This is supposed to be sermon time, not

business-meeting time, Reverend. If memory serves me, we reserve business matters for Wednesday evenings."

Straightening, the Reverend took a moment to gain his composure. Pursing his lips, he began thoughtfully, "Good people of Deliverance, the Lord has blessed us all in a mighty way. Before I go on with this morning's message, I want you to promise you will go home, get down on your knees, and consult the Lord about his will concerning the new steeple. Perhaps we don't need it—perhaps I'm wrong. But please give it prayerful thought this week. It is my firm conviction that something needs to be done, and done soon."

A young father got up, a severe black suit hanging on his lanky frame. "Times are hard, Reverend. No one is trying to duck responsibility, but I got five kids to feed and clothe. There just ain't anything left over at the end of the month." He sat down, frowning at his wife when she patted his knee in silent support.

"And well I know that, Jim. If the steeple weren't a hazard, I wouldn't be asking that it be replaced. I'm confident we'll all pull together and do what we can."

Faith made herself as small as possible, wondering why Nicholas didn't speak up. The Shepherds could help with the steeple and never miss it. Instead he sat straight as a statue, eyes fixed on the podium, showing not a sign of emotion other than a muscle working tightly in his left jaw.

"The subject isn't appropriate," Liza declared. "Now if you don't mind, I have a roast in the oven. Kindly get on with the sermon." She crossed her arms, then uncrossed them in search of her fanning hanky.

Vera bounded to her feet, knocking over a sheaf of organ music. Righteous indignation flared beneath her bright orange hat. A young boy darted from his pew to retrieve the fallen sheets. "Liza Shepherd, whatever has gotten into you! Why, Abe would've given the shirt off his back—"

"Sit down, Vera!" Liza's razor-sharp rebuke interrupted Vera. Drawing a deep breath, Liza said more calmly, "Abe is no longer with us. I handle the Shepherd money, and *I* say the steeple needn't concern us. It does not need to be replaced. Repaired, I grant you, but not replaced."

Vera gave a loud hrummph, reached for the sheet music, and sat down.

Defeat settled in the Reverend's eyes as he quietly opened the Bible and instructed in a crisp voice, "This morning's sermon will be taken from Philippians chapter 1, verse 6."

Faith breathed a sigh, relieved the exchange was over. Opening her Bible to Philippians, she read, "Being confident of this very thing, that he which hath begun a good work in you will perform it until the day of Jesus Christ."

Chapter Four

FAITH opened her eyes Monday morning
long before the rooster crowed. Nicholas had spoken with
Reverend Hicks after the service, and Reverend said he
could marry them Monday afternoon at two. Faith could
hardly sleep for excitement. By the end of the day she
would be married!

When finally it was time to get up, she jumped out of bed
and ran to the open window to look out. As far as the eye
could see, it promised to be a perfect day. The sun was
shining, the sky a brilliant blue. Not a cloud in sight, and
a subtle breeze rustled the lace curtains.

The stains on her Irish linen wedding dress were barely
visible this morning. A generous-sized bar of lye soap and a
scrub board had done the trick. She smoothed her dress and
took one last look in the beveled mirror above the bureau.

She'd never thought much about primping, but today was special. She wanted to look especially nice for Nicholas on their wedding day.

Brushing her hair until it shone, she then pulled it to the sides and secured it with pearl combs. It fell to her waist in gentle waves. She considered wearing it in a neat bun. The style would have been more to her liking, and much cooler, but the thought of Mother Shepherd and her taut braids changed her mind.

Pinching one cheek, then the other, she added a touch of color to her face. She'd watched Hope use the trick on many occasions. The feminine ritual had always seemed silly to Faith. Now she knew it was downright ludicrous. It hurt almost as much as the pointy shoes she was wearing. She longed to wear her comfortable brown leather boots that were hidden away at the bottom of her valise.

Turning, she opened the bedroom door. The musty smell from the parlor hung heavy in the air.

Mother Shepherd was sitting in her rocker by the kitchen stove, bent over her sewing. She was wearing a cotton frock just as drab and ordinary as the one she'd chosen for the wedding three days earlier. Once again that awful black shawl rested around her shoulders. No wonder she was so hot all the time.

"Wondered if you were going to sleep all day."

Faith glanced at the clock. It was barely six o'clock. "The wedding isn't until two this afternoon."

"Been changed. Reverend sent word he'd have to do it this morning. Got sick folks to attend this afternoon."

"Sorry," she murmured, resisting the urge to ask why she hadn't been told. Like the Good Book said, "Be slow to anger and sin not." She wanted Nicholas's mother to like her. Their marriage would never be harmonious if his mother disapproved of her. Liza would be her children's grandmother. . . . She quickly shook the thought aside. First things first. She needed to build a strong foundation with Liza, although it was clear the older woman didn't share the challenge.

"I see you're wearing the white dress." Liza eyed the still visible, but faint, spots. "You think it's appropriate?"

Hold your tongue, Faith. Be kind.

"Are the spots noticeable, Mother Shepherd?"

Liza bit off a piece of thread, switching subjects. "There's ham and biscuits on the stove. Your eggs got cold. I threw them out with the gravy."

So. The first shot sounded.

Faith eyed the cold biscuits. How would Jesus handle this? With kindness and tolerance. Her sister June would seek to win Liza over with a winning smile. Faith's inclination was to sass, which always brought swift restitution from Papa.

"I'm not hungry, thank you." Faith set her jaw. She would just be so nice Liza could do nothing but love her.

"What's wrong with your face?" Liza held the needle up to the light to thread it. "Looks like you've been pinching yourself."

Faith blushed. Drats. Liza wasn't making things easy. OK, tomorrow morning she would come down those stairs looking like death warmed over.

"Oh, for heaven's sake. Whatever you've been up there doing, best get a move on. Nicholas can't surrender another day's work on account of your lollygagging." Liza got up and disappeared into the parlor.

Faith eyed Liza sorely. She bet Liza pinched her cheeks too. She jerked her bodice in place, aware her cheeks no longer needed the additional color.

Faith hurried to keep up with Liza as much as the uncomfortable pointy shoes would permit. She glanced down at the shiny black leather, tightly laced to her ankles. The pointed heel made a woman's life miserable. A body could snap an ankle wearing such things.

Grabbing her white hat, she hurriedly pinned it atop her head as she went out the back door. It didn't matter that it set a tad too far to the left. No one in this house was going to notice.

Pausing on the porch, Faith took a moment to catch her breath. Nicholas emerged from the barn, smiling as he tipped his brown suede Stetson at her. He was wearing work clothes, though this morning they appeared to be clean.

Faith sighed.

No breakfast. Not a single mention of the extra attention she'd given to her appearance. Both Shepherds looked as if they were about to cut hay, not be major participants in a wedding.

She sighed again, then wadded the folds of her dress, expelled another weary breath, and stepped off the porch to join her future family.

Mother Shepherd was already in the buckboard, sitting in the middle of the bench. Faith wondered if she intended to make that her permanent position.

Without a word, Nicholas helped Faith into the wagon and they drove off. Faith thought it would have been nice to ride to the Reverend's house in a real buggy instead of a supply wagon. And she'd have preferred to have a church ceremony, not some indifferent recital in the Reverend's parlor. She studied the bluebonnets growing along the roadside and thought how they'd sure make a pretty bridal bouquet.

She might as well wish for the moon. She wasn't going to have a real buggy, a church service, or a pretty bridal bouquet. This buckboard was as good as it was going to get.

Nicholas suddenly strained forward on the seat, his eyes trained beyond a small rise. In the distance a thick cloud of ominous black smoke boiled upward. Faith saw him stiffen as his eyes scanned the smoke. Even she knew from the direction the wind was blowing, it wouldn't take long for the smallest ember to reach the town settlement.

Snapping the reins, Nicholas urged the team to a full gallop.

Faith gripped the side of the buckboard, holding on to the white hat. The pins flew from her hair, and the dark mass whipped freely in the wind.

"Nicholas—slow down! You're going to kill us!" Liza exclaimed. "What in heaven's name are you—" She fell silent when she spotted the deadly smoke.

Nicholas cracked the reins harder, racing the horses, the

buckboard bouncing over potholes and ruts. With each rut, Liza landed hard on the bench, her rigid posture unaffected.

Faith's heart pounded as the wagon sped closer to the flames. Thick smoke teared her eyes now. Each breath produced a sharp stinging in her lungs.

Angry flames lashed upwards, waist high to a grown man. The fire was spreading across the grassland as fast as butter melting on a hot biscuit.

Men from Deliverance were already battling the scorching blaze. In the distance, more could be seen hurrying to join in the fight. Nicholas slowed the horse, tossing the reins to Liza before the wagon came to a complete stop.

Bounding down, he ran to the back of the wagon and took out a handful of empty burlap feed sacks, then raced in the direction of the licking blaze.

"Over there!" Dan Walters shouted, pointing to a waiting buckboard. Two large wooden barrels sat on the wagon, brimming full of water. "Wet your sacks!"

Liza held the team steady, clutching her handkerchief to her nose.

Faith's eyes scanned the unbelievable inferno. Never in her life had she seen anything so powerful. Tossing her hat aside, she jerked the pearl combs free, then wadded her hair into a bun and secured it. Snatching the handkerchief from Liza, she bunched up the layers of her wedding dress and jumped to the ground.

The look on Liza's face would have been comical under other circumstances. Faith refrained from laughing, knowing full well the repercussions of what she was about to do.

But she couldn't just sit in some old wagon when a fire like this was going on!

Liza shot to her feet, yelling, "Young lady—you get back in this wagon and stay out of the way!"

Liza's voice was little more than an echo as Faith ran to help battle the blaze. She stopped long enough to scoop up a burlap sack Nicholas had dropped, then raced headlong to the water wagon. The once-clear water was now blackened with soot. Faith dipped the handkerchief into the barrel, quickly tying it across her nose and mouth. Murky water dripped down the front of her white dress, but already the smothering air was easier to breathe. She submerged the burlap sack, hoisting it up soaking wet and dashed to help the men.

Swatting flames with the devil's fury, Faith worked side by side with the men. Cinders and ashes flew. A spark caught the hem of her dress and she quickly doused it, but not before it had burned a good-sized hole. Drats. She glanced down at Mother Shepherd's smoke-blackened handkerchief and frowned. Double drats. For over thirty minutes Faith fought unnoticed alongside Nicholas before her luck ran out. Nicholas was so engrossed in the fire, he hadn't noticed her presence, or most certainly, hadn't expected it.

Passing him on the way to the water barrel, she made the mistake of speaking.

"Terrible fire—wonder how it started?"

He stopped in his tracks, staring at her in total disbelief. "What are you doing out here!"

"Putting out a fire!"

"Get back in the wagon—you're in the way!"

"No, I'm not! Nobody's complained so far!" She doused the sack in the water and brought it up, dripping.

"I'm complaining now!"

"Just a few more sacks." She'd fought the fire for over a half hour. That counted for a respectable amount of experience. Just because he'd just noticed her—well, that didn't mean she hadn't helped.

Nicholas's tanned face blotched with impatience. "Go back to the wagon, Miss Kallahan."

"You need all the hands you can get," Faith argued.

"You're in the way. Get back in the wagon!"

"Let me just take one more sack." She glanced at Mother Shepherd, who was now standing up in the buckboard, watching the exchange. Oh, Papa would blanch at her sass, but Nicholas wasn't being fair!

"Get back in the wagon!"

"The town will be lost!"

"Deliverance was here long before you came! It's up to the men to see that it stays that way!"

Faith stiffened her resolve. He had no right to tell her what she could and could not do! "An extra hand never hurts, Mr. Shepherd."

"A grass fire is no place for a woman!"

"A good wife—"

Nicholas's hand shot to his hip, and Faith wondered if he was going to physically pick her up and haul her back to the wagon. He wouldn't dare. "We are not married yet, Miss Kallahan."

Their eyes locked in a heated duel. "Mr. Shepherd," Faith began. "I am well aware we are not married yet, but when we do say our vows, I refuse to be another Shorthorn that you simply brand and put out to pasture. A wife's place is to be a helpmate to her husband—"

"Get back in the wagon," he ordered.

He hadn't heard a word she'd said! Faith rolled her eyes, more determined than ever to make her point. "Eve was created from Adam's rib. Not from his thick head. Nor from the tip of his boots. From his rib! That's how close I intend to be to my husband, Mr. Shepherd—a part of his rib!"

Nicholas paled, and for a moment she wondered if she'd gone too far. Then her eyes steeled. "You brought me here to be your wife—"

"To be my wife! Not to get underfoot!"

"Nevertheless, I am here. And I intend to stand by your side until death do us part, and that includes fighting this fire with you!"

Nicholas shot her a stern look. She knew what he was thinking. It was going to be a long life.

"Well? What do you say to that, Mr. Shepherd?" Her eyes widened as the muscular Swede rushed her. Squealing, she tried to step aside.

Nicholas lunged, and they tumbled to the ground. Holding onto her, he rolled her on the charred grass.

The jolt knocked the wind out of Faith. She had no idea

what possessed him to do such a bizarre thing! She was only trying to make a point! The moment she caught her breath she began kicking and screaming.

Nicholas trapped her in his arms, rolling her on the ground, effortlessly dodging her pointy-toed shoes.

"Mr. Shepherd! You get off of me this instant!"

Liza cupped her hands and shouted from the wagon, "Nicholas Shepherd, you get up from there! The very nerve—my son, wallowing on the ground with a woman—have you lost your mind?"

Nicholas grunted, dodging another kick. "Stop that kicking! I'll personally take those shoes off you!"

They rolled and tumbled through the charred debris as men sidestepped them on the way to the water barrels.

"I'll stop kicking when you get off of me!" Faith tried to squirm from beneath his heavy bulk.

"I'm trying to save your life!"

"Save my life?! You're being stubborn, that's what you're doing!"

Pinning Faith's shoulders to the ground, Nicholas said with a deadly calm, "Your dress is on fire, Miss Kallahan."

Her eyes narrowed. "My dress is what?"

"On fire."

Springing to her feet, she beat the flames out.

Nicholas rolled to his feet, and Faith avoided his eyes.

"The way you came charging at me like an old bull—"

"Get back into the wagon."

She studied the frenzied scene. Men were still fighting the fire, gradually controlling the flames.

Faith glanced down the front of her wedding dress. Even a double dose of Mother Shepherd's lye soap couldn't save it now. The once beautiful garment was now black with soot and scorched beyond repair. She tried to stem the tears but failed.

"Now look what you've done." Nicholas awkwardly brushed cinders from her charred dress.

In his own way, she knew, Nicholas was trying to comfort her. There were just some things a man obviously didn't understand.

"Yes. It's just a dress," she whispered. Her wedding dress. But it didn't look as if she'd ever be getting married anyway.

The fight was gone out of her. Tired and discouraged, she gathered up the scorched hem and walked slowly to the Shepherds' wagon. "You can use my sack if you want," Faith said, refusing to look over her shoulder.

Nicholas dashed off to join the other men.

As she climbed up into the wagon, Liza gave her a censuring look. Faith knew she'd seen her and Nicholas rolling around on the ground, and the thought left her stricken with shame. She reeked of smoke; she didn't care.

It was late in the evening before the last man dropped to the ground with exhaustion. Faith thanked God the fire hadn't reached Deliverance. Speculation about the cause ran rampant. Old Charlie Snippet, who helped out around the general store, swore it was a lightning storm that did it. Others blamed a couple of gamblers who rode into town early the night before looking for a game. They'd been upset when they found out Deliverance had no saloon. Whatever the cause, Faith was thankful the fire was finally out. She dropped to her knees to thank God for his goodness and mercy.

Worn out, the men headed home. They climbed aboard wagons and saddle horses and scattered in all directions.

On the way home, Nicholas was silent. Faith was too tired and too discouraged to offer conversation. Her wedding had been thwarted twice. She wasn't in the mood to discuss a third attempt.

When the wagon stopped in front of the house, Liza got out and disappeared inside without a word. Nicholas went to the barn to tend chores.

Faith poured a pitcher of water into the wash basin, then discarded the ruined dress and scrubbed herself clean before changing into her nightclothes. Worn out and humiliated, she crawled into bed. The feather mattress felt heavenly against her aching body.

She lay in a lonely bed, in a lonely house, wondering why Mother Shepherd treated her so coldly.

The smell of fried potatoes and bacon drifted to her. She sniffed, her stomach knotting with hunger. She hadn't eaten all day.

When she heard the back door shut, she realized Nicholas had come in from the barn. She heard Mother Shepherd's muffled voice as she shuffled around the kitchen. Faith dreaded the thought of morning dawning, a new day beginning. There was no telling what new disaster awaited.

Oh, Father, grant me more faith, more wisdom, some way to

reach Nicholas and his mother. Am I doing something wrong?
Am I disappointing you? Is my faith not strong enough? Give me
patience to try harder. Reveal your will, dear God. I'll follow as
best I can.

Tossing and turning, she finally drifted into a restless sleep.

The sharp rap of knuckles on her bedroom door jolted Faith
awake before dawn. It rattled the old rooster off the
window ledge, denying him his daybreak caterwauling.

"Breakfast," Mother Shepherd snapped.

At least she was speaking to her. Even if it was in one-
syllable barks. It was far more than Faith expected.

Yawning, Faith rolled out of bed. Wearing those torturous pointy shoes another day was out of the question. She
buttoned a red-and-black plaid shirt, pulled on denim bib
overalls, and put on her old boots. Looking in the mirror,
she admitted she wasn't exactly a flattering feminine image.
Well, she sighed, looking like a lady hadn't won her any
prizes yesterday.

Nicholas was seated at the head of the table when she
walked into the kitchen. Liza was taking a pan of biscuits
out of the oven. Nicholas briefly nodded to her, smiling.
Faith quickly took her seat across from Liza.

Mother Shepherd set the platter of sausage and eggs on
the table, her eyes fixed on Faith's attire. "Are we milking
this morning?"

Faith ignored the cutting remark. "Sorry I'm so late. I

slept longer than I expected. Is there anything I can do to help?"

Liza unbuttoned her collar and fanned herself. "I can manage my own kitchen, thank you."

Faith pitied Nicholas's predicament. He was a man in the worse possible situation, caught between two warring women, his mother on one side, his intended bride on the other. Liza Shepherd was set in her ways. Faith couldn't imagine her giving an inch, now or ever.

Faith, on the other hand, was young and cheerfully optimistic most times. But she had a fire in her spirit that Papa always said would cause some man a good deal of trouble.

Apparently his prophecy had come true.

"Well, are we going to eat or just stare at our plates all day?" Liza asked. "Nicholas, say grace."

Nicholas complied. "Thank you, Father, for our many blessings and for the food we are about to receive. Amen."

Faith was aware that Nicholas was staring at her over the rim of his cup. She refused to meet his gaze, keeping her eyes trained on her plate. Once or twice she saw him glance at his mother as if she puzzled him. His bitter words still rang sharply in her mind. "Get back in the wagon where you belong!"

Well, she didn't belong in a wagon. She belonged beside him. If that bothered Nicholas, they would have to discuss the situation and find a workable solution. If he wanted a kitchen wife, he'd wasted good money sending for her.

Nicholas pushed his unfinished plate aside and stood up.

His gaze focused on Faith. "There will be no wedding today."

Faith nodded, buttering a biscuit. The announcement came as no surprise. She was beginning to think there would never be one.

"Reverend Hicks has been called out of town for the remainder of the week. I've promised the Johnsons I'd help with their barn raising today. Hay needs to be put up while the weather's good, so the wedding will have to wait until a week from Thursday, if you're comfortable with that." For the briefest of moments, Faith thought he looked mildly disappointed.

"Yes, sir," she murmured.

Nicholas pushed his chair against the table. "If you'll excuse me, I'll hitch the wagon." He left the room, and a moment later Faith heard the front door shut behind him.

It was the time of day she'd come to dread. She and Mother Shepherd, alone. Whatever Nicholas's mother said, no matter how mean and petty, Faith vowed to be respectful and patient. Somewhere above, her heavenly Father would be watching.

Liza's mood caught her off guard. As the door closed behind Nicholas, she reached for the coffeepot almost pleasantly. Not a word mentioned about the fire or about Faith's improper behavior. She acted as if Faith were in another room as she quietly began clearing dishes from the table.

Picking up her plate, Faith pushed her chair back from the table. "May I help?"

"No, thank you. I've been clearing tables long before you

were born," Liza said. "Besides, you're hardly dressed for women's work."

Faith fought the urge to respond, then tempered her thoughts by reminding herself to respect her elder.

"You're absolutely right, Mother Shepherd. I'll just see if Nicholas needs any help hitching the wagon." A moment later she let herself out the back door, letting Liza wash dishes by herself.

She found Nicholas in the barn, checking the horse's shoe. When he looked up, Faith smiled, but he went on working.

"You should be in the house getting ready. You'll need to change clothes before we go."

She glanced down at her bib overalls. Perhaps she should; the overalls were a bit wrinkled, but they would get dirty anyway at the barn raising. She couldn't wait to get her hands into that project! Papa had always said she was as good with a hammer and saw as any man he knew. But as silly as it seemed to change clothes, she would meet Nicholas halfway. "I'll change right away." She glanced at the two beautiful horses she'd seen earlier, housed in a stall beside the wagon. "Can I ride one sometime?"

Nicholas glanced up, surprised. "Ride? You're welcome to take the buggy anytime you want."

"No." She moseyed over to pet the horses. Their noses felt wet and moist. "I want to ride one of these fine fellows if you don't mind."

He bent his head, mumbling, "Mama won't approve of it."

"I'll ask her very properly. If she consents, will it be all right with you?"

"If she consents, it will be a miracle," Nicholas grunted, hitching the harness to the wagon.

He might as well know right here and now he's not marrying a parlor lady, she decided. "I've always favored outside work over inside work."

"Yes, I've noticed that."

"And I love animals of all kinds. Don't you?"

"Not real fond of cats." He glanced up, a slow smile spreading across his features. Faith caught her breath, struck by his handsomeness. He winked. "But I guess if you want one, I can learn to live with it underfoot."

Her heart soared. She could finally have that kitten! "Thank you. That will make me real happy." Giving the horses' rumps a final pat, she moved away from the stall.

A short time later she came out of the house. Liza trailed behind, shaking her head because Faith had donned *clean* overalls.

Nicholas was hitching the wagon.

"Need some help?" Faith called. She trotted out to stand beside him.

"I'm just finishing up here." He scowled at her appearance. He tripped over her feet, trying to get around her.

He might as well know he was marrying a tomboy, too. When she saw his eyes narrow, she said quickly, "I changed my clothes—soiled to clean."

"Don't you own more than one dress?"

"Four or five of them," Faith admitted. "But I can't build a barn in a dress."

He straightened. "You are not going to build a barn."

Well, we'll see about that, Faith thought.

During the ride to the Johnsons' house the silence was so thick it could have been sliced with a knife. The only sound was the rhythmic clop of the horse's pace, passing acre after acre of Shepherd cattle.

Faith's head spun with every turn of the wagon wheels. She could almost read Nicholas's thoughts. Right now he was wondering how he was going to build a barn with her in his way. She didn't care; she was eager to have a hammer in her hand again.

She glanced at Liza. She was probably wondering how she was going to turn a tomboy into a lady. Not very easily. Papa had tried it and failed.

Faith sat up as she spotted a coiled rattler beside the road within striking distance. All Nicholas would need was to lose a good horse. That would surely ruin the whole day. Reaching behind her for the shotgun, she carefully eased it out of the holder. She'd take care of that creature before it did any harm. . . .

Liza turned around. "What on earth—?"

Springing to her feet, Faith blasted both barrels into the coiled reptile. The gun's kick nearly toppled her.

Nicholas jumped as if he'd been shot when the gun exploded.

Liza choked, swallowing the pinch of snuff she'd just stuck in her mouth.

Slapping her hand against her thigh, Faith squealed with delight. "Got it!" The same instant the horse reared. Wide-eyed, Nicholas fought to gain control.

The runaway horse tore off down the road, out of control for over a mile, trailing a cloud of dust the size of a Texas twister behind the buckboard. The old wagon rattled and shook their teeth, threatening to split apart as it careened over potholes and gullies. Liza's hairpins came loose, spinning recklessly in the wind.

Nicholas stood up and sawed back on the reins, using brute strength to bring the horse under control. Gradually the wagon rattled to a jerky halt. The three shaken occupants slowly climbed out.

Liza's braids dangled below her shoulders, her face flushed, looking mad as an old wet hen.

Color rushed to Faith's face. She probably should have warned them before she shot. . . .

Nicholas seemed surprisingly calm. "Is anyone hurt?"

Liza made a strangling sound, and Faith reached over and whacked her on the back. A wad of snuff popped out of her mouth.

"There," Faith soothed. "That feel better?"

Then Nicholas went up like a keg of dynamite. *"What* were you *thinking?"*

Faith stammered, "I-I didn't want the snake to spook the horse, so I—"

"You didn't want the *snake* to spook the horse?" Nicholas said a dirty word. So dirty it brought a blush to Faith's cheeks. He should be ashamed of himself. God would not think highly of that! "You took it upon yourself to fire a shotgun ten inches from my eardrum? Mama, are you all right?"

"WHAT?"

"ARE YOU ALL RIGHT?"

"I CAN'T HEAR A BLASTED THING!"

Well, that did it. She had only tried to help, and they were acting as if she'd committed a crime against the government.

"In the future, kindly refrain from lending your help!" Nicholas tipped his head to the side, trying to clear his ears. "Do you have any idea how idiotic that was?"

"I'm not stupid, Mr. Shepherd." Faith glowered. "I just didn't stop and think."

"In the future—"

"I know! Stop and think!"

Nicholas glowered at her.

"I said I was sorry. What more do you want?"

He pointed to the wagon seat. "I want you to sit on that bench—no thinking, no helping, nothing—until we get to the Johnsons. Do you understand?" His eyes snapped blue fire. Papa had never used that tone of voice with her. "And keep those trigger-happy fingers in your lap where I can see them!"

She nodded.

The three climbed back aboard the wagon, and Nicholas turned the team toward the barn raising.

Faith glanced at Liza. "Mother Shepherd, I'm sorry about your braids."

"WHAT?"

"The bouncing shook them loose." Faith reached over to fix them. "Let me put them back in place—"

"Don't touch me." Liza scooted as far as she could away from Faith.

Faith sighed. Poor Mother Shepherd. Everything Faith did was wrong. At this rate, they were never going to be friends.

Chapter Five

EXCITEMENT grew when the Shepherd buggy rolled to a stop at the site of the barn raising. Faith's eyes drank in the sight of buckboards, colorful Jenny Linds and various other conveyances. From the very moment Nicholas had mentioned there was going to be a barn raising, she had looked forward to the social event. She was eager to form new friendships in the community that was to be her new home. She hoped Nicholas would introduce her to women her age.

Young Brice Johnson and his bride, Elga, appeared to greet the new arrivals. The young couple smiled and shook hands, welcoming the Shepherds to their home. Levi Johnson, Brice's father, was the Shepherds' closest neighbor to the south. The two families shared water rights. Faith judged Elga to be two to three years her junior, pretty, with a tousled head of russet hair and sparkling goldish-brown eyes. Elga had been married less than a month, and she still glowed with matrimonial bliss.

Over protests, Brice helped Liza down from the buggy, then took the picnic basket from Faith. His blond, sunny good looks and amicable gray eyes reminded Faith of the air after a summer thunderstorm. Refreshing. If only Nicholas smiled that way once in a while, he'd be every bit as handsome as Brice.

Brice energetically pumped Nicholas's hand. "Glad you could come today. Can always use an extra hand."

The sounds of hammers and saws rang out as Faith trailed Nicholas and Liza through the milling crowd. Nicholas called to several families, who returned the greeting. Faith decided if he wasn't exactly a social butterfly, he was at least a well-respected member of the community.

"Need to talk to you about one of my bulls!" a man in the crowd shouted.

Nicholas waved, promising to get together later as he steered Faith in the direction of the blanket Liza was spreading under a large oak.

"Can't I help?" Faith protested when she realized he intended for her to remain with Liza for the day.

"Women have no place doing men's work," he said.

Her chin tilted with determination. "I've done it before. Once, June and I helped build a whole shed. Mr. Siddons was thankful for our help, said we had the strength of two men, and—"

Nicholas cut her off. "No wife of mine is going to build

a barn or a shed. Stay here, and stay out from under foot."

Faith bit her tongue, sorely tempted to remind him she wasn't his wife, but she could see his pride was at stake. He wanted his wife to meet community standards. Well, she resented that he hadn't seemed the least bit upset about their two delayed wedding attempts. When she opened her mouth to argue, he pointed her to the blanket and sat her down.

Handing her a paper fan, he motioned toward the women setting up the food table. "I'm sure Nelly Johnson will welcome some help."

"Woman's work," Faith muttered.

"Nothing wrong with woman's work," Nicholas said. "You can unpack our food basket. It'll keep you out of trouble."

Keep her out of trouble! Jerking her hat in place, she stared at his disappearing back, silently seething. What would it hurt if she handed nails? Or sawed a board to the proper length?

Fanning herself, she looked up to see Liza pulling balls of yarn and crochet hooks out of her sewing bag. Faith saw two hooks, and her heart sank. It was going to be a long day.

"Should I set out our food basket?"

Liza handed her a hook and a ball of thread. "No hurry. Here. Make yourself useful. Idle hands are the devil's playground."

Faith bet the devil himself wouldn't have to sit under a

tree and crochet on a pretty day like this. Removing her hat, she set it aside.

Puffy white clouds floated overhead as she made a knot in the yarn and placed it on the hook, listening to the voices of the men, who, on the count of ten, heave-hoed, hoisting the newly framed walls into place. How she envied their camaraderie. *God, I don't question your wisdom, but I sure wish you'd needed more men than women when I was born.* She would have relished the peppery smell of fresh-hewn wood in her hands, adored the feel of a smooth shiny nail.

A faint breeze rustled branches overhead as Faith laid aside her crocheting and sighed. In the distance, a group of children were playing a spirited game of crack-the-whip. Her eyes searched the crowd for Dan Walters and his brood. She finally located the young widower nailing window frames together at a nearby sawhorse. Jeremiah was standing beside him, holding baby Lilly in his arms.

Smiling, Faith waved, and the old hermit tilted Lilly's arm to wave back. Jeremiah's gaze lightly skimmed Liza before returning to the business at hand.

Faith heard Lilly fussing a short while later and quickly laid her handwork aside.

Liza glanced up. "And where do you think you're going?"

"The Walters baby is fussy. I thought I'd see if there's anything I can do to help."

"Dan's capable of taking care of his children."

"Dan's busy right now. I'll only be a minute." Before Liza

could stop her, Faith darted off, thankful for the break in the monotony.

She approached Jeremiah and Lilly. "Can I help?"

Jeremiah gratefully handed over the squalling infant. "Thanks." He sniffed the air, wrinkling his nose. "I believe the infant's soiled her didee."

Faith smiled, glancing at Dan. "I'm Nicholas Shepherd's fiancée."

"Yes, ma'am. I saw you in church Sunday morning." Dan's ruddy complexion looked like a boiled lobster from the heat and exertion. "Quite a service."

"Yes—quite."

"There's clean diapers in the wagon. Adam, show Miss Kallahan where they are."

"Faith," Faith corrected, then smiled. "Please call me Faith."

Dan paused, returning her smile. "Thanks. Faith it is."

Adam took Faith's hand and started toward the wagon. With each step, he counted. "One, two, three . . ."

It was only then Faith realized that little Adam Walters was blind.

Fifteen minutes later the baby was changed and settled on a blanket, quietly nursing a bottle. Jeremiah and Adam had gone off in search of other projects.

Faith sat on the sidelines, shooing flies from the baby as Dan hammered nails into wooden frames. His quick, efficient motions confirmed his carpentry skills, although Faith had heard Nicholas say Dan worked with the blacksmith.

"Have you built many barns?"

"A few." Dan glanced up, using a shirtsleeve to wipe the sweat off his brow. Unlike Nicholas, he seemed happy— almost hungry—for the conversation. "What about you? Ever built anything?"

"A shed once, and I helped my father around the parsonage."

"You're a preacher's kid?"

She nodded. "Papa was the best there is."

They struck up a friendly conversation that lasted until the dinner bell rang. Work ceased as men washed up, then gathered before a long row of tables laden with platters of fried chicken, boiled potatoes, steaming bowls of turnips, ears of corn, green beans, and poke greens. Heaping pans of crispy brown corn bread and bowls of thick, freshly churned butter were started around. Sitting on nearby tables, fat apple pies and rich chocolate fudge cakes awaited.

Levi Johnson gathered the group around. "Father, we thank you for this glorious day and the blessings you have given us. Thank you for friendships, family, and for the bountiful food you've placed before us. Watch over and protect us this day. We ask in Jesus' name, amen."

"Amen!" the crowd responded.

Families and friends broke into small groups to partake of the noon meal. Good-natured laughter filled the air as the hungry workers socialized over talk of weather, grasshoppers, and much needed rain. Faith busied herself helping

Dan feed the two smaller children. She filled plates with
chicken legs and small helpings of green beans and potatoes,
deliberately avoiding Liza's annoyed stare. Nicholas sat
beside his mother in silence, the Shepherds keeping a safe
distance from the others. Faith knew if she looked their
way, she would be obligated to join them, so she purposely
looked the other direction.

At one o'clock the bell sounded again. The men groaned,
patted full bellies, then pushed to their feet. Minutes later
the sounds of hammers and saws once again saturated
the air.

The Walters children refused to let Faith go. Adam, who
Faith had discovered was born blind, and the three-year-old
girl, Sissy, held tightly to her hand as Faith playfully tried
to pull free. Laughing, she agreed to stay, then settled them
on the blanket and told Bible stories about Jonah and the
whale, and David and the giant, Goliath. Clapping their
hands, the children stomped around the blanket, mimicking
tall giants, until Dan called for them to settle down.

"Has anyone ever read you stories from a make-believe
book?" Faith asked as she repacked the picnic basket. She
fondly recalled the large, colorful book of fairy tales her
mother had read to her when she was about their age.

Adam's sightless eyes lit with expectation. "Papa says we
cain't tell no lies."

Faith ruffled his hair. "I'm not talking about lies—
make-believe stories. Snow White and Rose Red,
Rapunzel, Faithful John?"

Adam and Sissy shook their heads in awe.

"Do you know how to tell make-believe stories?" Adam asked.

Faith nodded, placing his hand on each side of her head so that he could not only hear but also feel her answer. "What am I saying?"

Adam paused, thinking. He broke into a wide grin. "Yes!"

"Yes!" Faith hugged him tight. "That's very good!"

Sissy started prancing again. "I wanta hear stawies!"

As the barn's rafters went up, Faith recited fanciful tales about sisters who loved each other so much they made a vow that what one had she must share with the other; a beautiful girl with magnificent long hair, fine as spun gold; and a servant who strove to be faithful to his king. The children giggled, gleefully pretending to let down their hair for the other to climb down upon.

Sissy's head was nodding by the last story. Faith wiped her hands and face with a cool cloth, then settled her on the blanket beside the sleeping baby.

Disagreement erupted when Adam declared he was too old for a nap. Dan joined the spirited debate, but Adam eventually won out, claiming he couldn't sleep now because Jeremiah had promised to teach him how to spit. Dan looked at Faith, and they both grinned.

"Spitting is an art no boy should be denied," Faith proclaimed.

Dan nodded, playing along. "I think you're right." He pointed the child in the direction of the old hermit.

Hands on hips, Dan paused, studying Faith. "How did you get so good with children?"

Faith shrugged. "Mothering comes natural, I guess."

"Well," Dan said, reaching for the dipper in the pail, dousing his head with water. Sunlight caught the glistening drops cascading off his fiery hair. He wasn't a handsome man, but kindness radiated from every pore. Faith decided kindness was better than handsomeness any day of the week. Kindness and an even temper. "You should have yourself a whole houseful of children," he said.

Faith spotted Nicholas working high above in the rafters, and she wondered if she'd have even one. "Maybe I will, someday."

Dipping back into the water pail, Dan drank his fill. Wiping his mouth with the back of his hand, he gazed at Faith. "Heard you didn't get to say your vows the other day."

"No, one of Nicholas's cows was having trouble birthing. Then there was the fire yesterday."

"That's too bad. Suppose you'll be saying them real soon?"

"Suppose I will." Faith glanced back at Nicholas. "Next Thursday, providing the Lord's willing and the creek don't rise." Or there's another fire or cow in trouble.

Dan grinned. "Nicholas is a lucky man."

She blushed, fairly certain Nicholas didn't think so.

Faith settled on the blanket when Dan went back to work. Her eyes focused on Nicholas, still perched high atop the barn, nailing rafters. Powerful muscles stood out in his arms as he drove nails into two-by-fours. Faith shivered, wondering how gentle those arms would be holding a woman—one he loved and respected. Her gaze meandered through the crowd, and she waved at a few of the church ladies. So far everyone had welcomed her with an amicable smile and an open heart.

"Want to help?"

Dan's offer brought her out of her musings. "Me?"

He stood beside the frame he'd just built, extending a hammer to her. "You said you like to build things."

"I love to build things!" Jumping to her feet, she straightened her overalls. "Are you serious?"

"Serious as buck teeth. Come on. You can help me with the next one."

Faith stepped in closer, helping to hold the board Dan was about to saw.

"Ouch!" She jumped, shoving the piece of wood away as it broke neatly into two pieces. Dan bent down to retrieve the boards, praising her efforts.

"You'll be building a town next."

"I would love it!" She grinned, then picked up a handful of shavings and threw it at him.

Leaning down, he scooped up a handful of sawdust and threw it at her, and a friendly sawdust war erupted. Chips flew, coating hair, faces, and clothes. Faith spit, brushing the swirling fragments out of her eyes as she fended off the attack. She fell to her knees, laughing when a barrage of shavings assailed her.

"Faith Kallahan!"

Faith sprang to her feet, blinking shavings out of her eyes as she glanced up to see Nicholas scowling at her. Staggering to her feet, she blinked again, trying to see through the haze of sawdust. "Yes, sir?"

Hammers fell silent; saws suddenly stilled. The air hummed with tension as workers ceased their efforts. Inquisitive eyes rotated to the direction of the angry voice.

Nicholas, hands on his hips, face as black as a witch's heart, stood in front of her. Liza hovered at his flank, narrow lipped, eyes vibrating with condemnation.

Swallowing, Faith brought her hand up to cover her tripping heart, afraid it was going to thump right out of her chest. Dear goodness. What was she doing? How must a sawdust fight look to Nicholas? She'd forgotten herself and was caught up in harmless frivolity, but how must it look? She hadn't stopped to think about her actions; if she had, she would have realized they were inappropriate. Her eyes locked with Nicholas's and her heart skipped a beat when she realized he was going to make a scene. And by the look on Liza's face, she was about to take a willow switch to her.

She smiled faintly. "Hello, Nicholas. Did you want something?"

Nicholas's eyes turned to blue steel. Faith winced when she saw a muscle tighten in his jaw.

Stepping forward, he took her by the arm, marching her through the crowd. Color flooded Faith's face. She highly resented his barbarian treatment! Who did he think he was, treating her as if he owned her! She tried to wrest free of his clasp, but he only tightened his grip.

"Let go—you're hurting me!"

"You are making a mockery of the Shepherd name," he said in a tightly controlled voice.

"A mockery? I was only throwing sawdust—"

He hurried her along, refusing to listen.

When they reached the Shepherds' blanket, Liza wasn't far behind. "Young lady—"

"Mama!" Nicholas took off his hat and pointed it at her. "I will take care of this."

"But Nicholas, she's—"

"I will handle the matter, Mama. Sit down."

Hurt flashed across Liza's face, but she stepped back.

Nicholas's shirt was soaked with perspiration. Blond hair lay in damp waves against his forehead. For an instant Faith was moved by the urge to brush it back. She warred with conflicting emotions: Concern and compassion fought with the deep temptation to kick him in the shins. He was a most unpleasant man, determined to take his resentment out on her!

Then he spoke, and his cold, exacting voice sent any noble thoughts flying out the window. He was a mean, boorish brute who delighted in embarrassing her!

"I told you to stay here with Mama and keep out of the way," he began in a calm, calculated tone.

"Well, you see—Adam and Sissy needed help. I was only—"

He cut her off. "You were sawing a board!"

"One board!" she defended. "Before that I was helping

with the children. I fed them, diapered the baby, then told Sissy and Adam stories—"

His voice dropped to an ominous timbre. For one brief, elated moment she thought she saw jealousy flare in his eyes. Then it was gone. "You were not brought here to tend Dan Walters's children. And while we're having this talk, I don't want you socializing with Jeremiah."

"But I like Jeremiah!"

"What you like or dislike makes no difference. People will wonder why you are drawn to a drifter, a hermit. The man could be dangerous—he isn't a puppy or a kitten, Miss Kallahan, a stray in need of help. No one knows anything about him, or his past, other than he chooses to be alone."

"But the Lord expects us to be kind to all men."

"You are to keep your distance from Jeremiah. You were brought here to be a Shepherd. A Shepherd does not pick up every stray she runs across."

The air was electrically charged as she turned her back to him. Crossing her arms, she counted to ten. If she were a man . . . how dare he order her around in that tone! Papa had never so much as raised his voice to a woman, and he'd have no patience with a man who did.

Taking a deep breath, she dropped her voice. There was no point in making a spectacle of herself in front of the growing crowd of onlookers. "You don't have to remind me why I'm here."

"Has it ever occurred to you people will talk when they see you cavorting with Dan Walters?"

"Cavorting!" She whirled to face him. "Cavorting?" she

repeated. "I was helping Dan—if you recall, I offered to help you, but you told me to sit down and be quiet."

He snorted. "And look where that got me." He glanced at the curious onlookers, then lowered his voice. "Just do as I ask, please."

Liza spoke from the sidelines. "You should be ashamed of yourself, young lady. Have you no regard for Nicholas—"

Nicholas stopped his mother. "I've already spoken to Faith about the situation, Mama. This matter does not concern you."

Turning back to Faith, he repeated quietly but firmly, "You are to sit with Mother the remainder of the afternoon and behave like a lady. Do I make myself clear?"

Her chin lifted. "Do I have to crochet?"

"If that's what it takes for you to conduct yourself in an acceptable manner."

She looked away, crossing her arms again, staring into the distance. "I hate to crochet."

"Look." He lowered his tone. "All I'm asking you to do is act like a lady, and don't embarrass Mama or me. Is that too much to ask?" His dark tone warned her he'd brook no further nonsense. He turned and walked off.

"Apparently so," she murmured.

Nicholas glanced over his shoulder. "What?"

Faith opened her mouth to repeat her declaration, then clamped it shut, words from Ephesians ringing in her ears: *Wives, submit yourselves unto your own husbands, as unto the Lord. For the husband is the head of the wife, even as Christ is the head of the church: and he is savior of the body.*

Nicholas's tone took on a dangerous edge. "Was there something more you needed to say, Miss Kallahan?"

"No, sir." She refused to look at Mother Shepherd.

"You're certain?"

She turned her back to him. "Positive." Her obedience wavered when she added under her breath, "Except that you're not my husband yet."

Liza settled herself on the blanket, then reached for her handwork. "You're asking for trouble."

"Asking?" Faith released a pent-up breath of frustration before picking up her crochet hook. She seared a hole through Nicholas's retreating back. "Seems to me I've already got it."

Chapter Six

FATHER, *I don't mean to be a burden. I'm not proud of my actions of late. It seems no matter how hard I try, I'm short on understanding and long on criticism. Who am I to criticize Liza—or Nicholas, for that matter—when I have so many faults of my own? I truly want to marry Nicholas, and I believe that's your will. Why else would you send me here, among so many strangers? Even as ill tempered and disagreeable as Liza is, I want her to like me. Truthfully, I can be pretty ill tempered and disagreeable myself, and I'm not proud of it. I pray for your forgiveness and the ability to do better. I don't want to disappoint the Shepherds—and I never intentionally do things to upset them. Bless Liza, Lord. Send happiness into her life: She misses her husband so. I seek only to do your will, even if at times I miserably fail. Amen.*

Rising from the side of her bed, Faith quickly dropped back to her knees. *And, Lord, please tell Papa not to worry.*

Once Nicholas and I are married, I won't be such a bother.
I remain your faithful servant, Faith Marie Kallahan.

Hay was put up and the wedding scheduled for the third time. Faith followed the Shepherds to the wagon Thursday morning, dressed in a yellow-sprigged cotton with leg- of-mutton sleeves. The gown wasn't as pretty as the white Irish linen, but it was the next best thing she owned. The tatted lace she'd stitched around the collar made it seem like new, although she'd had it for years. The only other hat she had was a thick fur cap with attached earmuffs. Nice for blustery cold winters in Michigan, but useless in sweltering Texas heat.

After the way Nicholas had treated her at the barn raising, Faith wasn't fully able to recapture wedding-day anticipation. Still, she and Nicholas had an understanding, one she intended to honor. Nicholas and she were as different as daylight and dark, but perhaps, in time, there would be more acceptance of each other. The least she hoped for was tolerance.

A smile played at the corners of her mouth, and she felt more optimistic as she remembered the Good Book. If the Lord could heal the sick, raise the dead, and save the most wicked sinner from the fiery pits of hell, he could bless this marriage. All she needed was faith the size of a mustard seed.

Nothing was said on the ride to Reverend's house. Faith watched the countryside roll by, mesmerized by the hum of the wagon wheels. Texas was unbelievably big. Everywhere she looked fertile fields were dotted with cattle, grazing or bunched in herds, seeking the shade of cottonwoods, mesquite, or majestic oaks. She sat up straighter when she spotted one of those strange-looking creatures the elderly gentleman on the stagecoach had called an armadillo. The patterned, plated animal with brown armor on the top and side surfaces of its body darted across the road in front of the wagon.

"Do you see that—that monster?" Faith exclaimed.

"Don't go making a mountain out of a molehill," Liza said. "It's just an armadillo."

"Looks like an armored rat."

In another twenty minutes Faith spotted the church parsonage. She couldn't help comparing it with the Shepherds' dreary dwelling. The quaint white adobe, with porches running the length of the house, radiated warmth and love. Even the stable and chicken coop, with their bright whitewashed boards, captured the Hicks's cheerful spirit.

Though the wagon was still some distance away, she imagined she caught a whiff of the sweetest fragrance. As the rig rolled into the yard she spotted the source. Yellow roses grew in large clusters at the side of the porch. Vera had baskets of lush ferns hanging from every rafter. Lovingly tended flower beds overflowed with bird's-foot violets, but-tercups, and spider lilies. Pretty Indian blankets, their russet centers bursting into flared yellow tips, grew generously beneath two huge pecan trees. The heavy branches, like green-leafed umbrellas, provided a shady haven from the blistering sun. Faith longed to someday live in just such a house.

A chestnut mare, lathered and winded from a hard ride, waited by the front porch. A young man in denims and a blue shirt took the steps two at a time and pounded on the door.

"Mornin', Ethan," Nicholas said, helping Faith and Liza from the wagon. Nicholas and Faith started up the steps, Liza close behind.

"Mornin', Nicholas." Ethan paused long enough to acknowledge the ladies' presence. He quickly removed his hat. "Mrs. Shepherd, Miss Kallahan."

Liza nodded. "Something wrong, Ethan?"

"It's Sarah Jane. She's havin' the baby."

Vera came to the door and retreated quickly, then returned carrying a black satchel. Reverend Hicks followed, towering over his wife's short stature. "Hurry along, Ethan. Sounds like your young'un's anxious to make his entrance."

"Yes, ma'am!" Ethan jumped the porch rail and mounted his horse.

Scurrying down the steps to the buggy, Reverend Hicks had hitched and waiting, Vera turned to face the wedding party. "I'm afraid Amos will have to conduct the ceremony without me. Sarah Jane's in labor."

"That's quite all right, Vera," Liza acknowledged. "Lord knows there's no stopping a baby when it's his time to come."

Faith turned around to face Liza, surprised at the consideration in her voice. She sounded almost sympathetic. "I didn't know Mrs. Hicks was a doctor."

"She's not. You're in Texas now. Doc's likely to be out on another call, and Vera fills in for him. Many a woman calls Vera before they go for Doc. A mother couldn't be in better hands."

With such praise coming from Mother Shepherd, Faith knew Vera must be miraculous. Since arriving in Deliverance, she couldn't recall Liza saying anything complimentary about anyone.

Reverend helped Vera into the buggy.

"Thank you, dearest."

"You be careful, Mama."

"Can I be of help?" Faith asked. She didn't know much about birthing babies, but she could fetch water and clean linen.

"No, thank you, child." Vera picked up the reins. "Lord knows, I do appreciate the offer. I have everything I'll need in my satchel."

"This is one of those situations where too many cooks can spoil the stew," Liza volunteered.

The observation puzzled Faith. Mrs. Hicks was going to deliver a baby, not fix supper.

Vera and Ethan were about to leave when a frenzied rider, hollering and waving his hat, galloped into view. "It's time! It's time—the baby's a-comin'!"

Faith stepped back to allow the rider plenty of room as he sawed back on the reins, bringing his horse to a stop in a

boil of dust. As the grime settled, Albert Finney material-
ized.

Vera frowned. "Oh dear, Albert. Not Mary Ellen too.
Why, she's not due for another week. Albert, are you
sure?"

"Yes, ma'am!" Albert grinned. "I'm real sure!"

"Oh, dearie me." Vera bit her lower lip. "I suppose this
being your seventh, you would know."

"Yes, ma'am! You gotta hurry, she—"

"See here, Albert! I got here first!" Ethan declared. "My
Sarah Jane needs Mrs. Hicks's services—now!"

Albert frowned. "But Mary Ellen's about to pop! The
baby's not gonna wait!"

"First come, first served!" Ethan maintained.

"Mrs. Hicks, you know my Mary Ellen," Albert pleaded.
"When it's her time, it's her time! Ain't nothin' on God's
green earth gonna stop that young'un from comin'! Please!
My baby ain't gonna wait!"

"Mine ain't either!"

Faith expected the two men to end up on the ground,
going at it.

"Gentlemen, please! You're behaving like children!" Vera
interrupted. "I can only be in one place at a time."

"Then let's go!" Albert urged.

Ethan clenched his teeth, "I told you, Albert Finney! I
was here first! You're comin' with me, Mrs. Hicks."

"The two of you just calm down a minute," Vera
demanded.

Ethan backed off, grumbling, "Guess we could always draw straws."

"Draw straws!" Albert shook his head. "Ethan, we ain't talkin' about who's gonna go first in a horseshoe game! We're talkin' about my baby!"

"No need for straw drawin'." Vera glanced at Liza. "Liza, you're gonna have to help."

"Certainly." Liza sidestepped Faith and hurried back to the buckboard. She motioned for Faith to come along, and Faith blinked, looking to Nicholas.

He nodded. "Go on. Mama needs your help."

Faith wasn't sure what Liza expected of her as she hurriedly climbed aboard the wagon.

Liza picked up the reins, eyeing Faith. "I don't know if you've ever helped birth a baby, but if you're as good at it as you are at pulling calves, you'll do just fine."

Faith's eyes felt as big as silver dollars. "I—I don't know anything about babies—"

Liza snapped the reins, wheeling the wagon around in the direction of the Finney place. "You'll know more by tomorrow." The wagon careened forward. "Albert! Let's get moving!" Liza shouted. "We got ourselves a baby comin'!"

"Yes, ma'am!" Albert grinned, tipping his hat at the ladies as he led the way.

As the dust settled, Nicholas took off his hat, his eyes trained on the fading wagons. Reverend stepped down from the porch, craning his neck for a final look. "Well, we can't have a wedding without a bride."

"Looks that way." Nicholas was beginning to wonder if the wedding would ever take place. Three attempts, and he was still a single man.

Reverend chuckled. "Seems as if you and Miss Kallahan are having a hard time tying the knot."

The thought had occurred to Nicholas.

Reverend laughed, slapping Nicholas good-naturedly on the back. "Sometimes we don't understand why certain things happen. If God made it clear to us, I reckon we'd have no need for faith."

Faith. Nicholas took a deep breath. He prayed God understood Faith Kallahan's ways, because he sure was having a hard time coming to terms with them.

"You eat lunch yet?" the Reverend asked.

"Not yet."

Reverend Hicks opened the front door, motioning for Nicholas to join him. "I don't know about you, but the way I see it, if we can't pray over matrimony, we might as well pray over a good meal."

It was close to midnight before Liza and Faith returned. Light spilled from the kitchen window. Faith could see Nicholas sitting at the table, reading Scripture. When the wagon slowed, he got up to meet them.

"Baby get here all right?" He helped Liza, then Faith down from the buckboard.

"Easiest birthing I've ever tended." Liza yawned. "But I'm tuckered out. See to the buggy, will you, Nicholas?"

Easy? Faith thought, recalling how poor Mary Ellen had labored, it seemed, for hours. Not just for one baby but two. Albert had grinned from ear to ear when she handed him his newborn son. Moments later she handed him another baby—a girl this time. The proud new papa looked as if he might faint. Faith smiled. Twins would be a shock when you had six other mouths to feed.

"Supper's in the oven." Nicholas started for the barn with the horse and wagon. "Reverend Hicks insisted I bring home some of Vera's venison stew and cornbread."

Faith ate two bowls of stew before retiring to her bedroom. Exhausted, she opened the window. The night breeze felt good on her damp forehead. She lifted her hair, allowing the breeze access to her neck.

Stepping out of the yellow wedding dress, she caught her image in the mirror. Three attempts at the altar and still no ring on the third finger of her left hand. It was getting harder and harder to maintain that faith she had boasted to Aunt Thalia about. Then faith had been easy; now it took some doing to believe God had a plan for her and Nicholas Shepherd.

She knelt beside the bed, praying, but tonight for some reason, it felt as if her words went no higher than the ceiling. Papa used to say, "Even though it may feel like God isn't listening, that's when he's working the biggest miracles." She couldn't remember a time when Papa had told her wrong. He'd known the Good Book from cover to cover.

Lying in bed later, Faith's mind refused to shut down. As much as she loved children, what Mary Ellen had gone through tonight made her wonder if she ever wanted babies of her own. Liza had insisted it was an easy birthing, but it had looked difficult to Faith. Liza had taken over in a sure, competent manner during the births while Faith kept the sweat wiped from Mary Ellen's forehead and tried to keep out of the way. Mary Ellen had squeezed Faith's hand so tightly it still ached.

Just when Faith had felt certain there was no end in sight, cries from the newborns filled the room. In one glorious moment, the anguish was gone from the tired mother's face. All that remained was infinite love glowing in Mary Ellen's eyes as she held her babies for the first time.

Faith remembered something Aunt Thalia once read from the Bible. A Scripture about how the pain of childbirth, which can feel almost like dying, is but a clouded memory after the child is born. She sure hoped that was true in Mary Ellen's case.

She didn't think she'd be likely to ever forget such a thing.

After breakfast on Friday morning, Nicholas went to the woodshed. Faith had her heart set on joining him, but Liza made it clear she had different plans.

"Faith," she called out from the parlor. "I'll be needing your help this morning."

Drats. "Yes, Mother Shepherd," Faith replied, shocked that Liza would admit to needing anyone's help. She glanced up from dusting the parlor to see Liza slip a small brown vial from her apron pocket and take a sip.

Faith flattened her body against the wall. Had she seen what she thought she'd seen? Nicholas's mother chewed *and* imbibed spirits?

Peeking around the corner, she covered a gasp when she saw Liza tipping the bottle back and taking another healthy swig.

She drew back. Oh goodness. Did Nicholas know about this? Should she tell him? Her mind whirled.

Liza came into the parlor and pushed a basket of socks, thread, and a darning needle at her.

"Best get started. We haven't got all day." She frowned. "You do know how to darn?"

"Yes, ma'am," Faith replied, omitting the fact that she detested the chore. As Liza brushed past her, Faith bent close, trying to get a whiff of the liquor.

Liza pulled away, giving her a dour look. "What are you doing?"

"Nothing." Faith grinned.

The weather was beautiful outside. Faith couldn't stand the thought of being cooped up inside. She could hear the sound of the axe biting into the wood. She would much rather chop wood than darn any old day. She'd pricked her finger three times, and it was getting sore. No doubt about it. Darning was more dangerous than wood chopping.

It wouldn't be quite so tiresome if Liza would only talk to her. But the two women sat in the dark room, methodically darning as they listened to the ticking clock.

Faith's eyes roamed the parlor. Every piece of furniture was covered with sheets, even the two straight-backed chairs in which they sat.

The more Faith studied the coverings, the more she wondered why. "Mother Shepherd, why do you keep the furniture covered?"

Liza drew a tolerant breath, concentrating on her stitches. "I'll not have the sunlight fading the furniture. It's wasteful."

"Oh." *As if sunlight could possibly get through those drapes,* Faith thought.

An hour passed without the two women exchanging a word. Faith's toes curled in the pointy shoes she was wearing. She longed for her boots. She should have worn them—and her overalls. At least she would be comfortable.

Her thoughts switched from the furnishings and her foot discomfort to Mother Shepherd, trying to look beyond Liza's coarse exterior. Her eyes were probably once as deep blue as her son's. Faith's heart ached. Did Nicholas have the least suspicion that his mother had taken to strong drink? Perhaps it was only for medicinal purposes. . . . That was possible. There was a woman in Papa's church who contended that a tiny drink every now and then helped her rheumatism. Yes, that was it. Liza was using liquor as a medicinal remedy for whatever plagued her.

Remarkably, Liza's fair skin was barely touched by the Texas sun. Her hair, once blonde but now streaked with silver, could still be attractive if only she would loosen those unbecoming braids.

Faith was amazed to realize that Liza Shepherd wasn't that old—why, she might even be pretty with a little fixing. She stuck her finger and winced.

Drats. She'd rather spit nails than darn socks. Her boredom growing, Faith fidgeted in the chair.

"Must you squirm?"

The woman had barely spoken all this time, and now all she could contribute was, "Must you squirm?"

Faith tried to hide her frustration. "I'm sorry. . . . I need to use the necessary."

She wasn't lying; while she didn't need to go, she needed to *go*. The necessary was the only refuge she'd found to escape monotony.

"Well, don't sit there and squirm. Go do what you have to do."

"Yes, ma'am." Faith laid her basket aside, then stood and stretched like a lazy cat on a hot summer's day.

"And don't take all day. There's plenty of darning left to do."

Faith stepped off the back porch and reached behind the steps for the leather strap she'd been braiding on previous trips. Keeping to the well-worn path, she held the strap hidden in the folds of her dress. Her handiwork wouldn't be appreciated should she encounter Nicholas along the way.

She took refuge in the outhouse, bolted the door, then made herself as comfortable as possible. For over an hour she braided and prayed for patience, more faith, and more guidance. Papa always said, "Don't make a bit of difference where you pray. God hears you no matter where you are."

Well, she sure hoped he was listening now because she was giving him an earful.

I'm running real low on faith, Lord. I don't mean to be always complaining. I know there's folks a lot worse off than me. Guess I'm just feeling sorry for myself again. My fingers hurt from darning, and I've got a big blister on my little toe from those awful pointy shoes. I know Nicholas isn't as cranky as he seems. I caught him talking real gentle-like to a stray dog the other night. He didn't know I saw him, but he was awfully kind to the lost pet. And one night, he brought a new calf into the house and laid it by the stove. I thought Liza was going to faint. Said she'd just mopped the floor that day! But he didn't budge an inch. Said he wanted to keep a close watch on the heifer in case she got off to a rocky start. Now I ask you, Lord, would a mean man be that considerate? I don't think so. I think he must have other things on his mind, things that don't concern me but that make him the way he is. On the inside, I suspect, he is a kind man. If you'll just provide me sufficient faith to see this thing through, I believe it will all work out. . . . Bless Mary Ellen's new twins. They sure are sweet—

The sudden knock on the outhouse door startled her from her preoccupation.

"Faith?"

She sat up. "Yes, Mr. Shepherd?"

"Mama says you've been in there over an hour. Are you ill?"

"No. I'm fine." Faith felt color heat her cheeks. Of all the humiliating things Mother Shepherd could do! Sending Nicholas to the outhouse to fetch her back to darn those old socks!

An eternity passed.

"Are you coming out?" Nicholas's voice sounded weary.

"Do you need to come in?" Faith asked, wishing he would just go away. Couldn't a woman enjoy a personal moment?

More agonizing silence passed. She knew she'd have to answer him sooner or later.

"Mr. Shepherd? You still there?"

"I'm here."

"Go back to the house and tell Mother Shepherd I'll be there in a moment."

She couldn't come out with him standing there. He'd see the braided strap and be angry. It was one of those "man" things he'd warned her not to do. She exhaled a heavy sigh when she heard the sound of receding footsteps.

Supper that night was fried chicken, milk gravy, string beans, and biscuits and sorghum. Faith cleared the dishes from the table. It was one of the few times Liza consented to let her help in the kitchen. Nicholas excused himself and retired to the side porch. Liza retreated to the parlor to read the Bible.

Faith completed her kitchen chores. Pouring a fresh cup of coffee for Liza and one for herself, she proceeded into the parlor to join her future mother-in-law.

The kerosene lamp burned low. Liza was asleep in her chair, her reading spectacles slipped down the bridge of her nose. The open Bible was still in her lap.

Poor dear, Faith thought. *Drinking and chewing.* How could she help Liza, make her see those were only temporary solutions to whatever was troubling her?

Setting the coffee on a corner table, Faith turned up the lamp for a closer look. Liza's face, peaceful in sleep, looked softer tonight, almost vulnerable. Leaning closer, she sniffed. Not a sign of liquor on her breath. Faith quietly removed Liza's spectacles, placing them and the Bible on the table. Leaning down, she gently kissed the older woman's forehead. *Maybe someday,* Faith thought, *you will grow to like me.*

Gathering the cups, she slipped from the parlor. Out the kitchen window, she saw Nicholas sitting on the porch. No sense in wasting two perfectly good cups of coffee, she reasoned, deciding to join him. She could use some company. There were times when the silence that filled the Shepherd house was unbearable. Tonight was one of those times.

"Mr. Shepherd, I thought you might like some coffee." Faith wasn't sure of the reception she'd receive, but she was willing to risk his rejection.

Nicholas turned to look over his shoulder. She was surprised to see him smile. "Thank you, Miss Kallahan. Coffee would be nice."

Faith handed him the cup. "May I sit for a spell?"

Nicholas made room for her beside him in the swing, glancing toward the parlor window. "Mama asleep?"

"Yes, I just checked on her."

Faith sat down beside him. She knew it wasn't considered proper for them to be together without a chaperone. But Liza was just beyond the window and she felt her presence. By the look on Nicholas's face, he felt it too.

A million twinkling stars filled the sky. Sweet smells and subtle sounds filled Faith's senses; hay cut that morning, crickets, a bullfrog croaking a lonesome love song to his mate. Fireflies flickered in the darkened pasture.

Faith closed her eyes, enjoying the breeze as it gently brushed her hair.

"Miss Kallahan . . ." Nicholas paused. "I'm sorry about the string of unfortunate events. I fear you will think I'm trying to get out of our understanding, but I'm afraid I must once again postpone the wedding."

She sighed, wondering if he indeed regretted sending for her. "Whatever you think best, Mr. Shepherd."

"I have business to oversee. It will be another two to three weeks before we can recite our vows."

Faith kept silent. Three weeks. She wondered if she should offer to return to Michigan and save him the embarrassment of asking her to leave.

"Mr. Shepherd, have you ever been in love?"

Nicholas gazed at the stars, his eyes mirroring distant memories. "Love has passed me by, Miss Kallahan." He glanced at her. "And you?"

"Not really. There were no eligible men in Cold Water,

at least none I cared to fall in love with." She thought of Edsel Martin and shuddered.

"Faith—may I call you Faith?"

"Of course . . . Nicholas." She rather liked the feel of his given name on her tongue.

"I know the wedding delays concern you. They concern me, and I fear I have not been fair with you—that at times I've been preoccupied and even short when I should have taken time to explain my concerns." His tone gentled.

"This newest delay is because I have cattle to take to market. I'll be leaving for San Antonio first thing on Tuesday and have some business to take care of on Monday before I go. We could marry tomorrow, but I would rather wait until I got back." He smiled. "It hardly seems fitting to get married, then run right off."

"I understand." Faith resolved to be patient. When the time was right, they would marry. Trust, Faith, the good Lord kept seeming to tell her. And she would. "The cattle must come first."

"Well, normally they wouldn't. But this time of year they must."

Faith sat up straighter, encouraging conversation. "Why is that?"

"If I want top dollar, I have to get my herd to market before it's glutted."

"You mean before other ranchers beat you there and demand a higher price?"

He smiled. "Something like that. The more cattle bought, the more prices fall."

Faith could see he enjoyed explaining the procedure to her. She reveled in the secret knowledge that she wasn't nearly as green on such matters as she appeared. She'd always kept up on the stock reports, discussing them with Papa.

Though neither of them had moved an inch, it suddenly seemed they were sitting closer. She could feel the cloth of his trousers brushing her skirt. She wondered if he was aware of it, too.

"So, you'll drive the herd to San Antonio. Can you do that by yourself? You're just one man, and there are so many cattle."

"The ranch hands will help."

"Ranch hands? I've never seen anyone around other than you and Mother Shepherd."

"That's because the bunkhouse is at the far side of the land." He laughed. "Mama wants it that way."

Faith felt fuzzy with warmth. It was the first time she'd heard him laugh, and she loved the sound.

"Why would she insist on such measures?"

His eyes grew distant now. "Mama hasn't been herself lately. I'm worried about her. She has it in her head that our help pose a danger to her. She wants nothing to do with them."

"Are the men dangerous?"

"Most of the men are decent and hardworking. There are always a few who get out of line, but not many because they know they'll be sent packing when they do."

"I imagine it's hard for a man to get out of line in Deliverance. There are no saloons."

Nicholas chuckled, a manly sort of chuckle that made Faith blush. "San Antone has all they need. There have been a couple of times when a cowhand has come back with more cheap whiskey in his belly than pay in his pocket."

Faith wondered if she should mention Liza's brown vial. She decided against it; it would only cause him more worry. "What did Mother Shepherd want you to do about the men?"

"She wanted the bunkhouse moved." He chuckled again.

His mood was infectious. Faith joined in, and they had a good laugh over nothing. Neither meant disrespect toward Liza.

Faith regained her composure. "What happens when you sell the cattle in San Antonio?"

"A broker will arrange for the herd to be driven up the Chisholm Trail. There the cattle will be delivered to the buyer. Usually in Wichita or Abilene."

"I see." Faith paused. "Why don't you just cut out the middleman and drive the herd to the buyer yourself?"

He looked at her a long moment. "Very astute of you, Faith. Because it's a long, hard drive. For years we delivered the herd to the buyer. When my father was alive . . ." Nicholas stared into his empty cup. "Is there any more coffee?"

"Plenty." Faith gathered the cups and disappeared into the house. She glanced into the parlor and heard Liza's soft

snores. While the pot was heating, she thought of Nicholas
and the way he'd suddenly changed the subject at the mention of his father. Why?

"There's more," Faith offered when she returned and
handed Nicholas his cup.

"Thank you."

Sitting down, she gazed at the stars. It was a romantic
night. Was he mindful? "Are Texas nights always this
pretty?"

Nicholas gazed at the sky. "Seem to be."

"Have you always lived here?"

"I was born here—in this house."

"And your parents, were they born here too?"

Nicholas set the cup aside. "No, they're from Kentucky.
Father married Mother when she was sixteen. A year before
I was born, they loaded everything they owned into a
wagon and headed west. When they reached Texas, they
fell in love with the land. Papa staked his claim, then built
the herd with hard work and a lot of blood and sweat."

Faith smiled, warmed by the knowledge that he was
opening up to her. It filled her heart with joy. She set the
swing in gentle motion. "No brothers or sisters?"

"Just me." Nicholas closed his eyes, and she could see
him relax. The dim kitchen light shadowed his face, and he
looked like a small, tired boy. "The folks wanted more, but
no others came along."

"Nicholas?" she asked gently. "How did your father die?"

Nicholas stiffened. A seemingly endless moment passed.
Faith wished she hadn't asked. Papa always said she talked

too much. She was beginning to think he was right. Some people needed more time to heal than others. At least that's what Aunt Thalia always said.

Exhaling a deep breath, Nicholas said softly, "Papa was shoeing a mule. No one's sure how it happened, but Gus, a ranch hand, was in the barn pitching hay. He said something must have spooked the mule. Said the animal went wild—Papa tried to get out of the way. The mule kicked him in the head. When Gus got to him, Papa was dead."

Faith shut her eyes, in touch with his pain. "I'm so sorry." They sat in silence as the lantern in the kitchen sputtered, then went out.

"Mama took it hard," Nicholas admitted. "She's still taking it bad. That's why I appease her moods."

Faith reached over and laid her hand on top of his. At least he'd noticed them. "I can imagine how hard it must be for her."

"She'd been with him most of her life. Papa used to laugh and say he'd practically raised her. She hasn't been the same since he died."

Faith looked at the strong, rugged man that sat beside her. Even in the depths of his pain, his concern was for others. Faith was grateful the Lord had allowed her to see a softer side of this man.

Aware that she was still holding his hand, she let go and smoothed her dress. It wasn't proper for a lady to be so forward.

Nicholas stretched, then got to his feet. "It's late—Faith,

when I get back from San Antonio, we might saddle those two horses you favor and take a ride. Would you like that?"

Faith thought of those two splendid Appaloosas and beamed. "Very much so."

He offered his hand and helped her up. "Will you be comfortable while I'm gone?"

"I'll be fine. If you don't mind, I'd like to spend time with little Adam Walters." The child had been on her mind since the barn raising. If she could help the sightless boy to experience the world more fully through her eyes, that would make her very happy.

"Dan Walters's boy?"

"Yes—do you mind? I thought with my teaching experience I might be able to help."

"No, I don't mind. The boy's a bright child—just let Mama know what you're doing."

"I will—and Nicholas?" Faith allowed him to open the screen door for her. She gazed into his eyes, picturing their clear blue in the darkness. Her stomach quivered.

"Yes?"

"Thank you for sharing your thoughts with me."

"I was just about to thank you for the same thing." Their eyes met briefly and a silent message passed between them. They could be friends.

As Faith approached the staircase, she turned to Nicholas. "Be careful while you're gone."

"You do the same." He disappeared into his room, softly closing the door behind him.

Chapter Seven

FAITH sat between Nicholas and Liza on the way to the Saturday-night community dance. She'd wished a hundred times she'd been more thoughtful, shown more discretion at the Johnson barn raising, but tonight would be different. She was on new footing with Nicholas after their talk on the porch; she would guard her behavior, although she enjoyed Dan's company and adored his children. When she thought of how excited Adam was when she'd told him stories, she felt she had to share it with someone, so she'd sat up late last night writing long letters to Hope, June, and Aunt Thalia, extolling Dan and his children. God did indeed work in mysterious ways, for if he hadn't sent her to Deliverance, she might never have known the joy of reading to a sightless child. She'd never met anyone who was blind, unless she could count old Mr. Gunnison, who Papa had said could see a little even if he contended he was blind as a bat. Papa said Mr. Gunnison overly enjoyed attention.

As usual, silence prevailed as the wagon bounced along the rutted trail. Faith searched the countryside for signs of trouble, relieved when she saw nothing but a radiant gold-and-blue sunset, though there were clouds looming in the east. The thought of lively music and tasty food quickened her excitement. It had been a long time since she had enjoyed a social evening.

She studied Liza from the corner of her eye, wondering why she'd wanted to come tonight. Faith couldn't imagine her cutting a feisty jig on the dance floor. Yet she appeared to have taken more care than usual with her appearance tonight. Faith bit back a smile, recalling how Jeremiah had started sprucing up lately. He'd looked right dapper at the Johnsons'. Clean shaven, smelling of soap and water instead of donkey. And he was wearing new clothes. Was it possible Jeremiah was smitten with Liza?

A laugh bubbled in Faith's throat when she thought of the unlikely pair: dour-faced Liza and good-hearted Jeremiah. She laughed out loud, remembering how she'd complimented Jeremiah on his new haircut. He blushed, dismissing the compliment as if it embarrassed him. Had Jeremiah ever been married? Did he have children of his own?

Faith glanced at Liza. Had she ever once laughed or had fun? What had Abe Shepherd been like? Debonair? Jovial? Rowdy and fun loving? Cranky, like Liza? The picture sitting on the parlor table portrayed Nicholas's father as a handsome man with a handlebar mustache and a brisk twinkle in his eye.

She laughed out loud again and jumped when Nicholas elbowed her and gave her a stern look.

"Sorry," she muttered, straightening the skirt of her dress. But the thought of Jeremiah and Liza together was funny.

The air was close, with an occasional flash of light in the east. Faith loved a good thunderstorm with jagged lightning and gusty wind. As a child she used to stand in the rain, arms outstretched, experiencing God's awesome power.

Jeremiah stepped off the porch when the Shepherd buggy rolled to a stop in front of the community hall. If Faith was surprised by his improved appearance at the Johnsons', she was thrilled with his appearance tonight. He was clean shaven and wore a sedate lightweight brown suit and white shirt. He looked different, distinguished, not at all like the shaggy recluse who had given her a ride into town on his mule.

Jeremiah reached for the horse's bridle, smiling. "Looks like we're in for a good soaking."

"We can always use rain." Nicholas set the brake, then wrapped the reins around it. "Surprised to see you in town tonight, Jeremiah."

Jeremiah smiled, his eyes openly admiring Liza Shepherd. "I never miss the opportunity to be with a pretty lady." He lifted a hand to help Liza down. When her foot touched the ground, she broke the contact, primly adjusting her dress into place, refusing to meet Jeremiah's eyes. "May I say you look fetching tonight, Mrs. Shepherd?"

Liza's eyes narrowed. "Don't you have anything better to do with your time than annoy folks, Mr. . . ." She paused, her face going temporarily blank.

"Montgomery." Jeremiah supplied. "Jeremiah Wilson Montgomery. And I have a variety of interesting ways to spend my time, but I would rather make the effort talking to you."

Adjusting her shawl, Liza sidestepped him and disappeared into the brightly lit community hall, where the sounds of fiddles and guitars filled the air.

Faith stepped from the wagon, wondering why Liza was so bent on acting ugly. Jeremiah was only trying to be sociable, and Liza did look . . . well, nice tonight . . . softer, less daunting. The particular shade of green she was wearing complimented her . . . made her hazel eyes look more . . . human-like.

Faith softened as Nicholas took her arm and they climbed the wooden steps. The polite contact sent her heart racing. At times he acted as though he didn't like her, much less want to marry her. At others he seemed polite, almost gentle. His moods were a puzzlement.

The brightly lit hall was crowded. Faith spotted the town's eligible women quickly. They surged toward Nicholas, smiling and gesturing. A young, very pretty, brown-haired woman waved to him from across the room.

Nicholas smiled at her, acknowledging her greeting. Faith was startled when she felt a twinge of jealousy.

A group of ranchers who were gathered around the punch bowl called to Nicholas, motioning for him to join them.

Settling Faith on a bench, he said quietly, "Please try to remember your place."

Faith's eyes focused on the colorfully dressed dancers whirling around the floor. Her foot automatically tapped to the beat of the lively music. "My place is to sit here on this hard bench all evening?"

"That isn't amusing, Miss Kallahan."

"Neither is being the dance wallflower, Mr. Shepherd."

"We're here for you to become better acquainted with our neighbors, not necessarily to dance." Nicholas straightened. "I'll be nearby if you need me."

Faith didn't doubt that. Between him and Mother Shepherd, she would be watched like a hawk.

Nicholas wandered off as Faith settled her skirts, prepared to endure a long evening. A quick search of the dance floor confirmed her suspicions: There were few men her age in attendance. A lanky youth with a rash of angry-looking pimples looked her way, but she quickly averted his gaze. Tonight she was intent on behaving properly. She would not give Nicholas or Liza one morsel to fault her. She located Liza conversing with Vera Hicks and two other ladies gathered around the refreshment table. Jeremiah was standing to the side, talking to the Reverend. Faith giggled, wondering if Liza was aware she had an admirer . . . no, she wouldn't be. Having an admirer would border on frivolity, and no one could accuse Liza Shepherd of having a frivolous bone in her body. Actually she was downright rude to Jeremiah, and Faith wondered why. Jeremiah was the epitome of politeness. Until recently he could have taken more care with his appearance, but Faith had been taught to look deeper than the outside. She knew Liza would be horrified to know how intently Jeremiah's intelligent eyes followed her around the room.

A small group of men and women stood at the back of the hall, discussing the needed new church steeple. Their remarks caught Faith's attention. She strained to hear their conversation.

"One good wind and it's gonna come down," a stout-looking man proclaimed.

"We're still hundreds of dollars short from being able to replace the steeple," his wife said. "Everybody's given all they can." Eyes swiveled to Liza, who was ladling herself a cup of punch.

"Looks to me like someone ought to just open up their moth-eaten pocketbook and donate a new steeple." The woman's voice dropped to a whisper. "The Shepherds have all the money they'll ever need. Why Nicholas doesn't put his foot down with Liza puzzles me. If Abe were alive, it'd be a different story, I'm here to tell you."

"Now, Geraldine," her husband patted his wife's arm. "If it weren't for Nicholas, the Brunson family wouldn't have a roof over their heads. Wasn't he the one who paid to have their house built back after the fire? As I recall, Liza didn't like it, but Nicholas did it anyway."

"Yes, and remember Liza paid for Whit Lawson's little girl's leg braces. Poor little mite would have been a cripple if Liza hadn't stepped in," a silver-haired woman added.

"Liza was a different woman then. Abe was alive."

"If the Shepherds are so blamed charitable, why don't they offer to replace the steeple?"

"Well, we all know Liza's a good woman and serves the Lord. Seems a new steeple isn't high on her list of priorities these days."

The women looked at each other and tittered. "Doesn't seem like anything's high on her priorities these days," one observed.

The woman's statement was met by a round of good-natured laughter, and Faith wanted to go to them and tell them to stop whispering about Liza! Faith couldn't imagine why Liza didn't want to help with the steeple, but maybe she had her reasons.

Why *didn't* Liza buy that steeple? Seemed to Faith the Lord had poured out a blessing on the Shepherd family the likes of which most common folks had never seen. Papa would say, "The more God blesses a body, the more responsibility that person has to use his gifts wisely."

A disturbance drew Faith's attention to the doorway, where Dan was just coming in. Baby Lilly was screaming at the top of her lungs. Adam trailed behind Sissy, dragging a lumpy bag, which Faith assumed contained diapers and bottles.

Faith started to get up and help the new arrivals but quickly sank back down to the bench, remembering Nicholas's warning to keep her place. If she disobeyed, he would be angry.

Dan weaved toward her, holding Adam's hand and maneuvering Lilly on his right hip. The crowd moved back,

allowing the noisy family plenty of leeway, a few shaking
their heads in sympathy. Sissy spotted Faith and started running, dragging Adam along with her. The sightless boy
tripped over his feet, and the bag spilled to the floor. Faith
caught her breath as she heard the sound of breaking glass.

Before she thought, she was up, running to help the child.
Milk bubbled out of the sack and pooled in a widening
puddle on the floor.

Dan stooped down to pick up the broken bottle amid
baby Lilly's deafening cries. "Stay back, Sissy! You'll cut
yourself!"

Faith searched the room for Nicholas, relieved to see he'd
barely looked up at the commotion. Taking a deep breath,
she reached for the baby. As long as she didn't have fun,
he'd have no reason to be upset with her. If ever a man
needed help, it was Dan Walters.

Jiggling the baby up and down, Faith tried to calm her
as Dan accepted a towel and mopped up the spilled milk.
Adam and Sissy darted into the crowd, ducking between
unsuspecting legs and creating general havoc.

Faith's heart went out to Dan as he sank down on the
bench, trying to catch his breath. His discouraged thoughts
were reflected in his eyes: The Walters family had been at
the dance for less than five minutes, and the room already
looked as if a cyclone had hit it.

Faith sat down beside him, lifting Lilly to her shoulder.
The baby's cries dwindled to soft mews, and she began to
suck her fist.

"Maybe she's hungry." Faith glanced at Dan. "Do you have a bottle?"

"Not anymore. They were all in the sack."

"Well, I'm sure we can come up with something." She smiled. "Raising children isn't easy."

Sighing, Dan leaned back, bracing his head against the wall. He closed his eyes, and Faith knew he was relishing a rare quiet moment. "I do the best I can, but they need a ma."

Mary Ellen handed Faith a fresh bottle and smiled. "I always pack a spare, just for Lilly."

"Thank you, Mary Ellen. I don't know what I'd do without you." Dan grinned sheepishly.

Faith gently cradled Lilly's soft mound of carrot-colored hair as she fed her. The infant smelled of soured milk. Faith wished she could give her a good bath and sprinkle cornstarch on the heat rash dotting the baby's face. "You must miss your wife very much."

Dan laughed softly. "I miss her so much at times that I don't think I can stand it."

"You had a good marriage?" The question was intensely personal, and Faith hoped he wouldn't think her brash. They barely knew one another, certainly not well enough to confide their personal lives, yet in an odd way, she felt as if Dan were the only person in Deliverance she could talk to. The town women were polite, but they kept their distance. Nicholas ignored her, and Liza spoke only to criticize or reprimand.

"The best," Dan conceded. "Carolyn was real young

when we got married . . . barely fifteen. We ran off. . . .
Her pa had a fit . . . threatened to turn a double-gauge shotgun on me, but Carolyn stood between us and vowed he'd
have to shoot her first." Faith pretended not to notice the
moisture that suddenly filled his eyes. "I surely did love that
woman." He glanced up. "I may be out of place askin', but
what's a pretty lady like you doing marrying a Shepherd?"

"A Shepherd?" Faith frowned. He made it sound worse
than a medieval curse.

"Oh, Nicholas is a good catch, I suppose . . . but he's
older than you—"

"Not much. He's thirty-four."

"Thirty-four?" Dan shook his head. "I thought he was
older."

"No," Faith conceded. "He just acts that way." Recog-
nizing her disloyalty, she blushed. "I'm sorry. Sometimes
I speak before I think. Nicholas is just very serious minded
and worried about his mother. He feels a responsibility to
Liza."

Dan snorted. "Surprised Liza is gonna let him get married.
She's kept him on a choke chain since Abe died."

Faith's eyes were drawn back to Nicholas, who was standing at the punch bowl. The pretty brown-haired lady he'd
smiled at earlier had him cornered. Nicholas's laughter
floated to her.

Sitting up straighter, she watched the exchange, amazed
by the difference a smile brought to his face. He lit with
animation as he talked, eyes sparkling. The transformation
was startling.

"Dan, who's Nicholas talking to?"

Dan's eyes traced her gaze. "That's Rachel. . . ."

"Who's Rachel?"

"Rachel . . . the woman Nicholas almost married. Hear tell, folks around here thought they'd tie the knot when they were younger, but she ended up marrying Joe Lanner." Dan lowered his voice. "Lanner drinks, and he gets real mean when he's under the influence. . . . She ought to leave him, but she won't."

About that time Nicholas threw his head back and laughed uproariously at something Rachel said.

Faith stiffened. "Is he still in love with her?" She had a sinking feeling he was—he'd never laughed at her remarks that way. A man didn't look at a woman the way Nicholas was looking at Rachel if he didn't feel something.

"You'd have to ask him. Story goes Rachel got tired of waiting for Nicholas to propose, so she up and married Lanner."

The woman, married or not, was standing rather close to Nicholas. Where was that Shepherd sense of propriety?

"You didn't answer my question." Dan's voice broke into her thoughts.

"I'm sorry. . . . What was the question?" Baby Lilly had settled down and was now dozing on her shoulder.

Dan was about to repeat the question but winced instead at the sound of chairs overturning. "Sissy!" he roared, coming to his feet. "Come here!"

The frisky three-year-old darted out the front door and

made a beeline for the street. Annabelle Grayson latched on to the girl's shirttail to thwart the escape.

"I'm doing my best, but I guess I'm not hard enough on them," Dan confessed, sitting down. "Well, what about my question?"

She knew the one he meant. The whole town was buzzing about her situation. "It isn't that I wanted to be a mail-order bride, but my sisters and I didn't have a choice." She briefly explained the circumstances that had brought her to Deliverance. "Aunt Thalia can't afford to feed three more mouths forever, and the meager funds I made teaching school wouldn't support my sisters and me. So we answered an ad, and very shortly all three of us had offers of marriage."

"You answered an ad?"

She nodded. "It seemed the only sensible solution."

"I can't picture Nicholas running an ad. . . . What's the name of the journal?"

Faith told him, wondering at his sudden interest. "Would you like the address? I'm sure I have it somewhere. . . ."

Dan shrugged. "I've never heard of running an ad for a wife. . . . Cold Water has no eligible men?"

Faith thought about Edsel Martin and shivered. "Not really."

Dan shook his head in sympathy. "Real shame. A nice lady like you deserves the love of a good man."

Faith smoothed the baby's hair, silently agreeing. Just then Nicholas laughed again, and she bristled. Nicholas Shepherd was seeming less and less the likely candidate.

"Well, you're lucky to have part of Carolyn still with you. Lilly's a beautiful child."

"Yes, ma'am, she is. Looks exactly like her ma."

Lifting Lilly to her shoulder, Faith gently patted her back. "You've got your hands full. How do you handle three children and work every day?"

"Old Man Dickson's real understanding. He lets me bring the young'uns to work with me on the days I can't find anyone to look after them. The town ladies have been real good. Many a night I've come home to find supper waitin' on the table and the wash ironed and folded."

Adam darted toward the food table, tripping over Eldorene Hardy's foot. Eldorene's punch went airborne, landing in Lawrence Hardy's lap. Lawrence sprang up wide-eyed, muttering under his breath as he gingerly fanned the wet front of his britches.

Sissy raced to the punch bowl and grabbed the ladle, wielding it recklessly. Sticky red punch showered the occupants standing close by.

Faith could see the pride fairly oozing out of Dan as he watched the chaos. "Them kids are sure independent, got to hand it to 'em. Being blind don't stop Adam from doin' anything he sets his mind to."

"Yes," Faith agreed faintly. "He's spunky." The community hall was a shambles, chairs overturned, punch staining the once pristine white tablecloth, cookies ground underfoot, but Adam was independent, all right.

Dan shoved slowly to his feet. "Well, guess I better corral the young'uns. Can I get you a cup of punch?"

"No, thank you. I'll just sit here with the baby." Faith doubted there was a drop left in the bowl anyway.

"Well, much obliged." Dan wandered off in the direction of the sound of more shattering glass.

As Dan left, Jeremiah excused himself from Reverend Hicks and walked in Faith's direction. She smiled as he approached.

"What's a pretty little thing like you doing sitting on the sidelines?"

Patting the bench beside her, she motioned for him to join her. "I am behaving myself," she announced. "What's a handsome gentleman like you doing all alone? I should think the eligible women would be fawning over you."

Jeremiah chuckled, his eyes traveling to Liza. "Do you think a certain beautiful lady would box my jaw if I asked her to dance?"

Liza? Beautiful? Faith strained for a closer look at the dour-faced woman chatting with a group of women. Well, maybe she had been, once. Or maybe Jeremiah just needed spectacles.

Jeremiah's focus centered on the baby. "Heard her crying a minute ago. . . . Seemed a mite out of sorts."

"She's hungry, and her bottles are broken. Mary Ellen brought a spare, but Lilly drank it all."

Shaking his head, Jeremiah watched Dan trying to break up a food fight between Sissy and Adam. "Spirited children."

Faith nodded. "Real spirited."

Jeremiah settled down on the bench. "Well, at least Dan's

determined to keep them with him. He'll have to learn discipline, but he's not much more than a boy himself."

Faith nodded. "It's a shame Adam's energy can't be channeled. He's a bright boy."

"Exceptionally bright." Jeremiah reached in his pocket and took out a pipe. "Do you mind?"

Faith shook her head. "Papa always said it was the devil's habit, but I always kind of liked the smell of tobacco smoke."

Jeremiah opened a pouch and tapped tobacco into the bowl. "Bad habit, all right. Tell me about yourself, Miss Kallahan. You appear to be a highly intelligent young woman. Have you a formal education?"

She nodded. "Papa saw that his children were educated. My sisters and I were lucky. My mother graduated from one of the first women's colleges."

Jeremiah drew on his pipe. "I understand you've taught school?"

"Only for a couple of years; then Papa died. But I loved it, loved the children and seeing them learn."

Jeremiah puffed, sending billowing smoke spiraling toward the ceiling. The smell of tobacco floated pleasantly in the air.

"It's a real shame there's no one here in Deliverance who can teach Adam Braille."

"Braille?" Faith brightened. "Are you referring to the Frenchman Louis Braille . . . the man who invented the Braille system?"

"The same." Lighting a match, Jeremiah touched it to the

tobacco, drawing deeply, whorls of white smoke mush-
rooming over his head. "Have you heard of him?"

"Heard of him! He was a dear friend of my grandpapa—
Grandpapa Troy." She remembered how Grandpapa had
said Louis had been blinded at the age of three in an accident. While studying in Paris at the National Institute for
Blind Youth, he'd witnessed an army officer demonstrate
a military code for night communications. Grandpapa told
how the code used dots and dashes but was too complex
and inconvenient for the blind to use. The Institute's
founder had developed cumbersome texts with large raised
writing, but that, too, proved too complicated. When Louis
was only fifteen years old, he improved the dot system,
teaching it throughout his life.

"You don't say." Jeremiah drew on the pipe thoughtfully.
"Then I'm sure you recognize the potential a child like
Adam has."

"Yes, but I'm afraid I don't know anyone who teaches
Braille." Louis Braille first published his dot system in 1829,
but few, if any, in the rural communities taught it.

"Yes, yes," Jeremiah concurred, "Louis Braille's tech-
niques are different . . . but I would imagine an illustrious
person like yourself could pick them up easily enough."

Faith glanced over, and suspicion nagged her. From the
moment she'd met Jeremiah, she thought there was more
to the man than what appeared. Talking with him now, she
detected a vein of intelligence and knowledge far superior
to that of most men she knew. Did Jeremiah have a secret
past? A past he kept well hidden beneath a scruffy exterior?

"Yes, I suppose one could learn Braille. . . . Have you personal knowledge of Braille's teaching?"

"Me? Oh, no. I've only read about his work."

"Really?" Faith eyed him suspiciously. "Do you have access to magazines and journals concerning the subject?" She couldn't imagine that he would, but his eyes belied his protestation.

"Oh . . . suppose I might be able to come up with something. . . . Why do you ask?"

Faith winced at the sound of silverware clattering to the floor. "What you say is true. Adam is exceptionally smart, and he was very responsive when I told him stories. A whole new world would open for him if he were able to read for himself. If you could provide material on the subject, perhaps I could teach Adam Braille. I would be happy to donate my time."

"That would be most gracious of you, Miss Kallahan."

"I would enjoy the challenge. Will you help?" Was that a mischievous twinkle in Jeremiah's eye?

"I'll certainly do whatever I can, but I can't promise I'll come up with anything. . . ."

Faith was elated at the thought of applying her teaching skills. She'd have to discuss the plan with Nicholas and Liza, of course, but surely they couldn't object to such a noble gesture. Her spirits sang. The outings would relieve her from household chores, and she'd do almost anything to get out of darning.

"Please see what you can find out, Jeremiah, and let me know."

123

"I'll do whatever I can, but right now I think you have bigger problems." Faith saw what he meant. Old Man Zimmer was threading his way across the room, his faded blue eyes zeroing in on her.

Rollie Zimmer was deaf as a board and missing every tooth in his head. He stopped in front of her, holding an earpiece to his right ear. "WANNA DANCE?"

Faith glanced at Jeremiah.

"COME ON, GIRLIE! LET'S YOU AND ME CUT A JIG!" He handed Jeremiah the horn, then grabbed Faith's hand and jerked her to her feet. Faith shot Jeremiah a frantic look as he reached for the baby. Shaking his head, he motioned for her to dance.

When they reached the dance floor, Rollie jumped straight up in the air and clicked his heels. He landed flat on his feet, his weathered face splitting into an impish grin. "HOWDY!"

"Howdy," Faith murmured, aware that every eye in the room was on them. She located Nicholas and smiled lamely. He wouldn't care if she danced with Methuselah.

The music started, and Rollie whirled her around, then caught her in a breathless dip. Inspired, Faith tried to follow his lively steps. He jigged and jagged across the floor, pulling her along with him. She felt pins fly out of her hair when he suddenly paused and spun her around in the middle of the floor like a toy top. The room tilted, she staggered, flailing the air as she tried to regain her balance.

"YOU'RE A GOOD DANCER, HONEY PIE!" The old man energetically gave her another spin.

Faith blushed, wishing the dance floor would open up and swallow her. By now the other dancers had cleared a path, laughing at the funny spectacle. She, with her hair loosely flying, trying to match the spry old man's steps. She flew past Liza and witnessed her mortification at the unseemly exhibition.

Suddenly a large arm firmly encircled Faith's waist, halting the fiasco. She looked up to meet familiar cool blue eyes.

"May I cut in, Rollie?"

"EH?"

"Cut in—dance with my fiancée!"

"EH? DIDN'T SAY NOTHIN'! I'M DANCIN'!"

Nicholas leaned closer and shouted in Zimmer's good ear. "I WANT TO DANCE WITH MY FIANCÉE."

"WELL, WHY DIDN'T YOU SAY SO?" Rollie relinquished his hold on Faith, his ferretlike eyes spotting Widow Cumming sitting on the sidelines. When she saw his intentions, she bolted from the bench and headed for the front door. Rollie followed, hot on her heels.

The music slowed to a calming waltz. Nicholas lightly held Faith in his arms at a proper distance. She was surprised to find he danced flawlessly, gliding her effortlessly around the crowded floor. She wondered who had taught him the art. Beautiful Rachel, perhaps?

"Thank you," she murmured, remembering her manners.

He gazed down on her, amusement creasing the corners of his eyes. "For what?"

"For coming to my rescue. I . . ." He smiled, distracting

her. Her stomach did somersaults. Why didn't he do that more often?

"I must say, you and Rollie made a pathetic sight."

She bit back a grin. She liked him immensely when he wasn't so serious. "I don't suppose we'd win any contests."

He drew her closer, renouncing propriety. "I can't imagine anyone letting you enter one."

Faith felt strangely right in his arms. She could smell the tangy scent of soap, the sun-dried scent of his shirt. She quickly located Liza and grinned when she saw that Jeremiah had her cornered.

Resting her head on Nicholas's broad shoulder, Faith sighed. Perhaps the evening wouldn't be so boring after all.

Thank you, Lord. Faith. That's what I've needed, to hang on in faith. I'm believing that you're going to keep helping Nicholas to come around.

Chapter Eight

LIZA placed a steaming bowl of gravy on the table, then took her seat. Nicholas said a prayer, and the day's routine began.

With Rachel's image still vivid in Faith's mind, she had dressed in the blue gingham this morning. She might as well have worn a burlap sack for all of Nicholas's interest.

The memory of Rachel's beauty haunted Faith. Rachel was so pretty, and Nicholas had once been in love with her. Was he still?

Well, one thing Faith was grateful for—if Nicholas didn't acknowledge her appearance this morning, he certainly wasn't going to notice the brown boots hidden beneath the hem. She couldn't wear those pointy shoes one more day.

Faith took a bite of biscuit, reviewing her talk with Jeremiah the night before. Teaching Adam to read excited her.

She had always eagerly embraced a challenge—especially when nothing but good could come of it. In this particular situation her direction wasn't quite clear, but her mind was made up. If Jeremiah could provide a channel by which she could purchase the Braille teaching material, she would teach Adam to read.

She had a small nest egg from her teaching funds. Aunt Thalia had insisted she keep the money she earned, so she'd set aside as much as she could spare from her daily expenses. She could think of no worthier cause for the money. She'd spent the better part of the night praying and asking God's guidance. Knowing she'd have the Shepherds to deal with, Faith had searched her mind for all possible arguments. She took comfort in knowing that, regardless of the outcome, her priorities were in proper order.

Last night Jeremiah had planted some powerful images in her mind. Little Adam, unknowingly, strengthened those thoughts. The idea of teaching Dan's son to read Braille quickly escalated. One little boy . . . then maybe another child, and then another. How many blind people lived in the area? Perhaps adults would come; perhaps she could start a school. . . . She pondered the creation of an institution that would serve hundreds of others.

She had been tempted to share her enthusiasm with Nicholas and Liza during the ride home last night. But Liza had seemed on edge. She sat in her usual place between them, fanning and grumbling about how close the air was. Faith wasn't sure if Liza's annoyance was due to Jeremiah's obvious attraction to her, or to Rollie Zimmer's spectacle on the dance floor. Whatever the reason, Faith hadn't mentioned her talk with Jeremiah.

She must wait for the proper time to discuss her idea of teaching the blind. . . . Studying Liza's and Nicholas's stoic faces, she feared there might never be a proper time. Her excitement couldn't be contained another moment. She had to tell someone before she burst!

Lifting her napkin, she blotted her mouth with the stiff muslin. "Nicholas, I've been thinking. . . ."

Nicholas and Liza lifted their heads in unison.

Faith's courage momentarily flagged, then revitalized. "Is this an appropriate time?"

Liza frowned. "We don't discuss trivialities during meal-time."

"My thoughts aren't trivial, Mother Shepherd." Faith tempered her inclination to scream.

Nicholas calmly poured cream into his coffee. "Mama, let her speak."

"Nicholas, we—"

"Let her speak, Mama." Nicholas nodded to Faith. "What is it, Faith?"

Faith hoped her gratitude showed in her eyes. "Thank you. Jeremiah and I had a talk last night. If it's all right with you and Mother Shepherd, I would like to teach Adam Walters to read." When objection flared in Liza's eyes, Faith hurried on. "Of course, I'll have to speak to Dan, but I'm hoping that if I'm successful in obtaining his permission, then I might teach other blind in the area to read."

"Hogwash and dishwater."

Nicholas pushed the cream pitcher aside. "You surely have a way with words, Mama."

"Don't use that tone with me, Nicholas Shepherd! You'll be taking your breakfast outside to eat with the dogs!"

"We don't have dogs."

"Well, let me tell you—if we did, you'd be eating with them. I'll not tolerate disrespect!"

The conversation was disintegrating. Faith didn't intend to be dissuaded from her purpose. Her mouth opened, intent on saying something she'd no doubt regret. But Aunt Thalia's calming words of biblical wisdom reverberated softly in her spirit. *Be slow to anger, and sin not. . . .*

Biting her bottom lip, Faith moderated her tone, "My family always shared conversation at the dinner table—"

"Well, this isn't dinner," Liza said.

"I'm *going* to teach Adam to *read.*" There. She'd said it. Faith waited for the explosion.

To her relief, none was forthcoming. Liza's mouth dropped open; Nicholas simply eyed her with curiosity.

She could see they both clearly thought she had lost her mind.

"In all my born days—are you addled? Dan's boy is blind." Liza shook her head. "How do you propose to teach a blind child to read?"

Faith blushed. "I'm going to learn Braille and then—"

"Braille? Those dot things?" Liza shook her head again. "Doesn't make a bit of difference what you learn, you can't open that boy's eyes."

"By using Braille, Mother Shepherd, Adam can learn to read. And not just Dan's son, others can too."

"What others? I don't know any others."

"Maybe not in Deliverance. But there are undoubtedly many in Texas, and once the blind school—"

Nicholas interrupted. "Are you saying a blind child can be taught to read?"

"Yes," Faith said proudly. "And taught many other things. Learning to read is only the beginning."

Liza looked faint, sitting back in her chair to fan herself.

"You call this method Braille?" Nicholas asked.

"Yes, Braille."

"And how is it you seem to know—"

It was all the encouragement Faith needed. Sliding to the edge of her chair, she explained. "Grandpapa was born in Coupvray, near Paris. As children, he and Louis Braille played together in the village. When Mr. Braille was very small, he was blinded in an accident."

She was pleased to see that Nicholas was listening closely. She relayed the story of Louis and how he had developed the Braille system.

"Grandpapa took great pleasure in telling of his boyhood friendship with Louis. As the years passed, they didn't spend as much time together, but they continued to correspond with each other. They did so until Mr. Braille died in '52."

"If this Mr. Braille was blind, how was he able to teach others like him?"

"Blind leading the blind," Liza muttered.

"Mother." Nicholas sent her a censuring look.

"No—she's right, Nicholas. In a sense, that's exactly what happened."

"How did Louis Braille teach blind children to make sense of a bunch of dots on a piece of cardboard?" Liza exclaimed.

Faith was more than happy to tell her. "It only took Louis five years to develop the system. From what I've read in journals, Mr. Braille created his dot system using six dots. From sixty-three possible arrangements of the dots, he devised an entire alphabet, punctuation marks, numerals, and later even a means for writing music!"

Faith knew Liza would never admit to it, but even her curiosity was obviously kindled. "From a bunch of dots?"

"Not just dots. Each letter, numeral, or punctuation mark is indicated by the number and arrangement of one to six dots in a cell, or letter space, two dots wide and three dots high."

Liza's skepticism returned. "Dots, spots, or knots! The blind can't see to read them."

"That's true. But Braille books are pressed from metal plates. The sightless read Braille by feel—running their fingers over the dots."

"I think you were out in the sun too long yesterday." Liza reached for a second biscuit. "And just how far will running fingers over a bunch of dots help that poor Walters boy?"

"Plenty," Faith defended herself. "Louis Braille was an outstanding student, excelling in science and music. In fact, he became famous in Paris as an organist and as a violoncellist. Not to mention a *church* organist."

Liza's eyes softened with respect. "He learned to play organ in the church?"

Faith nodded. "Yes, and other blind children can be taught to do the same, and more."

Nicholas studied her. "But you said you'd need to learn this Braille?"

"My, yes. Coupvray was long before my time. When Mother was a baby, her parents immigrated to this country. I was born in Michigan. Grandpapa used to tell us stories about Louis Braille. I was always fascinated by Grandpapa's good friend and paid attention to every detail. But I've never had access to a Braille book. I intend to exhaust every opportunity to find one. With Jeremiah's help, I know I can learn."

"Jeremiah! What could that old coot know about Braille?" Liza snapped.

"I don't know—but I have a feeling he knows more than he's saying. He's promised to do all he can to help me."

Liza cleaned her plate and pushed back from the table. "Helping little Adam Walters is one thing, but a blind school—that's a horse of a different color."

"Blind children should have the same advantages as sighted children."

"An entire school for one blind child? That's nonsense."

"The school wouldn't be just for Adam. We could invite others."

Nicholas laid his fork aside. "You know, Mama, there are some other blind people I know about. What about Gregory

Hillman, and that Bittle girl? Are you thinking you'd teach children and adults, Faith?"

"Yes, children and adults!"

"Nonsense! A school costs money, money the town doesn't have. Nicholas, talk some sense into her."

After a moment's thought, Nicholas said, "A blind school makes more sense than a steeple. You would need a building—I suppose we could look into the Smith place."

Faith could barely contain her excitement. "The Smith place?"

"It's been abandoned for years and getting to be an eyesore. It could serve as a school," Nicholas conceded. "The old schoolhouse has plenty of room. Until the blind school has enough pupils to keep you busy, perhaps the school can be used not only for the children but, if you're willing, also for teaching adults who don't know how to read. Lord knows, there's enough men and women around here who can't read a thing." He smiled. "I think your idea is sound, Faith."

Liza was predictably quick to spoil the mood. "And who's going to pay for cleaning up that eyesore, not to mention acquiring the property?"

Faith glanced to Nicholas for support. "Wouldn't the town help—?"

Liza cut in. "Help, help, help. That's all I ever hear. Why is it when people holler help, what they really mean is money! Why don't they just come right out and say what they mean? Money. You know why. Because a fool and his money are soon parted."

Faith was sorely tempted to stand up and fight for her cause, but she declined. Papa said you shouldn't kill a fly on a friend's head using a hatchet, and though Liza wasn't exactly a friend, she did control the Shepherd purse strings.

Faith allowed the subject to drop. But she wasn't about to forget it. If she could teach Adam and others like him to read, that's what she was going to do. The Lord had laid the mission on her heart, and she gladly accepted it.

When breakfast was over, Nicholas excused himself and left the house. Faith knew he was getting ready for the upcoming cattle drive. For the first time she resented Liza for having such a hold on her son, and Nicholas more, for allowing it. She'd had Nicholas on her side until Liza threw on the wet blanket.

"The morning's near spent," Liza said, clearing the table. "We have chores."

Faith reached for an apron. "I'll feed the chickens."

"Don't stay out there all day."

"No, ma'am. I won't."

Faith barely finished sprinkling feed in the chicken coop when Liza rounded the corner. Her unexpected visit startled Faith. The hens set to cackling and flapping their wings. Faith snickered, thinking how Liza could intimidate even the least of God's creatures.

"It's butchering time. There's pig's feet waiting to be put up," Liza informed her. "I need your help in the kitchen."

Pig's feet. Faith's heart sank. That would take all day. She hated pig's feet. The mere sight of those boney-looking hoofy paws made her sick.

"Yes, ma'am." She set aside the feed bag, latched the weathered gate, and followed Liza into the house.

As she entered the kitchen, she tried not to look at the huge pan of feet. Jars lined the counter. Did Liza intend to feed an army? She would be stuck in this kitchen forever.

Liza sat down across from Faith at the table, and the two women set to work.

Faith stuffed pig's feet into jars until her fingers ached. Still, her pan was half full. Liza finished her share with remarkable speed.

She eyed Faith's pan, sighing with impatience. "I'll wash more jars. You fetch more water."

Faith drew two buckets of water from the open well and hurried back inside. Though her heart wasn't in it, she knew the harder she worked, the quicker she could escape the kitchen and those hateful feet.

Liza washed and dried the remaining canning jars. Stuffing the last foot into a jar around noon, Faith drew a sigh of relief. Her fingers ached, not to mention her sore back.

It took both women to carry the cumbersome load to the stove.

As the water started to boil, Liza picked up a basket of dirty laundry. "I'll be doing wash. Don't let the pan boil dry."

"Yes, ma'am."

Faith was amazed how quickly her enthusiasm rekindled about the school for the blind. She would just explode if she didn't tell someone.

Hope and June. They were happily married now, without

all the problems she faced; still, they would understand her excitement about the school.

Her sisters would be delighted to hear of her grand adventure. Faith glanced at the pot of boiling pig's feet. Liza's "don't let the pan boil dry" sounded in her mind. The pan looked just fine, she determined, before going to her room for the stationery Aunt Thalia had given her.

Sitting back down at the kitchen table, she wrote Hope first.

My dearest Hope,

It is with great sadness that I write, for I sorely miss you. You are always in my thoughts and my prayers. Have you any word from June or Aunt Thalia? I pray for a letter. I suppose it takes a good many days for such correspondence to reach Texas. This land is so big; most of the time I feel as though I've gone to another country.

There are so many times my heart aches for the three of us to be together again, with Aunt Thalia, in Cold Water. I often wonder if Deliverance will ever be my home . . . a home like the three of us shared, with laughter and happy times. There is very little laughter and virtually no happy times here.

I have no intention of doubting the good Lord's ability to know what is best for me, but I admit that at times my faith falters. I wonder if I have made a mistake in understanding his direction. Deliverance seems to be anything but a place where I belong.

Dreary is a word that describes my present situation. Now that I think about it, the calamity started mere miles before I arrived. The stagecoach broke down just outside of Deliverance. A kind man named

*Jeremiah was generous enough to bring me into town on the back of a
donkey. . . .*

*I am yet to be a bride, though several attempts have been undertaken.
You will not believe the obstacles; still, I will share them with you.
Perhaps in doing so, we may have ourselves a hearty laugh or two.
It's far more uplifting than crying, which I'm often tempted to do.*

Faith then wrote all about the wedding delays, her spoiled
dress, and Mary Ellen's birthing twins. As she wrote, she
sometimes wiped away a tear, and sometimes giggled.

*Now Nicholas informs me the wedding must be postponed yet another
two weeks. He is leaving soon to drive cattle to San Antonio, where
they will be sold and herded up the Chisholm Trail to somewhere in
Abilene or Wichita. Nicholas is a puzzling man, but one I think I
could grow to love. At times he seems tied to his mother's apron
strings, but I think he only appeases her because he's worried about
her. If I didn't believe that, if I didn't believe there was still hope for
us, I would be on my way back to Michigan this very moment.*

*I know this letter must leave you disheartened. But blessings do
abound. There is a very nice young widower, Dan Walters. His
struggles are many. But he's taken time to be very kind to me and is a
perfect gentleman in the truest respect. His wife died giving birth to his
daughter. The baby's a darling nine-month-old named Lilly. Dan says
she is the image of her mother. Dan also has two other children. Sissy,
who's three years old and full of vinegar, and Adam, as rambunctious
as any five-year-old, except that he is blind. He has been since birth.*

*But don't be sad, my precious Hope. This is where the good news
starts. I have the utmost intentions of learning Braille, and as quickly*

as possible. Jeremiah, the hermit I told you about, is trying to help me get some Braille books. I want—I have a burning need—to teach Adam to read. Perhaps that is my calling, the true reason God has brought me to Deliverance. After all, the way things are going, it's beginning to look like a wedding isn't the purpose for my journey. Ha. Yes, you may laugh. But not hysterically.

Hope, whatever the Lord has me do, I willingly rejoice in his labor. When I think of Adam and all of the possibilities, my heart sings. I think of the Scripture "and a child shall lead them." Perhaps, though Adam's eyes are now darkened, he will yet be able to shed light, giving hope and a measure of deliverance to others with the same affliction. You can see how desperate I am to be even the smallest part of that miracle. And not just for Adam, though I love him dearly. There are many who live in darkness, longing for a brighter way. I have this dream of starting a school to help all the blind who will come learn how to read.

My dear sister, I ask that you unite with me in prayer concerning this matter. I know that you will, and God's will shall be done.

I truly wish that Nicholas would stand up to his mother more. He has the patience of Job with that woman. Although I pray every night for God to give me more patience, I still find it very hard to still my fiery tongue.

Faith penned a similar letter to June. Writing to her sisters eased the homesickness she'd been battling for days. She addressed and sealed each envelope with care. It felt so good to share her feelings with someone who would understand.

She suddenly sat up straighter, catching a whiff of a foul odor.

The pan! Faith sprang from her chair and dashed to the stove. The pan was bone-dry. Jars exploded, sending a plume of steam and pig's feet spiraling toward the ceiling. Feet belched from the pan like hot ash.

Throwing her arms over her head, Faith ducked as thousands of boney particles rained down on her. When the explosion died off, the room turned deadly silent.

Horrified, she viewed the carnage. Shattered glass from broken jars littered counters and floors. Pieces of pig's feet hung from the ceiling. Nothing could be salvaged. Not even the pan.

Smoke stung Faith's eyes; the odor was sickening.

Fanning with a dish towel, she glanced outside and groaned when she saw Liza coming toward the house, empty laundry basket tucked beneath her arm.

Sinking into a chair at the kitchen table, Faith braced herself for the approaching storm.

It was likely to be a dandy.

Chapter Nine

DUSTING the oak sideboard, Liza's hands suddenly stilled. Picking up a small picture frame, she smiled. "Good morning, Abe. I miss you, darling." Her fingertips lovingly traced the features of her beloved's face smiling back at her. Abe. Husband, lover, best friend. When would the awful pain ease? Friends said, "Time, Liza. Time will heal your loss." But time had failed to change anything. Would she ever go to bed at night without automatically reaching for the comfort of Abe's arms? He had been her protector, her mentor, the reason she got up every morning. And he was gone.

Evenings she used to look up from her handwork and see him sitting beside her, reading a journal, spectacles riding on the bridge of his nose. Tonight when she looks up, she will see his empty chair.

She kept the furniture covered now, unable to cope with memories. Abe had made every single piece; worked for years to build whatever she wanted. She couldn't bear to look at the furnishings now; it just inflicted fresh wounds.

She had prayed—oh how she had prayed—that when it was time, God would take Abe and her together in order to spare the other agony. It was a selfish wish; she knew that. God had called Abe first. Now only she remained to look after their son.

Nicholas was a dutiful boy, but a son couldn't take his father's place. Not in matters of the heart.

Alarmed, Liza's hand came to her throat as the familiar thump vibrated in her chest. She needed to see Doc about her worsening condition, yet she was frightened, afraid Doc would tell her there was something horribly wrong: She was going to die.

At times she felt she'd welcome death. Since Abe had died, Liza thought of the grave more as a friend than an enemy. Dying didn't concern her, for she knew in whom she believed. Her concern lay with Nicholas. If she were gone, who would see to his needs? Who would love him, care for him? She'd prayed daily for the Lord to send a good woman into Nicholas's life—a woman, not a scatterbrained child from Michigan! Her heart skipped erratically. *Oh, Abe, I'm in desperate need of assurance that our child will have someone to rely on when I'm gone—and God has sent a twit.*

Liza wanted a home for Nicholas, a wife, children. She wanted to die with the certainty that he was happy, surrounded by those he loved. But Nicholas no longer believed in love. She saw the way he looked at Rachel, as though still convinced that she was the one woman who would have made him happy. Liza didn't for a minute agree with him. Rachel's passive nature would never mix with Nicholas's proud spirit Actually, Faith was more suited to Nicholas's nature. . . .

Odd how that just came to her. Of course, those pig's feet. . . . A grin hovered at the corners of her mouth. Land sakes . . . all those pieces of feet clinging to the ceiling. Her smile died.

Liza knew her "condition" made her impossible to live with lately, but she still had a clear mind—most of the time. More often than not, her conversations with her son ended in arguments. Lately, Nicholas had been predisposed to silence; she supposed it was an effort to keep the peace.

Her fingers tenderly retraced the photograph of her smiling husband, arm in arm with his son in the field. The photograph was old and tattered, like her heart. Abe was very handsome. . . . Nicholas looked so much like his father. She bit back tears, aching to hear her husband's voice, the sound of his silly laugh. . . .

Tears rolled down her cheeks, and her heart thumped. Emptiness settled in the pit of her stomach as she blindly set the picture down and dusted around it. All the tears in the world wouldn't bring Abe back. He was gone. When was she ever going to face it?

She missed Nicholas. Faith was startled by the admission, but it was true. She missed Nicholas. This strange man she'd agreed to take as a husband had been gone for over a week, and the days were endless without him.

Though Nicholas had barely acknowledged her presence, when he was around, the house seemed warmer, more bearable.

On the rare occasions when she experienced his smile or enjoyed his laugh, she was filled with the outrageous need for him to like her. She enjoyed seeing him read his Bible at night by the fire, looking so strong and confident. And she was sure his submissive way toward Liza was out of kindness, not weakness. Given the slightest encouragement, she might easily fall in love with this tall, somber man.

Nicholas practiced his faith more quietly than most men, yet it ran true and strong in his veins. True, there were times it seemed mother and son were set upon by the devil himself, determined to suck every shred of Christian joy out of their lives.

And yet . . . he could be kind. She smiled when she recalled how Nicholas had pulled her aside just before leaving. Concern colored his eyes, and he'd instructed her in a strong, confident voice, "You take care of yourself—don't be delivering any calves or shooting any snakes while I'm gone. Be in before dark, and if Mama gets on your nerves, go visit Mary Ellen. You hear?"

She'd nodded, feeling all warm inside. It had sounded almost as if he cared—honestly cared—about her welfare. He was such a puzzlement: stern one minute, irresistible the next.

Faith had known other Christians like the Shepherds.

Papa had called them suffering Christians. Those who accepted Christ but took no joy in living. All was law, and Christianity a sentence to be practiced conscientiously until God called them home. Faith felt that Christians should be the happiest folks around. What loss God must feel when his children failed to live a rich, full life.

Rinsing a skillet, Faith laid it aside. Perhaps Nicholas liked her more than she thought. There'd been times lately when he had acted like a smitten suitor. When other men had shown her attention—particularly Dan—Nicholas's mouth tightened, and he made her stop whatever she was doing and join him. The corners of her mouth turned up. She shouldn't take delight in his insecurity, and she certainly didn't encourage it; but she had to admit she rather enjoyed Nicholas's attention.

Dan was always grateful for her help. Considering the failed wedding attempts, Faith wondered if God had maybe sent her to Dan . . . to be a mother to his children rather than an unappreciated guest in the Shepherd house.

Folding the dishcloth, she draped it over a drying rack, then bent to pick up a stray piece of pig's feet she'd missed the day before. She never would have dreamed the chaos those exploding jars of pig's feet could cause. She'd thought Liza would faint when she saw the kitchen. But after her first bewildered stare, she had begun to grin, then chuckle, and before they knew it, the two women were laughing until the tears trickled down their cheeks. Faith shook her head. There was no figuring that woman out. After their laughter died down, Liza had said, "Of course, you'll have to clean it all up. Nicholas will be disappointed; he loves pig's feet." A grin hovered around the corners of her mouth. "To tell the truth, I've always detested them. But the neighbors know how much Nicholas likes them, and they supply him with all he can eat." Then, before Faith could say a word, she had turned around and left the kitchen.

Straightening, Faith focused on the small tin of snuff sitting on the counter. Such a tasteless habit. Why did Liza insist on chewing? Reaching for the tin, she quickly disposed of it. Perhaps Liza would rid herself of the habit if temptation weren't so readily at hand. If Faith could find that brown vial Liza kept in her apron pocket, she'd throw that away too!

She called to Mother Shepherd in the parlor. "Would it be all right if I took the buggy into town this morning?" Closing her eyes, she held her breath, waiting for the answer. It would be her first outing alone since she'd arrived in Deliverance, but if she didn't escape Liza's critical eye for a few hours, she was going to scream. She would hitch the buggy and go into town. She needed a few personal items from the mercantile, and while she was at it, she wanted to visit the land office to inquire about the Smith house. Nicholas and Liza hadn't approved her starting the school for the blind, but they hadn't forbidden her to start one either.

Liza poked her head around the kitchen doorway. "Why do you want to go into town?"

"Well . . ." Faith worried her teeth against her lower lip. She could fib. She could pretend she desperately needed something personal from the mercantile, and Liza wouldn't know the difference unless she went out of her way to check with Oren Stokes.

Papa's voice echoing Leviticus rang in her mind: "Ye shall not steal, neither deal falsely, neither lie one to another."

Drats. "Well . . . I thought it might be neighborly to stop by Mary Ellen's and see if she needed help with the new babies."

Not exactly her intended purpose for going into town, but neither was it an outright lie. She could easily stop by the Finney place.

Liza took a hanky from her bodice and fanned herself. "Nonsense. Mary Ellen can see after her own children. Have you seen my box of snuff?"

"No, ma'am." Faith's cheeks burned with the falsehood. *Forgive me, Lord; it's for her own good.* She stepped aside as Liza entered the kitchen, the older woman's eyes searching for the familiar tin.

Faith clasped her hands behind her back and trailed behind her. "I was thinking that Mary Ellen and her family might enjoy a fresh-baked cherry pie."

Liza's muffled voice floated down to her as she rummaged through a drawer. "Flour and sugar don't grow on trees, Miss Kallahan."

"But cherries do, Mother Shepherd." Liza had seen enough canned cherries in the pantry to feed a horse. "May I go?"

"Oh, very well." Liza closed the drawer. "You may take

the buggy, but don't be wearing out your welcome, you hear?"

"Yes, ma'am. Thank you! I won't be long!"

Faith ran to change into a dress with Liza's strident voice close on her heels. "Can't imagine what happened to my snuff lately. I've bought three cans this week!"

It was past noon by the time Faith hitched up the buggy, then tucked the fresh-baked pie into a secure corner. The crusty brown pastry was still hot to the touch. Climbing aboard, she picked up the reins, aware that Liza was standing in the doorway, watching her departure.

"You be back here before dark!"

"Yes, ma'am."

Snapping the reins, Faith set the horse into motion. The animal trotted briskly out of the barnyard as Liza stepped out on the porch, cupping her hands to her mouth. "And don't be running the wheels off that buggy!"

"Yes, ma'am! No, ma'am." Faith leaned out the side and waved. "I won't!"

Glorious sunshine beat down on the top of the buggy. Faith drew a deep breath, inhaling the sweet scent of honeysuckle growing wild along the roadside. Free at last! The horse stepped high as if he, too, welcomed the unexpected freedom.

The buggy rolled by fertile pastures and running creeks. Faith waved at a farmer in a nearby field, busy putting up hay. The tangy scent tickled her nose and made her sneeze. The farmer rested on his scythe, tipping his hat to her as the buggy raced by.

Mary Ellen was hanging wash when the Shepherd buggy rolled to a stop in front of the small dwelling. Chickens milled around the front stoop. Two coonhounds lay beneath the porch, cooling their bellies against the packed dirt.

Leaving her basket of wash, Mary Ellen ran to greet her. Children streamed out of the house, and the dogs set up a loud ruckus.

"Glad you stopped by!" Mary Ellen brushed a piece of hair out of her eyes. "It gets real lonely with no one but the kids to talk to."

Faith handed her the cherry pie, then patted a youngster on the head. "I can't stay long, but I'll be glad to do anything I can to give you a rest."

Time flew as the women chatted and folded diapers. Faith hadn't wanted to put the babies down, but she knew if she was to complete her mission in town and be home by dark, she couldn't linger. It was close to two when Faith climbed back into the buggy.

As she entered the land office, a cheerful-looking lady glanced up from behind a battered wooden desk. The gold nameplate read "Evelyn Williams." Evelyn's friendly blue eyes immediately put Faith at ease. "You're Nicholas's new bride."

"Not yet, but I'm trying." Faith grinned.

The matronly woman chuckled, shoving her considerable bulk to her feet. "Heard you two are having a hard time tying the knot."

"I never realized getting married could be so hard." Faith

149

briefly explained the three delays and how Nicholas had now taken his cattle to market.

"Well," the woman said with a wink, "Nicholas is a man well worth waiting for. Why, half the women in Deliverance have been waitin' on him."

Faith frowned. "For what?"

"For him to make up his mind who he's gonna marry!" Twinkling eyes scanned Faith, and Evelyn's smile widened. "Looks like he's picked a real beauty."

Faith blushed, clearing her throat. No one had ever accused her of being a beauty. Hope was the only Kallahan who could claim that distinction. "I've come to inquire about the Smith house."

"Bert and Betty's place?"

"Yes, ma'am . . . I was wondering what the state planned to do with the homestead."

Evelyn grimaced. "Land sakes, don't rightly know. Are the Shepherds interested in buying it?"

"No," Faith said. "And I'd appreciate it if you wouldn't mention my interest just yet." No use stirring up a hornet's nest with Liza if she didn't have to. "I've been thinking about starting a school, and the house looks ideal for what I have in mind."

Evelyn frowned. "Town's got a school."

"Not this kind of school. I want to start a school for the blind."

"A school for the blind?" Evelyn's brows bunched tighter. "A school for the blind. Well, guess there's a few in the area who'd benefit by a school for the blind."

"There might be lots."

"Yes . . . there's Dan Walters's boy. Land sakes, that boy's got ants in his britches! He'd not sit still long enough to learn anything!"

"Adam's exceptionally bright, Mrs. Williams. He just needs his energy channeled. I want to teach Adam, and others like him, to read and write and cipher as good or better than children with sight." Faith could feel her excitement rising every time she thought about it. To be able to make a difference enthralled her. "And if at first there aren't enough blind students, then I can teach adults in the community to read and write."

"Yes, guess you could. There are a few around here who'd like to learn to read. The Bittle girl's blind, you know—old enough to go to school now—and Gregory— he'd like going to school. Sixteen years old now, hard to believe."

Evelyn stepped to the file drawer and rifled through a stack of folders. Moments later she extracted a file, her eyes scanning the contents. She glanced up, smiling. "Looks to me like Bert's place can be bought for back taxes."

Faith's smile faded. Back taxes. Her heart sank. She had her teaching money, but that probably wouldn't be enough. Nicholas and Liza hadn't said she couldn't start the school, but she knew without asking that Liza would never back the project. She swallowed. "How much?"

Evelyn shook her head, still perusing the sheet of paper. "Doesn't say . . . but I'll find out." Slipping the file back into the cabinet, she shut the drawer. "Come back Saturday, and I'll have the information for you."

Faith smiled. "Thank you . . . and Mrs. Williams?"

"Call me Evelyn, dear."

Faith nodded. "Don't forget what I said about not mentioning my visit to anyone."

Evelyn brushed her concern aside. "I'll not say a word, but you'll have a difficult time keeping something like this from Liza very long."

Faith was in a good mood when she left the land office. In a few days she'd know for certain whether the Smith house could be purchased. She had no idea where she'd get the money, but she planned to pray long and hard about it. If the school was meant to be, God would provide the means. Faith brightened when she spotted Jeremiah unloading a wagon in front of the mercantile.

Waving, she ran to meet him as the hermit heaved a large crate off the wagon. For a man his age, he still had remarkable agility.

He smiled as she approached. "You look pretty as a rose in January. What's put the bloom in your face this fine day?"

Faith could barely contain her enthusiasm. "I was just talking to Mrs. Williams at the land office. She says the Smith place might be bought for as little as back taxes! Isn't that wonderful! I can start my school for the blind there."

Setting the crate on the steps, Jeremiah pulled a handkerchief out of his pocket and mopped his forehead. The late afternoon sun bore down on the town. "Sounds reasonable enough—if a body had the money for the back taxes."

Faith sat down on the lower step of the porch to visit. "It might not be so much. Mrs. Williams will know the exact amount in a few days."

Jeremiah removed his hat, wiping the brim with a kerchief. "It's a worthy goal you're attempting, but a mighty big undertaking you've set upon, young lady. Have you talked to Dan about your idea? Might be he won't allow Adam to attend your school."

"What father wouldn't want to see his child educated and offered a better life?"

Reaching the back of the wagon, Jeremiah lifted another crate onto the sidewalk.

"Don't suppose you've mentioned your plans to Nicholas or Liza."

"I mentioned it," she admitted.

"And?"

"No use getting them all upset until I see if the Smith place is affordable." She sat up straighter. "Have you been able to locate Braille teaching material?"

Jeremiah glanced away. "I wired a friend . . . he might be of help, when everything else is in place."

"Well." Faith sat back. "If all goes well, I plan to start teaching Adam by fall. And I'm going to send out letters to the other people Nicholas told me about, inviting them, too. I can teach folks to read while the blind school is getting started." As she spoke, she realized she'd just decided. There was no use delaying the project.

"Fall, huh? That's pretty optimistic thinking, young lady. Aren't you forgetting something?"

Faith looked up.

"What if Nicholas doesn't want his wife running a school for the blind? What if he forbids you to open the doors?"

Faith hadn't considered the possibility. Nicholas was a God-fearing man, and God-fearing men were committed to do all within their power to help others. . . . Besides, Nicholas had encouraged her. But Liza hadn't. What if Liza forbade her to teach? Would Nicholas stand by her if Liza opposed her?

"Guess I'll cross that bridge when I come to it," Faith admitted. She fervently hoped she wouldn't have to cross it at all.

Jeremiah paused, resting on the side of the wagon. "Lot of work to be done before a school can materialize. You'll need three paying students just to open the doors."

Faith stared off into the distance. Dan was preparing to shoe a horse in front of the livery. The rhythmic clang of his hammer against the anvil filled the air. "And it'll take a lot of hands to repair, paint, and fix up that old house."

Jeremiah nodded. "We're not just talking about donated time. You'll need food, cots, blankets, supplies. Then there are Braille books, wood for heating and cooking, kerosene for the lanterns. . . ."

Faith listened as the list went on and on. Everything Jeremiah said was true, but she held fast to the belief that God had sent her to Deliverance for a purpose, and that purpose was looking less and less like she was intended to be a help-mate to Nicholas.

Sighing, she got to her feet. "There's still a lot of work to be done, but my mind is set, Jeremiah. When Nicholas gets back, I'll ask his help."

"That should be interesting." Jeremiah turned to load another crate.

Faith brushed dirt off the back of her dress. "I have to be going. I promised Liza I'd be home before dark." She brightened. "Would you like to eat dinner with us?"

When Jeremiah met her suggestion with a wry look and a quick shake of his head, she giggled, thinking of Liza's reaction should he accept such an invitation.

"Well, perhaps another time."

Jeremiah nodded. "Perhaps . . . if hell ever freezes over."

A week later, Liza made her purchases at the feed store and started home. She felt faint from the heat. Mopping her forehead, she wondered what was wrong with her lately. The sudden waves of heat ignited her body, as if she'd been soaked in kerosene and had a lit match thrown on her. She was jolted awake in the middle of the night, drenched in sweat, her heart pounding. Was her heart giving out? Yes, that was it. The Lord had heard her prayers. Once Nicholas married, God planned to call her home.

She looked in the opposite direction as the wagon rolled past Doc's office. She couldn't tell a man her problems. He'd laugh and tell her to go home and rest. Rest. She hand-fanned her face as another hot spell assaulted her. She'd like to see him rest with the fires of Hades licking at his britches. She could consult Vera, but Vera would tell Molly, and Molly would tell Etta, and the whole town would know her problems by morning.

The wagon passed the mercantile, and she quickly averted her head. Jeremiah. That old fool. Why had he started coming around? For years he had avoided people, but lately he was everywhere she looked. He dressed decently these days; his hair was cut to a respectable length. Her lips thinned. He must have his eye on Widow Blackburn. The old fool.

The wagon rolled past the land office, and wheeled out of town. Liza's heart hammered against her ribs. She felt as if an invisible hand had hold of her throat. She had to get home to be by herself!

Whipping the horse, she pushed the animal on. The wagon flew around the bend in the road, and the Smith house came into view. Faith's buggy was parked at the front stoop!

Sawing back on the reins, Liza slowed the horse. What would Faith be doing here? She was supposed to be helping Mary Ellen churn this morning.

Clicking her tongue, she turned the horse up the rutted lane.

Faith was down on her knees, humming as she scrubbed the worn floor. Plans for the school were moving much faster than she had expected. Evelyn had given her permission to clean the old house this morning. Even if the house never became a school for the blind, Evelyn agreed the town eyesore needed a good cleaning. Faith was thrilled. It was a monumental task, but once the town saw how the blind school was beginning to take shape, Faith hoped more people would get excited about it.

She was badly in need of able-bodied men to repair the outside, and Evelyn promised if the men came, the women would soon follow. She could use all the help she could get. Right after she helped Mary Ellen churn butter, she had left and gone directly to the land office, thinking Evelyn would have the information on the taxes. Instead, Evelyn had handed her a key and told her she was free to start cleaning whenever she wanted, predicting the money and help would come in.

Faith suddenly froze at the sound of Liza's strident voice.

"What is the meaning of this?"

Scrambling to her feet, Faith brushed damp hair back from her forehead. "Mother Shepherd! What are you doing here?"

Liza's eyes coldly assessed the bucket of suds.

Faith swallowed and hurried on. "I—I thought the place needed cleaning."

"You thought an empty homestead needed cleaning?"

"I . . ." Faith knew that sounded ridiculous. "Evelyn gave me permission."

"Why would Evelyn give you permission to trespass on the Smiths' property?"

"I'm not trespassing."

Liza's eyes narrowed. "Does this have something to do with your insane idea to open a blind school?"

Faith sighed. "Mother Shepherd, it's not an insane idea. Jeremiah's promised to help, and I—"

Liza cut her off sharply. "Get into the buggy."

"Mother Shepherd—"

"Into the buggy, young woman! You are making a laughingstock of the Shepherds! I won't have it!"

Faith had never once shown disrespect to an elder. Papa would've taken a switch to any one of his daughters who dared to talk back to a senior, but she didn't think he'd object to her standing up for herself.

"No."

Liza's brows shot up. "What did you say?"

"I said no . . . ma'am." Faith met her glacial stare. "I don't mean any disrespect, and it troubles me to disobey you, Mother Shepherd, but I've been given permission to start work on the school, and I intend to see it through."

"Have you lost your mind? Just where do you think you're going to get the money to start this school?"

"Well, I've been praying. . . ."

"The Lord isn't a fool, young lady. He doesn't answer every whim a headstrong young woman throws at him— and if you've got it in your mind the money's coming from Nicholas, you can just get it right out again! People around here think we're made of money! All this talk about new steeples and blind schools—it's enough to make a body want to scream. Now pick up that bucket and get in the buggy. I'll hear no more talk of this school for the blind. Do you understand me?"

"Yes, ma'am." Faith didn't move.

"Well? Pick up that bucket!"

"No, ma'am, because I'd just have to set it down again." Faith felt faint. She'd never stood her ground in such a bold manner, but the school was important—so important she was willing to fight for it.

Liza's face suffused with color. "Do I have to take a switch to you?"

Faith blushed. "No, ma'am. If you would only listen to reason—"

"Very well." Liza pinned her with a final look. "You will either pick up that bucket and come with me, or you needn't come home at all."

The threat hung between them.

"I can't do that," Faith said softly.

"You will do it, or you will be sent packing, young lady. You are not Nicholas's wife yet. This . . . this blind school is a matter that will require considerable thought—you can't just come in here and turn our lives upside down."

"I'm not starting the school today, Mother Shepherd. I'm only cleaning—"

"Don't sass me. Either get up and come with me now, or don't bother coming back to the house."

Faith mulled the ultimatum over in her mind. Where would she go? She couldn't go back to Aunt Thalia's. Aunt Thalia would turn her over her knee for certain when she learned Faith had deliberately disobeyed an elder, but she couldn't stay and live in a household where she wasn't wanted, either.

Liza tapped her foot. "Have you forgotten your purpose, Miss Kallahan? You were bought—purchased, by my son. Have you forgotten that?"

Faith recoiled from the spiteful words. *Purchased?* The hateful word was hostile, repugnant. God had sent her to Deliverance; Nicholas had sent for her, and Liza had no right to ask her to leave. When Faith married Nicholas, she had every intention of being an obedient wife. To Nicholas, not Liza. Was that what was bothering Liza? Was the school for the blind the real issue, or was it the knowledge that her son would soon belong to another woman that incited her?

"Are you going to answer me?"

Faith dropped to her knees and started scrubbing, closing her eyes against the sound of Liza's audible gasp. She had no idea where she would go, but she wasn't going back to that cold tomb the Shepherds called home.

"Very well. Your belongings will be on the front porch when you decide to pick them up. You had best find another place to stay, Miss Kallahan. You are no longer welcome in my house."

"What about Nicholas?" Faith murmured, afraid to look up.

"My son will do as I say." Liza turned to walk off, then turned to give Faith a cold stare. "I'll expect the buggy to be returned immediately."

Biting back tears, Faith scrubbed harder. The floor was old and chipped, but with work it would come clean. She looked up only when she heard Liza's buckboard rattle out of the yard.

Dear Lord. What would she do now? She had just been thrown out of the Shepherd house. She had failed God; she had failed Nicholas.

Burying her face in her hands, she sobbed.

Chapter Ten

I'M already missing home, Rusty."

As foreign as homesickness was to Nicholas, the realization was clear: He wasn't looking forward to the long trip. He was going to miss Faith. The thought was even more sobering when he conceded he barely knew the woman. Yet he was going to miss her. Her infectious zest for life, her spontaneous nature, her radiant smile had brought sunshine into the Shepherd household, something sadly missing for longer than he cared to remember.

"Well, it won't be long before the cattle are ready, Boss." Rusty whistled, steering a stray heifer back into the herd.

For six weeks the men had worked hard before Nicholas joined them, searing hot branding irons into the cattles' sides, marking them Shepherd beef. Sunup to sundown, the men worked, readying the cows for the cattle drive.

Nicholas smiled, missing his comfortable bed and hot meals already. The roundup was taking longer than Nicholas liked. For the past few days he'd worked the back range and shared a cabin with Rusty Treson, the trail boss. This morning the two men rode to the main bunkhouse. The men were up and saddling their horses, loading their Winchesters and securing bedrolls. Cook, Gabby Masters, was busy stocking the chuck wagon with beans, flour, cornmeal, coffee, lard, salt pork, bacon, and beef jerky. The drive was finally under way.

Thirteen days later Nicholas took off his Stetson, wiping sweat from his forehead as he eyed the hardy group. He studied the men, proud of his help. The men knew their jobs and always gave him a full day's work. There were a couple of tenderfeet in the crowd this year, but by the end of the drive, they'd be seasoned drovers. One cattle drive, even a short one, could determine a man's calling in life.

Nicholas's features sobered as he faced the cowboys. "You each know how much I appreciate the job you're doing. You've put in long hours and had little rest. But we still have our work cut out for us. Tonight's activities are bound to cause problems, but you men need a break from the tedious work. Have a good time, but remember, you're paid to work, not to play."

Nicholas knew that a few hours of relaxation would see them back, rested and brimming with enthusiasm. "Bear in mind the rules. No one comes back drunk, and everyone is to be in his bedroll by ten o'clock."

A good-natured groan went up.

"Ten o'clock," Nicholas reiterated. "There'll be a brief prayer service at sunup."

"How about extendin' the time to ten-thirty, Boss?" Gabby Masters grinned. A gold tooth glistened in the predawn light.

Nicholas gave the weathered old cook a good-natured frown. Nicholas couldn't recall Gabby ever leaving camp. "You know what's expected of you, Gabby. Just keep the biscuits and gravy coming."

Rusty spoke up. "We'll be on our best behavior, Mr. Shepherd. I guarantee it. Ain't that right, boys?"

A few nodded; some mumbled as they adjusted their spurs, tightened their chaps, and mounted their horses.

"Let's head 'em out!" Nicholas ordered, his high-spirited Appaloosa stirring up a trail of dust as he led the way.

This year's herd was larger than usual. The cattle plodded along with riders ahead, behind, and on both sides. Gabby, eating a lot of dust, followed behind the herd with the chuck wagon. At the end of the day, there wasn't a man in the pack who wasn't ready to climb out of his saddle and chow down. Gabby set up camp at the edge of a small, clear stream. By the time the men had washed up, supper was waiting.

The hungry drovers lined up at the chuck wagon.

"I've eaten more dust today than a cyclone," one of the men joked.

"A meal, fifteen minutes of shut-eye, then I'm headin' into town!" another declared.

Cook piled tin plates with salt pork, steaming beans, and biscuits. Gabby's generous helpings were guaranteed to stick to a man's ribs.

Nicholas poured scalding hot coffee into a tin cup, then leaned against a rock. He hoped the drive would end in San Antonio in a few days, maybe less. Faith filled his thoughts. Were she and Mama getting along? He grinned, taking a sip of the biting coffee. He sure hoped so.

The women reminded him of two ornery bulldogs staking out their territory. It had been slow coming, but now that he wasn't around, maybe they'd get along better. Mama needed to accept Faith; after he and Faith were married, she would be a comfort to Mama. He pictured them sitting in the parlor, stitching handwork as they talked about whatever women talked about. Later Mama would fix that tea she favored—maybe put a few of those lemon cookies on a fragile plate, and the two women would warm to each other.

He felt a twinge of guilt, realizing he hadn't been fair to Faith. He should have taken time to court her, let her get to know him. But with Mama acting so strange, hay to be put up, and the cattle drive, he'd neglected his intended bride. He planned to change that when he got home.

Pitching the remainder of his coffee into the fire, he decided to join the men in town.

As the cowboys crawled into their bedrolls later, they fell asleep listening to the night watch sing to the herd. A few weary snickers sounded from nearby bedrolls. Even Nicholas had to smile. No matter how off-key a cowboy sang, his voice had a soothing effect on the herd.

Camp had been asleep not more than an hour when the wind suddenly rose. In an instant, bolts of lightning lit up the churning sky. Thunder reverberated through the ground, and rain fell in blinding sheets.

"Watch the herd!" Nicholas shouted, and the men ran for their horses.

Cattle moved about restlessly. *Father, don't let the herd spook,* Nicholas prayed as he rode the perimeter of the camp. The storm passed, and the weary men spent the remainder of the night rounding up stray steers. The electrical storm would throw them yet another day behind schedule.

The men, worn out from lack of sleep, broke camp before dawn.

"Just look at all that mud." Rusty took off his gloves, eyeing the swollen river. "Think we should try and cross it?"

"We're not camping here another three days. Better warn the men." Nicholas took off his hat, studying the churning rapids. They'd crossed worse, but he didn't like to test the animals.

The chuck wagon mired down twice in midstream. Cowboys tied ropes from their saddle horns to the rig, using the horses' weight as leverage. Cooking utensils banged and rattled as the wagon rocked back and forth but refused to budge.

Gabby shook his fist, hollering, "Don't you cockleburs bust up my pots and pans! I'll have your skins in a skillet!"

The men kept at it until the wagon broke free from the mire and surged onto the bank. Gabby inspected every last pot and pan before saying with a grin, "Thank ya, boys. Right nice of ya."

"Never rile the cook!" one of the tenderfeet observed dryly.

"Pretty smart feller, for a knucklehead." Gabby ignored the men's good-natured ribbing as they tipped their Stetsons and galloped off.

Toward dusk a lone rider rode up. "Got a man down!"

"What's wrong?" Nicholas turned his horse, trying to hear the drover.

"One of the tenderfeet broke his leg!"

Spurring his horse, Nicholas rode ahead. Dismounting before the horse came to a halt, he ran to a young man lying on the ground, writhing in pain. The boy's leg was shattered, the bone poking through the skin.

Nicholas shook his head. "It's going to have to be set."

The boy cried out in pain.

"Gabby, Rusty and I will hold him down. You pour some whiskey on that wound. We don't want it getting infected." Nicholas scouted the area until he found a two-inch stick. Wedging it between the boy's teeth, he apologized. "Sorry to have to do this, son. It's going to hurt."

Gabby made a splint and then poured a shot of rotgut down the screaming youth's throat.

"As bad as it is," Nicholas muttered, "it could be worse. God was looking after you. You could have lost your leg. Rusty, have someone take him back to camp."

"Sure thing, Boss."

Nicholas hated to lose the cowhand. Shorthanded or not, the help's welfare came first. That was Abe Shepherd's cardinal rule and one Nicholas was glad to follow. Whether they realized it or not, many of the men were like sons to him. He would never sacrifice their safety for his own financial gain.

A few miles farther up the trail, Nicholas spotted one of his men on a ridge a couple of hills away, signaling with his Stetson.

Rusty rode up beside him. "Trouble?"

"Riders, eyeing the herd from a distance."

Signaling back, Rusty let the cowboy know they'd gotten the message.

That evening they made camp beneath a scattering of mesquite trees a few miles south of San Antonio. A full moon hung overhead like a huge lantern. Millions of stars twinkled in the darkness as the tired drovers fell into their bedrolls, dropping off to sleep to the sound of lowing cattle.

At dawn Nicholas and the trail boss rode into town to meet the buyers. Nicholas groaned when he learned the cattle buyers from Abilene were delayed.

"That could take another week!"

"Can't be helped," the man told him. "Been delayed by rain and swollen streams."

Nicholas had no choice but to stay until they arrived.

Three days passed. When the buyers finally arrived in San Antonio, they sent a rider to camp. Nicholas and the men drove the cattle into the stockyards and finalized the purchase. The cattle brought a high return, and though Nicholas was pleased, his thoughts were not on profit. They centered on home.

That night he spread his bedroll on the ground. Though Nicholas was tired, sleep would not come. Instead, his mind was on his approaching wedding. Now that the cattle were sold, he could take care of personal matters.

Rolling to his side, he stared at the stars. Faith was a Christian woman, strong in her faith.

Under Mama's influence, she would be domesticated. Her fiery spirit tested his patience, but he wouldn't want her any different. She was well mannered, and though he hadn't thought so at first, he realized now that she was pretty, real pretty, with a cloud of dark hair and those striking violet-colored eyes.

Desire stirred, a feeling he didn't often acknowledge.

Yawning, he closed his eyes in weariness. Home. He was going home. It was comforting to think Mama and Faith would hit it off while he was gone. Why, he could almost smell the biscuits baking in the oven. . . .

"She's *what!*"

Nicholas took off his hat and hooked it over the peg beside the door. Liza kept her back to him, beating flames from a pan of biscuits she'd just taken out of the oven. The stench of burnt bread hung heavy in the air.

His gaze roamed the empty kitchen. "Faith's gone?"

Liza bounced a burned biscuit off the stove. "I sent her packing."

"You *what?*"

"Are you deaf? Since when did I have to start repeating myself? You were born with two good ears—use them." Liza slammed the pan of biscuits on the table. "I told you, I sent her packing. Believe me, that isn't the half of it. She's moved in with Mary Ellen."

Nicholas's face fell. What nonsense was Mama babbling this time?

"Don't stand there like some love-struck pup! Sit down. Supper's ready."

Nicholas sat down, trying to assess the situation. Mama was mad; Faith was gone. What had happened? "What do you mean, you 'sent her packing'?" He couldn't imagine Mama acting so unchristian. Had she taken permanent leave of her senses?

Liza scraped blackened crust from her biscuit and added butter. The butter wadded into a gooey ball. She pitched it aside. "I've made a mess. Hand me a dish towel."

Nicholas handed Liza the towel. She took a long time wiping butter from her fingers. He waited.

"What happened? Where's Faith?"

Dissolving into tears, Liza buried her face in the dishcloth. "She was awful to me, Nicholas. I had no choice but to do what I did. She took it upon herself to clean the Smith house—after all we said about not wanting to get involved with her foolish talk of a blind school. Does she think we're made of money? I begged her to wait and talk it over with

you, but she refused. She's gone—moved in with Albert
and Mary Ellen Finney."

"Finneys?" Nicholas glanced around the room, bewildered. "Why would she do that?"

Liza worried the end of the dishcloth, shrugging.

"Mama. Why would Faith move in with Albert and Mary
Ellen?"

"Well, she just left—taken a shine to those twins. That's
all she wants to do—look after those babies."

Nicholas didn't believe that for one minute. Faith was
definitely a Good Samaritan, but to leave his house to help
with babies?

"Are you sure about that, Mama?"

Liza took a deep breath, dabbing the dishcloth at the corners of her eyes. Her face was mottled from crying. "I think
I would know. You don't see her, do you?"

Nicholas fixed his gaze on his mother's face.

Liza averted her eyes and wiped the table around her
plate. "I tried to stop her, Nicholas—she—she just won't
listen to me!"

Nicholas frowned. Faith and Mama didn't get along, but
Faith had never disobeyed Liza, not in his presence.

"Used my sugar, my flour, and my cherries, the week
before. Said she was taking a pie to Mary Ellen."

"So?"

Liza folded and refolded the damp material. "So, what?"

"Did she take a pie to Mary Ellen?"

"I doubt it. She's wily, I tell you. Plain wily."

Frustrated, Nicholas ran a hand through his hair. Faith

didn't have a wily bone in her. How could the situation have gotten so out of hand? "Mama, what do you think she did with the pie—how could you let this happen? Have you prayed about this?"

"Of course I've prayed about it. Faith lied. Said she was going over to help Mary Ellen with the babies, and she knew all along what she was going to do. Nicholas, I told her to leave and not to come back. I should have known better than to let her go that day. . . ." She suddenly softened. "You're right; it was my fault. I'm sorry I didn't watch her more closely."

Nicholas stiffened. "What is going on here! You told her to leave?"

"I did—it was a horrible thing to do, but when I found her cleaning that old house, intent on that blind school, I just exploded. Told her to leave, she wasn't welcome here any longer." Burying her face in her hands, she wept. "Lying, sneaking around behind my back—I'll not have it, Nicholas."

Nicholas's insides churned. "Exactly what did you say to her, Mama?"

Tears rolled unchecked down Liza's cheeks, and it was obvious she was starting to get worked up again. "I told her she wasn't welcome here any longer."

Nicholas's heart sank. For a brief moment he felt his loyalty shift to Faith. Why would Mama do such a thing? She had no right!

"Over there cleaning that house like a woman possessed. Oh, you'll hear it all from the town gossips. Molly and Etta will tell the whole town! Then come Sunday morning they'll sit like saints in the amen corner, shouting hallelujah at the top of their lungs."

Nicholas stared at Liza in disbelief. "Mama, stop it—Molly and Etta are your friends."

Liza's eyes darkened. "I don't have friends, Nicholas! Can't you see that? Haven't since Abe died—not one friend has stuck by me. When Abe was alive, we had more couple friends than we could shake a stick at, but now . . . now, I have nobody." She flung her hands to the ceiling. "They've all drifted away—every last one of them." Spent, she buried her face in the dishcloth and sobbed.

"I'm sorry, Mama, that you feel you don't have friends. I happen to think you do; you just haven't cultivated them lately, but I fail to see what this has to do with Faith."

"She lied to me, Nicholas!" Liza shouted, pounding a fist on the table.

Nicholas stared at her. Her face was flushed a bright red. Tiny beads of sweat trickled from her forehead, and she looked as if she were going to burst. He'd only seen her this angry on rare occasions. Her distress went deeper than Faith.

"Mama." His tone tempered. "Have you done as I asked and seen Doc?"

Liza exploded and evaded the question, "What's Doc got to do with anything? There's nothing wrong with me! Faith Kallahan is the problem here. Not me!"

"I'm trying my best to understand the situation," Nicholas

snapped. "Did Faith tell you she wasn't going to the Smith's house?"

"Of course not!"

"Well, then, she didn't lie."

"Oh, for heaven's sake! It's blazing hot in here." Liza sprang from the chair and jerked the window open wider. "Hot as Hades in this kitchen."

"Faith didn't lie," Nicholas repeated.

"Maybe it wasn't an out-and-out lie." Liza hesitated, holding her handkerchief to her throat. "But she deliberately led me to believe she was going to help Mary Ellen. She didn't say a word about going to the Smith house—she knew I would forbid it!"

"So, she did go to Mary Ellen's, and then she went to clean an empty old house that's been nothing but a community eyesore for years." Nicholas's patience was wearing thin.

"She defied me. I refuse to be treated with such disrespect— How can you defend her, Nicholas? A stranger? I'm your mother!"

"And from what you say, Faith was only scrubbing a dirty floor—hardly grounds for a firing squad."

Liza reached over and thumped him soundly. "Are you sassing me?"

He winced and silently asked God to give him patience. "No, Mama, I'm trying to make sense of what you've done. I'm not defending Faith; I just find it hard to believe she would disobey you without a reason."

"Well, she did. She wouldn't budge an inch from that bucket—even after I threatened to take a switch to her."

"A switch? You threatened to take a switch to her? At her age?"

"Yes, a switch! If she's bent on sass, then she needs a good switching."

Like the occasional thump on the head Liza found necessary to inflict on his noggin!

Liza folded the dishcloth and laid it aside. "I gave her a choice: Come home and forget all about the blind school, or stay and finish that floor. If she chose the floor, then I told her not to bother to come home at all. She scrubbed that old floor as if she hadn't heard a word I said. Even after I reminded her she'd been purchased to—"

"Purchased!" Nicholas roared. He sank down in a nearby chair. "You told her she'd been *purchased?*"

"Well? Wasn't she? Have you forgotten who paid for her ticket out here?"

Nicholas got up to look out the window. *Purchased.* How must that make Faith feel? Purchased, like beef on the hoof. He had been disrespectful to Faith; Mama even more so.

Liza rearranged the sugar bowl. "Nicholas, have you seen my snuff? I can't find it."

"Good."

"Nicholas!"

Nicholas held his tongue. He was too angry to talk sense. Mama was out of hand. He was personally taking her to see Doc first thing in the morning. Meanwhile, he needed time to think this mess through.

Liza was muttering under her breath now, fanning. "Came straight home, packed Miss Kallahan's belongings, and set them on the front porch, I did. It was after dark when Albert came for her things. Told me not to worry about her; she'd be all right with them. I just bet she will. She'll be going full steam ahead with those blind-school plans."

Liza wiped her forehead. "At least Albert was thoughtful enough to return the horse and buggy. Miss Kallahan would not likely have thought about it."

Nicholas turned from the window, trying to temper his rage. "I can't believe you've done this."

"I haven't done anything. It was Faith Kallahan's doings, not mine. I've done nothing that any good mother wouldn't do." Liza pushed back from the table and got up. "Most likely she's over there cookin' supper for the Walters family. You've seen the way Dan looks at her."

The declaration was like ice water in Nicholas's face.

Liza sniffed. "Supper's getting cold. Sit down. You're worn out from the long trip."

Nicholas was more heartsick than tired. "I've lost my appetite." He snagged his hat from the peg and went out the back door, slamming it behind him. The lace curtain gyrated wildly.

He entered the barn and quickly climbed the ladder to the loft. Exhausted, he lay back on a bale of hay, allowing familiar sounds and smells to calm him. How had his life gotten so complicated?

The thought of Faith in another family's house stung. The thought of her with Dan hurt even more. He had seen the way Dan looked at her, relied on her. Was Nicholas falling in love with her? No. Would he ever be able to love again? Did he know Faith well enough to love her? He'd loved only one woman, Rachel. But he'd had to let that sentiment die once she was married. Now he felt sorry for her, and guilty that she was married to a man who treated her badly. He was sorry she didn't have the life she deserved.

His thoughts returned to Faith. Why wasn't he happy to have her out from under his feet? Nicholas started a slow burn. *I paid for her ticket out here; she's promised to me.* The angry thought jarred his senses. He was no better than Mama, using hateful thoughts to justify his shortcomings. *Father, forgive me. My thoughts are so muddled on this situation.*

Why should he let Mama send Faith away? Why didn't he march into that kitchen right now and tell Mama that since she was the one who'd told Faith to go, she had to be the one to bring her back?

Faith was told to leave; how could she just waltz back into his house?

She should never have left; she should have stood her ground until he got back and could straighten this thing out.

Had she been looking for a reason to leave? Was that reason Dan Walters? Mama's words rang in his head: *over there cooking the Walters's supper.*

Well, he'd see about that! He'd saddle his horse and bring Faith back to the Shepherd ranch where she belonged. Then he'd deal with Mama's absurd accusations and get to the bottom of all this nonsense.

Climbing out of the loft, he saddled the Appaloosa, his thoughts on his mission. His hands suddenly paused.

Regardless of Mama's interference, Faith had chosen to move in with Mary Ellen. What if she had been looking for a reason to leave? Liza's rash demand and Faith's decision, no matter how warranted, made him feel like a downright fool now that she'd left him.

Jerking the saddle off the horse's back, he sat down, torn. What would make him look the bigger fool in the town's eyes? Faith's remaining with the Finneys, or his going after her?

Dropping to his knees, he prayed. *Father, give me guidance. Forgive my pride; give me the strength to do what's right.*

Getting to his feet, he swung the saddle back on the horse and mounted, then slid back down and jerked it off again.

The answer was obvious. He wouldn't go after her even though he wanted to. And, God help him, he did want to. If she had a shred of decency, she would come home, try to straighten this out—at least consult him about it! If she didn't . . . well, it would just prove that she didn't want to stay with him after all. Mama had no right to humiliate Faith, but Faith had no right to humiliate him. A man had his pride.

Exhausted, he curled up on a bale of hay, shivering in the night air. It wasn't the most comfortable place to sleep, but he had his pride. Let Mama wonder where he'd spent the night. She should never have sent Faith away.

So much for his mail-order bride. He rolled into a tighter knot, prepared to endure a miserable night.

Liza paced the kitchen floor, occasionally parting the curtains to look out. Where was Nicholas? He'd been gone for hours, and there wasn't a sign of light in the barn.

Dropping the curtain back into place, she resumed pacing. She'd gone too far. Her acid tongue had betrayed her one too many times. Nicholas had never spoken to her in such a shameful way. The sound of the slamming door echoed in her mind. She glanced around the empty kitchen, feeling the full brunt of her loneliness.

Bursting into hot tears, she wondered how Nicholas—her own flesh and blood—could treat her so badly. What evil possessed him to side with Faith Kallahan? He barely knew the woman. How dare he choose an ungrateful mail-order bride over his own mother?

He had deserted her. She had lost him. Just like she'd lost Abe. Only her son's abandonment hurt more; he had a choice. He'd angrily slammed out, leaving her to wonder if he'd ever come back. Abe was never coming back; she understood that, but Nicholas—he couldn't leave her. She would have nothing, nothing to live for.

Liza sobbed, certain she was losing her mind. Had Abe lived, would he have left her too—in the most wretched time of her life? She couldn't think straight anymore. It was as if the world had gone crazy.

The way she'd been acting, she wouldn't blame Nicholas if he left and never came back.

Kneeling, she prayed for forgiveness. *Help me, Father, help me.*

She rocked back on her heels, burying her face in her hands. *Oh, Abe, what should I do?* If only Abe were here to protect her, comfort her, hold her close. Where could she go for refuge? Bitterness rose in her throat. *Why, God, why did you take Abe and leave me? Worthless me, who can do nothing but cry and sweat and hate the world!*

Where had her little boy gone? Where was the laughing child she'd once cradled in her arms, sprinkling butterfly kisses on his tiny forehead as she gently rocked him to sleep? Her little boy was gone, and oh, how she missed the sound of tiny feet scurrying through the house.

Wiping her tears, she got up and looked out the window. She missed the boy, but she was proud of the man he'd become. Nicholas was so like Abe . . . so like her Abe.

Everyone was gone now. Abe was dead. Nicholas had walked out. And Faith . . . she'd shoved her away, too . . . and Nicholas would never forgive her. The image of Faith sitting in the middle of the Smith floor, trying to restore the dirty wood to decency, tore at her conscience. What harm could scrubbing an old floor cause? She had been irrational, cranky, and unreasonable. What had she been thinking?

"Oh, Lord," Liza cried out to the empty kitchen. "What's happening to me? What have I done?"

She felt insufferable heat rising in her chest, a hellish fire that ignited her. For a moment she thought she might not catch her breath. As quickly as the fire imprisoned her, it released her, leaving her exhausted and drenched in perspiration.

Taking a deep breath, she dried her eyes, then lifted her head with dignity. She would not give in to this strange malady, or the others inflicted upon her.

She would not.

Chapter Eleven

MISS Kallahan? Will you read to me?"

Faith let the front curtain drop into place. Adam had caught her looking again. She'd been hoping—no, praying—Nicholas would come. But she'd looked down that road until she couldn't look anymore. He wasn't coming; she must accept this cruel twist of fate. Could this be God's will? Why was she brought out here—to be rejected by the family who'd asked her to come? Was there some other purpose for her being in Deliverance, or should she return to Cold Water? She sighed. Would she ever understand God's will? Accept it she could, but understand?

When she'd discovered that Dan was having trouble finding someone to care for the children while he worked, she talked to Mary Ellen about the situation. Mary Ellen said Dan needed Faith's help more than she did, and to go on over. It was a way to feel useful, so she'd gladly offered Dan her help.

She enjoyed spending her days taking care of Dan's children, but it was becoming increasingly difficult to keep her thoughts away from Nicholas. How could she miss the Shepherd home so? It had never really been her home—though it was the only home she'd known in Deliverance. Then there was Liza. She had always been so difficult. And Nicholas.

Was she at fault in some way? Had she not tried hard enough to win Nicholas's love? Should she have tried harder with Liza? *Father, forgive me if I have not followed you closely enough, paid enough attention to what you wanted me to do. I just don't know what to do now. I wait on you. Please give me patience, and help me to know what you want me to do.*

Did Nicholas think about her? Not that he should be concerned about her welfare. She had disobeyed Liza, and for that she was sorry. In retrospect the school for the blind was a worthy cause, but her stance may have been too rash. It looked like that stance would cost her her marriage to Nicholas. The thought saddened her. In the short time they'd had together she had come to respect him—at times even like him. Most assuredly she'd looked forward to their occasional talks.

Now she was faced with a dreadful decision. If Nicholas didn't come after her—and she felt certain he wouldn't—she would be forced to return to Cold Water. Perhaps she would even have to marry Edsel Martin. She shuddered.

Daniel was asked to face mere lions; would the Lord ask her to face Edsel?

"Miss Kallahan, would you read to me?" Adam repeated patiently. His sightless eyes stared expectantly back at her, and she was reminded that her situation was not without blessings. And, she had made a choice. She could have gone home when Liza demanded it. Now she had to live with her choice.

Faith didn't know what was going to happen, or when, but for as long as she remained in Deliverance, she intended to make herself as useful as possible. She would help Mary Ellen with her children, and Dan with his. Oddly enough, word was spreading about the school for the blind. Many were offering to help; even some donations were dropped off at the Finneys'. Where was her faith, the faith she'd promised God to uphold?

Her thoughts returned to the child by her side. "Of course, Adam. What would you like to hear?"

"That story about that boy that killed that big old giant with one tiny stone."

"Go get the Bible. I believe I left it on the stand next to your bed."

Adam knew his way around the house with amazing accuracy. Within a few moments he returned, carrying the book. Lifting him onto her lap, Faith gently placed his fingertips on the pages, urging him to familiarize himself with the paper's texture. "Feel how smooth and worn it is?"

Adam nodded, running his fingers over the pages. "It feels like mommy's dress."

"I'd never thought of it that way, but yes, the soft parchment feels like fine silk or soft cotton." Faith rewarded him with a hug. God had given him much to overcome in his five short years. Inability to see and the loss of his mother. On the other hand, Dan was more than a father to his children, he was a friend. Faith saw how hard he worked to try to hold the family together.

Papa would have liked this righteous man Dan Walters. He would have said Dan was the salt of the earth.

"The pages are worn because your papa reads the Bible every day."

Adam nodded. "Uh-huh. And he tries to live by it, but he says sometimes it's powerful hard."

Powerful hard, Faith thought, recalling Liza. Sometimes nearly impossible.

Sissy and Lilly napped on the nearby couch as Faith retold the story of David and Goliath, Philistines, swords, five smooth stones, and a sling. When she finished, Adam turned to her, cupping her face in his small hands.

"Are you pretty?"

"Some say my eyes are an unusual shade, but no, I wouldn't say I'm pretty." She laughed. "Maybe passable, on a good day." Papa said eyes revealed a person's soul. If Adam could see her eyes, would he see a woman who longed for a child just like him? "Adam, do you understand color?"

Adam shook his head. "Papa's tried to 'splain them to me, but he's not very good at it."

"Would you like for me to try?"

"Would you?"

"Of course. Let's see—where should I start?"

Adam quickly decided. "'Splain me the color of *your* eyes."

Faith smiled. "Better yet, why don't I let you *see* the color of my eyes."

Adam cocked his head. "I *can't* see!"

"Maybe not with your eyes, but you can see with your hands."

The expression on the child's face clearly said she must be teasing.

Taking his right hand, she placed it on her left cheek. "Tell me what you see, Adam."

Adam carefully ran his fingertips over her cheekbones, frowning. "I see . . . lumps." He grinned.

"Now my eyes."

His fingertips lightly traced her eyelids, the tips of his fingers exploring her lashes, the shape of her nose.

"My eyes are violet," she said.

"Violet?"

"Violet is a cool color, like the lilacs blooming next to the porch step."

"Those smelly things?"

"Those *lovely* smelling things." He was so like a man. "Do you know the feel of cool, Adam?"

Adam shook his head.

Lifting him off her lap, she took his hand, and they walked outside and down the path to the icehouse. A draft of cool air washed over her as they entered the building.

Holding tightly to her hand, Adam edged closer. "I know where we are!"

"Yes, we're in the icehouse." She led him to a block of ice, then carefully took his hand and ran it across the cold, moist surface. "This is how cool feels."

Adam broke into a wide grin as he ran first one hand, then the other, over the icy surface. "Cool," he murmured. "Cold!"

"Very cold!" Faith laughed. "Now, let's feel warm."

"Like the stove? Papa said the stove's *hot!*"

"And Papa's right!"

Returning to the kitchen, she guided him to the cookstove. As trusting as a puppy, he allowed her to hold his hand above the burners. Heat radiated from the cast iron. "This is hot."

"Hot." He nodded. "Once I burned myself on hot, real bad."

"That can happen. Hot is best left alone." She opened the warming oven and took out a biscuit. Placing the bread in the child's hand, she said softly, "This is warm. Yellow is a warm color. Butter is yellow; sunshine is yellow."

They both turned as the back door opened and Dan walked into the kitchen.

"Papa!"

Grinning, Dan ruffled his son's hair as he made a beeline for the washbowl. "What are you two up to this fine day?"

"Faith's teaching me how to see colors!"

"She is!" Dan glanced at Faith appreciatively. "I've tried to explain colors to him, but I guess I don't do a very good job."

Faith dished up his dinner as he toweled dry.

"Where are the other young'uns?"

"Sissy and Lilly went down for naps earlier."

"I got tied up at the livery. Thought I wasn't going to get a dinner break at all."

Faith set a plate of chicken and dumplings in front of him, watching him eye the fat dumplings swimming in rich gravy with an appreciative sigh. "That sure looks good. Haven't eaten this good since Carolyn was alive."

They bowed their heads, and Dan said grace. Picking up his fork, he dug in. "Have you eaten?"

Faith nodded and poured coffee into a thick mug. "The children and I ate earlier."

Dan's eyes met hers across the table. "Much obliged. It's real nice to have a woman in the kitchen again." He took a bite of dumplings, then observed, "You know, I promised Carolyn I wouldn't pine away—I'd remarry someday, give the children a mama."

"I shouldn't think Deliverance has a shortage of women who'd be proud to look after them." Faith glanced away, careful not to acknowledge the tender look in his eyes. He was a good man, and he needed a wife more than any man she knew. Why hadn't God chosen her to be that wife? There could never be anything but friendship between them. If Nicholas didn't want her, she would return to Michigan. She would not shame Nicholas by marrying another man here in Deliverance.

The past week had opened her eyes regarding marriage. Vows could be bought and paid for like a sack of grain, but she discovered that she needed—wanted—more. She wanted to be in love with the man she married. If she were to explore a relationship with Dan, love would come. He was far too good a man not to love. As she'd cared for them these past days, his children had started to feel like hers. And Dan, well, he would make some lucky lady a wonderful husband. But she couldn't stay.

She and Dan had talked about their individual situations. He understood her insecurities, her doubts, her fears that Liza would never allow Nicholas to marry her, her dread of Edsel Martin. The wistfulness in Dan's tone when they talked about marriage had wrenched her heart. More than once he'd asked for the address of the journal in which Faith had placed her ad. She always steered the conversation to safer ground, fearing it was his subtle way of conveying that he, also, was in the market for a wife. Perhaps—perhaps if it weren't for shaming Nicholas. . . .

"There are a few women around, but none that I'd marry," Dan continued, buttering a piece of bread. "Jenny Petersen's looking to get hitched, but Jenny's got a temper like a chafed bull." He took a bite of chicken. "'Course, there's always Maggie Lewis, but Maggie's like her ma; she clings to a man like a summer cold. And not real trustworthy, either. I couldn't count on Maggie to get the kids in out of the rain." Dan bit into the bread. "Nicholas stopped by the livery this morning."

He'd changed the subject so quickly that Faith wondered if he'd read her earlier thoughts. She calmly took a couple of cookies from the jar and put them on a plate. "Oh?"

"Asked how you were doing."

She worked to keep her tone impartial. "I trust he's fine and his cattle drive was successful?"

"Fit as a fiddle, and richer." Dan reached for the sugar bowl. "Asked about you—did I say that?"

"Yes, it's always nice to hear you're being thought about." Nicholas might *ask* about her, but he'd certainly shown no interest otherwise. She set the plate of cookies in front of Dan. "What brought Nicholas to the livery today?"

"Said his horse was limping, but I couldn't find a problem." Dan looked up, grinning. "I think he's snooping."

"Snooping?" Faith scoffed at the unlikely assumption. The last thing Nicholas Shepherd would do was *snoop* on her. "Dan, I need to ask you something."

"Sure." He motioned with his fork for her to sit down.

Taking a seat opposite him, she folded her hands, studying them thoughtfully. "What does . . . well, this is a rather difficult question." Papa had done his best, but there were a few things he'd neglected to explain—like, what a man wanted in a woman, what he expected. Obviously, she didn't possess a single thing that attracted Nicholas.

Dan appeared curious. "What's the question?"

"Men. What do they want in a woman?" She bit her lower lip when she saw a red blush creep up the back of his neck. Was she being frightfully forward?

She didn't mean *what* did they want; she was old enough to know all about the birds and the bees, and she'd seen enough tomfoolery with friends to know that you didn't give a man everything he *wanted,* at least not without the sanctity of marriage. What she meant was: What did a man look for in a woman? Beauty? Loyalty? A hard worker? She shook her head, answering her own question. Nicholas certainly wasn't looking for a hard worker to make him happy. He had a bunkhouse full of men who were paid for that service.

Stirring cream into his coffee, Dan studied the question. "You mean, what makes a man fall in love with a woman?"

"I suppose that's what I mean."

"We're back to talking about Nicholas, aren't we?"

"Yes," she admitted, then released her breath in a disgusted whoosh. "I might as well be as freckled as a turkey egg the way Nicholas fails to notice me."

"A turkey egg?" Dan shook his head, sobering. "I don't think any man would think of you as a turkey egg. I've caught Nicholas looking at you a few times out of the corner of his eye."

"But his other eye was on Rachel."

"Rachel?" He frowned. "She's married to Joe Lanner, although I don't know of a person who'd fault her if she decided to leave him."

"I overheard someone in the mercantile say Joe mistreats her. Is that true?"

Dan nodded, taking a bite of dumplings. "She refuses to admit it, but she shows up every week with a new bruise or broken bone. Says she falls, but no one believes her. Joe Lanner should be taken out and hung from the highest limb. A man's got no right to treat a woman that way."

"Well?"

He glanced up.

"You haven't answered my question."

Pushing back from the table, Dan took a deep breath, loosening his belt. He'd eaten as if it were his last meal, but Faith was proud he enjoyed her cooking. "Let's see. What does a man want in a woman? That was the question."

"Yes, except for the obvious."

"Except for the obvious—well, I guess he enjoys a pretty face—but if she were as ugly as sin, guess that wouldn't matter as long as she had a kind heart and a humble spirit.

"A fine figure helps, but she could be fat as a hog, and if her man loves her, it wouldn't make an ounce of difference. There'd just be more to love—but you've got no problem there. You're a handsome woman, slim as a reed.

"I guess when it comes right down to it, a man wants someone who'll share his life, be his best friend, bear his children; and it wouldn't hurt none if she could make dumplings as good as his mama." He winked. "And you got *no* problem at all in that area."

She waited for him to go on, fascinated. When he didn't, she frowned. "That's all?"

His sincere chestnut brown eyes met hers. "What I'm sayin' is, Nicholas would be a fool to let you go, so stop your frettin'. Nicholas is a lot of things, but he's not stupid. He knows he's got a rose; it'll just take a while for his pride to allow him to admit it."

Faith fiddled with the end of the tablecloth. "Maybe Liza won't let him admit it."

"Nicholas is his own man. He's been real good to Liza since his papa died, indulged her more than he should, but

193

that doesn't mean she runs him. It may look that way; but I've known him all my life, and he doesn't do anything he doesn't want to do."

Faith wasn't as sure about Nicholas's independence. From all appearances, Liza ruled the Shepherd roost.

Tuesday morning Faith was down on her hands and knees polishing the banister at the Smith house when she looked up to find Nicholas standing in the doorway. Her heart shot to her throat. He looked so handsome standing there, tanned, wearing a blue shirt that matched his eyes, his tall frame filling the opening.

Dropping her gaze, she went on polishing. "Is there something I can do for you?" It was the first time she'd seen him since he'd gotten back from the cattle drive, and the moment was awkward.

A muscle worked tightly in his jaw as his eyes fixed on her. "One of Dan's bulls is out."

No pleasant "How are you?" or "I'm sorry you and Mother disagreed." Not even an "I think we should pray about this." Just "Dan's bull's out."

She kept her eyes trained on the banister. "Did you tell Dan?"

"I'm not going into town. You tell him this afternoon, when he gets home." She winced at his apparent willingness to be on with his business.

Deliberately keeping her voice pleasant, even though she wanted to bite his head off for caring so little about her, she said nicely, "I'm not going to be seeing Dan today; I'm going back to the Finneys'. Can't you put it up for him?"

"It's not my bull."

"It's not mine, either." *Nor my stubborn pride,* she reasoned. Pride goeth before a fall, the Good Book says. Papa would take a switch to her for her impertinence, but Nicholas's outward calm infuriated her! Wasn't he going to ask why she'd left? Didn't he even *want* to hear her side of the story?

The air was electrically charged with raw, masculine power. Faith kept her head bent, carefully working the rag along the railing, thanking the good Lord that Nicholas was a Christian man, able to keep his anger in check.

Pride might prevent him from saying he was disappointed and angry with her, but she could see it in his stance—stiff, unyielding. And in the stubborn set of his jaw. Why didn't he just put the bull back himself? Why bother her at all? He certainly hadn't troubled himself to come around all week. Why now?

"Tell *Dan* his bull will be in the north pasture."

"Thank you. I will tell *Dan* his bull is safe the moment I see him, which may not be until tomorrow," she returned in a voice as stiff as a bullwhip. When she glanced up, he was gone.

Dropping the rag, she sat back on her heels, fighting tears. She would not cry! She wouldn't. Nicholas Shepherd was a stubborn man who would go to his grave lonely and alone!

She reminded herself of that when she bumped into the arrogant rancher a few days later. She'd used the last of the cleaning supplies and several of the church ladies had promised to help with the cleaning Saturday morning.

Nicholas was rounding the corner of the livery when Faith collided head-on with him. Packages flew in all directions as she dropped to her hands and knees, her head spinning. She sat for a moment, trying to orient herself. Color flooded her face when she realized the noisy collision had drawn a crowd.

Strong hands latched on to her waist and effortlessly lifted her up, allowing her feet to dangle in midair. For a moment she stared into amused cobalt blue eyes.

"Shopping again, Miss Kallahan?"

Aware of the chuckles around her, she gritted her teeth and ordered, "Put me down."

"Why, of course, Miss Kallahan." He stood her back on her feet, none too gently, then knelt to pick up the scattered packages. Stacking parcels like cordwood in her arms, he stepped back, removed his hat, and affected a mock bow. Faith felt like a ninny. Every time he saw her lately she was either on her hands and knees or in the process of getting there.

"Might I be of further assistance?" he inquired.

Hugging the packages to her chest, she hurried off, sourly eyeing him over her shoulder. "May I be of further assistance, Miss Kallahan," she mimicked. Oh, she'd tell him *exactly* how he could be of further service if she weren't afraid of the Lord's wrath. The—the arrogant buffoon!

Saturday night, Community Hall was unusually crowded.
Faith arrived late with the Finneys.

She caught herself searching the crowd for Nicholas. Liza
was standing on the sidelines, vigorously fanning herself as
she visited with friends. Faith's gaze traveled the room,
stopping when she found her point of interest. He was
standing in a group of both men and women. Rachel was
standing beside him, smiling as she listened with rapt attention to what he was saying.

Envy sliced through Faith's stomach, and she prayed for
understanding. Nicholas was free to talk to whomever he
wanted, but Rachel wasn't. She was a married woman, yet
she'd heard Liza mention that Joe refused to attend socials.

Seeing the Walterses arrive, Faith hurried over to help
out. Taking Adam's and Sissy's hands, she ushered them to
the bench lining the wall and seated them.

"My belwee hurts," Sissy complained.

Adam instinctively turned his head in the direction of the
refreshment table. "May I have some punch?"

"I'll bring you a cup," Faith promised, recalling the chaos
he could incite when left to his own devices.

When the children were settled with cups of punch and
a cookie in each hand, Dan pulled Faith toward the dance
floor with a teasing light in his eye. When she protested,
Vera Hicks offered to hold Lilly, promising she'd keep an
eye on the two older children.

Faith realized it would only cause a scene if she refused
Dan this dance, but she didn't feel right about it. The whole

room would be watching, including Nicholas and Liza, and the last thing she wanted to do was cause the Shepherds further humiliation. Thanks to Molly and Etta, the town was already buzzing with the news that she had moved off the Shepherd ranch.

She could hear the murmurs and speculations now. "Does Faith Kallahan intend to throw Nicholas Shepherd over for Dan Walters?" "Didn't Nicholas bring Faith to Deliverance to be his bride?" "Is her insistence on opening the blind school causing the problem?"

Before Faith could make a polite refusal, the band struck up a lively reel, and Dan swung her onto the dance floor.

"Really, Dan, I'm a little tired tonight!" she called out as the fiddlers instituted a lively rendition of "Turkey in the Straw."

"You'll get your second wind soon!"

Faith whirled, then began the allemande left, threading her way through the dancers. When her hand came in contact with a solid steel grip, her heart tripped like a drum, but she kept her head low, trying to keep her composure.

"I trust you're enjoying yourself, Miss Kallahan?" Nicholas inquired as they passed.

"Exquisitely so, Mr. Shepherd. And you?" She smiled, determined to be pleasant if it killed her.

"Couldn't be better. Thank you for asking." They continued to allemande, completing a full circle.

A moment later they passed again. Faith bit her lip; she would not fire a return volley. He was only trying to antagonize her, and she wasn't about to fall for it.

"Mrs. Lanner looks lovely tonight, don't you agree?" She bit her tongue hard. Drats and double drats! Did she have to say that?

As they rounded a corner and were forced to join hands to dance through a tunnel of widespread arms, Nicholas returned quietly, "Funny, I was just about to comment on Dan's appearance tonight. He looks mighty dapper."

They reached the end of the archway where he gracefully twirled her, then caught her to him. She landed against the solid wall of his chest. Their eyes met, and for a moment she couldn't catch her breath.

His eyes made his point. "At least Rachel is obedient to her husband."

"As I will be," she volleyed, aware the conversation had just taken a personal turn, "but surely you've forgotten." She leaned closer and whispered, "I'm not married yet."

He whirled her a second time, and she moved on. Seconds later she was back.

"Perhaps if you weren't so stubborn, you would be," he observed nicely.

"Perhaps if *you* weren't so *thickheaded,* you would have asked to hear my side of the story." She smiled prettily, locking hands with him as they joined other dancers to form a bridge.

The caller shouted for the dancers to change partners. Faith whirled with first one man, then another, until the caller reversed the instructions and she returned to Nicholas's waiting arms.

"You, Miss Kallahan, have gone back on your word."

"And you, Mr. Shepherd, are allowing your mother to control your life."

"Nonsense."

"Truth." If only he'd come after her, she would have apologized from the bottom of her heart! She wouldn't promise to give up on the school for the blind, but she would listen to his concerns and address them.

They whirled, then whirled back to face each other.

"Don't deny it. You have your cap set for Dan—have had since the day you got here," he accused.

"I do not!" She stopped, tripping a row of dancers close on their heels. Men reached out to steady women who staggered clumsily to regain their balance. How dare he accuse *her* of disloyalty! Dan was a good friend, and she didn't like Nicholas talking bad about him. Had Nicholas asked, she would gladly have explained her relationship with Dan, but now, *now* wild horses couldn't drag it out of her. "Sorry, Papa," she muttered, "but you've never dealt with a man like Nicholas!"

Nicholas drew her closer, his eyes riveted with hers. "May I remind you *I* brought you here to marry me, not Dan Walters?"

"It's the money, isn't it?" She sighed. She had never seen two stingier people in all her born days, these Shepherds. "Well, I'll pay you back."

He scoffed. "Where would you get that kind of money?"

"I'll use my nest egg!" she shouted.

He blanched, and she realized she'd struck a nerve.

Lowering her voice, she apologized. "I'm sorry . . . it's

just that I feel I owe you an explanation—" She wavered as Nicholas took her arm and ushered her off the dance floor. Dancers looked momentarily confused, but quickly confiscated a couple standing on the sidelines to replace the void.

Bursting outdoors, Nicholas marched Faith to a corner of the porch where a lantern burned low.

"Let me go!"

"You are, undoubtedly, the most stubborn woman I've ever had the misfortune to meet!"

"And you are the most stubborn man." She tried to rub feeling back into her wrist.

Nicholas started to pace. "Is this any way for a grown man and woman to act?"

"You started it."

Her anger gradually dissipated as Papa's voice singed her conscience. "Faith Marie! That temper's going to earn you a good switchin'!"

"Sorry, Papa," she muttered. *Forgive me, Lord.* "But he just makes me so mad."

Nicholas turned. "What?"

Faith jerked the bodice of her dress into place. "I was talking to *Papa.*"

Running a hand through his hair, Nicholas paced the length of the porch. Faith supposed he was sorting through his thoughts. She turned to face the road, crossing her arms. Well, he had a powerful lot of sorting to do. Did he intend to marry her or not? Was he going to stand up and tell Liza that he meant no disrespect but he was the man of the house, that he'd brought Faith here to marry her, and he darn well was going to live up to his end of the bargain? Or was he not?

"Faith. Are you interested in Dan?" Nicholas asked the question so softly, reluctantly, Faith wasn't sure she'd heard it correctly.

"Am I interested in Dan?"

He looked up, and their eyes met in the moonlight. A soft breeze tossed his hair, making him look boyish. Her anger melted.

"No," she whispered, then wiped a strand of blowing hair out of her eyes. Clearing her throat, she repeated more firmly, "No. I like Dan, and I love his children, but there's nothing romantic between Dan and me."

Relief flooded Nicholas's features but vanished so quickly she wasn't sure it had ever been there. "Are you certain?"

She looked down at her hands, at the empty space, third finger, left hand. "I'm certain. I came here to marry you. If that can't be, then I want to go home, back to Michigan." She closed her eyes, waiting, praying he would say there was no need for that. That he didn't want her to go.

But he didn't.

The silence stretched. Overhead a hoot owl called to its mate. The moon slid behind a cloud, shadowing the honey-suckle-scented porch. It seemed like an eternity before he finally spoke.

"They'll be wondering what's keeping us."

Nodding, she whispered, "Well, we can't have that, can we."

She turned to leave and suddenly felt his hand on her arm.

Turning her gently to face him, he gazed at her for a very long time. "I'm sorry if I've been anything other than a gentleman."

Her voice caught as she took a deep breath, reminding herself that love and respect must be earned, and she didn't warrant either from this man. Papa would have been deeply ashamed of her behavior, and in the stillness of the soft summer night, she regretted her outburst on the dance floor. The Lord would be even more disappointed with her. How could Nicholas love a woman who embarrassed him? "You haven't . . . been so bad."

Cupping her face between his large hands, he gazed at her, then kissed her lightly. The kiss was simple, reserved, mysterious, but so utterly galvanizing that it struck a cord deep inside Faith. Why did happiness flood her very being with the touch of his lips? Could she possibly be falling in love with this man? She knew God's plan for her life was perfect, without flaw, but, oh, how her faith needed reassurance.

How was she to take that kiss? she wondered, as Nicholas took her arm and ushered her inside. Was it his way of saying good-bye?

Chapter Twelve

N

O one can leave Deliverance until after the Founder's Day celebration."

Faith glanced up from packing to see Mary Ellen standing in the doorway. Her friend's unexpected appearance startled her. "Good morning. I thought you were in the kitchen."

"I was, but I knew I had to talk you out of leaving today. It's Founder's Day." Mary Ellen stepped into the small cubicle and slid her hand across the dark blue calico folded in Faith's valise. "Carl Lewis's sister is here from San Antonio, Oren's brother's visitin' from Dallas—no one would miss the celebration."

"But, Mary Ellen," Faith protested.

"Don't do this, Faith. Don't leave in haste. Wait a few more days, and see what Nicholas does."

Faith shook her head. "I've taken advantage of your hospitality for over a month. It's time for me to go home."

"You've been a godsend." Mary Ellen's sober look vanished and her sunny smile returned. "Stay, if only for the day. I'm not even sure if the stage operates on holidays."

Faith felt stricken. It had taken days to convince herself that the time had finally come to leave. She'd seen Nicholas twice since the community dance—once at the mercantile, and last Thursday afternoon when she was crossing the street to attend Bible study. On both occasions they'd nodded politely and gone about their business. Sundays, Nicholas and Liza attended church services but left immediately after the sermon. Nicholas gave no indication of the slightest interest in her.

"Powder your nose; then help me get the food ready. Then we have to get the children into clean clothes." Mary Ellen gave Faith's shoulder a pat and ran to the bedroom door. "Albert, get the buckboard ready. We're going to a celebration!"

For weeks everyone in town had taken part in planning the anticipated event, scheduled to take place today. Faith knew Nicholas and Liza would be there, and Rachel as well. She just couldn't bear to run into those people again. She had to leave now. She'd wrestled with the issue, and it wasn't clear what God would have her to do. She just couldn't face a public situation where she would see Nicholas and Liza.

Then again, she really hadn't gotten the go-ahead from God to leave. . . . Oh, it seemed that every way she turned

she faced insurmountable problems! Yet in her spirit,
through all the chaos, she felt as if God was telling her to
wait . . . to hold on.

"Mary Ellen, if I do go to the celebration today . . ."

"No 'if'—you're going."

"OK, I'm going. But I must go by and help Dan get the
children ready. I told him I would help before I caught the
stage."

"Yes, I know you promised to help him. We'll drop you
at his house on our way."

The two women busied themselves gathering the food for
the day's picnic. Faith was caught up in the excitement of
the hectic household. She refused to worry about Nicholas
and his relationship with her today.

She arrived at Dan's shortly before noon. For weeks now
Sissy and Adam had talked about the Founder's Day festivities. Adam's voice filled with excitement as he chattered
about the annual fireworks display. As she watched the
excitement that radiated from a child who would never
experience the spectacular display of brilliant colors and
splendid designs exploding in midair, Faith realized how
many blessings she took for granted.

Adam and Sissy burst through the doorway, clamoring for
the washbowl.

"Papa said we're going to a sellobration!" Sissy shrieked.

"We're going, we're going, we're *going!*" Adam chanted.
"Faith, will you help me see the fireworks colors?"

"You bet I will, Buster!" Faith paused long enough to
embrace the little boy.

"Hey, my name's not Buster!" Adam grinned. "But you can call me anything you want—long as you promise to come with us!"

"I wouldn't miss it for the world!" Faith realized that was true, and she silently promised herself that tonight, somehow, someway, she would make Adam *see* the fireworks. She'd find a way to describe every detail, every magnificent, glorious, colorful burst. Though young Adam had been to previous Founder's Day displays, tonight she'd make certain he experienced the performance through her eyes.

The Walterses' buckboard rolled into town around twelve-thirty as the stage was just departing the depot. Faith's mouth dropped open, and she looked at Dan.

"Mary Ellen said she didn't think the stage ran today."

He shrugged, grinning. "We all wanted you to stay."

As the wagon drew closer to the church, Faith caught sight of the much discussed steeple. Liza still wasn't going to give money to replace it. But as she looked more carefully, she thought that with a little paint and some nails it would last for another few years. An idea hit her. She liked the townsfolk; most had made her feel wanted and welcomed. If she couldn't bring a school for the blind to Deliverance, she could leave a small legacy behind when she left.

She would fix the steeple. She and Dan. She was sure Dan wouldn't mind. Between them, they could have that old bell tower looking like new. It would mean she would have to stay in town a few more days, but what would that hurt? After all, she'd promised to head the steeple committee in exchange for the women's help cleaning the Smith house.

Dreams for the school for the blind were gone, but she could still fulfill her duty. Once the steeple was repaired, she would be free to purchase her stage ticket. It would take every cent of her nest egg, but it was worth it.

The quaint Church of Deliverance was nestled in a shady grove of pecan trees. It was one of those rare summer Saturdays when the weather was comfortable. Reverend Hicks stood at the front door, shaking hands as his flock packed into the small church.

Faith noticed Joe and Rachel Lanner's pew was empty today. Nicholas and Liza were already stationed in their usual front seats.

Faith followed Dan and the children into their pew and sat down.

Liza briefly turned to look over her shoulder as the Walters entered the room. For a split second, she met Faith's gaze. Faith's heart turned over. Liza looked very old and tired this morning, her eyes sad. Could it be, Faith wondered, that Liza regretted her reckless conduct? Bowing her head, Faith asked the Lord for forgiveness for both her and Liza. Neither had been acting as God wanted. If Liza would show one ounce of encouragement, Faith would gladly set their differences aside. Faith still believed God had sent her to Deliverance for a purpose. *I will never fail you. I will never forsake you.* Lifting her eyes ever so slightly, Faith offered Liza a tentative smile.

Liza nodded toward her, then turned in her seat as the service began.

Children squirmed throughout Reverend Hicks's oratory

about how Deliverance had been founded by a small band
of Ute Indians. The tribe had fallen ill from a strange malady, and J. W. Delivers had fed and cared for the ailing
tribe. All died except the chief. In gratitude for Delivers's
kindness, the chief had proclaimed that the land belonged to
Delivers. The town sprang up some twenty-five years later.

Even baby Lilly got restless during the long talk, squirming
on Dan's lap. He bounced her up and down on one knee,
trying unsuccessfully to quiet her. Faith finally reached over
and took the fussy infant. Lilly immediately stuck her fingers
in her mouth and surrendered to a peaceful sleep.

Faith looked up to see Nicholas watching the exchange
with eyes as cold as granite.

After the service, the congregation gathered for the
long-awaited celebration. With all the colorful blankets
spread on the ground, the churchyard resembled a giant,
multicolored quilt.

Activity was everywhere. Hardworking farmers and
ranchers who seldom saw each other gathered to discuss
crops and herds. Others tossed horseshoes or swapped tales
so windy that the Reverend jokingly said next year they'd
follow Founder's Day with a Liars Festival.

Children, like miniature whirlwinds, ran in every direction. Little boys in their best knickers and white shirts
played snap-the-whip or engaged in marbles, using shiny
agates and cat's eyes. Little girls in their frilliest dresses, with
matching pinafores and bonnets, skipped rope or played
ring-around-the-rosy. Their hearty laughter filled the air.

Women chased rowdy toddlers while others preferred to

sit in the shade, issuing idle threats. Single girls discreetly scouted for potential suitors, smiling and charming their way through the groups of young men whose ears flamed a bright red under all the attention. Women, young and old, traded recipes and gave advice on gardening, canning, and dressmaking. Conversations grew more animated as several women huddled to share the latest bit of gossip.

Adam was full of the need to help. Faith steadied his hands as he poured lemonade into glasses. When each glass was filled, he was thrilled with his accomplishment. A huge grin wreathed his face.

Dan gathered his brood and said grace, then Faith filled plates with fried chicken, baked beans, corn on the cob, and sourdough bread. Lilly got a bottle. A fine-looking chocolate cake and browned apple dumplings awaited them for dessert. During the past month, as Faith helped cook for Dan and for Mary Ellen, she was delighted to learn that although she still didn't like cooking, she was pretty good at it.

"Thank you for helping me, Adam." Faith smiled at the child as they cleaned up.

"Ahhhh, weren't nothin' to it." He grinned broadly.

"And what, young man, did you do to help Faith that was so special?" Dan asked, playfully ruffling the boy's carrot top.

"You want to tell him, Adam? Or should I?" Faith asked.

"You tell him." Adam's freckled face blushed a russet red.

"Your handsome son filled every last one of our glasses with lemonade!" Faith said. "And without dribbling a single drop!"

Dan patted Adam's shoulder. "Is that right?"

"Yes, sir." Adam beamed. "But Faith helped me."

"All I did was guide your hand, just a little. You did the rest. Pouring was the hardest and most important part."

Dan winked his appreciation at her. Father's pride glowed in his eyes at his son's latest success. Faith knew exactly how he felt. She was feeling a bit of pride herself.

"I suppose we should show this young man our appreciation," Dan said. "Don't know about the rest of you, but as for me, there's nothing quite as satisfying on a hot day as a cool glass of lemonade."

"I absolutely agree," Faith replied. "I suggest we make young Adam king for the day and seal his new title with a round of applause." They fashioned a crown of twigs and placed it on his head.

Faith, Dan, and Sissy clapped so loud and long that they drew attention from the crowd. Even Lilly made a couple of decent swats with her chubby little hands, squealing loudly. Faith could see by the sparkle in Adam's sightless eyes that he truly felt like a king. The young boy reveled in even the slightest accomplishment. An ache gripped Faith's heart when she thought about the school for the blind that would never be. Adam was so bright, so starved for knowledge. Little Adam Walters would someday make his mark in this life, she'd wager on that—and Papa never let her wager. Ever.

Midafternoon, musicians gathered to provide lively tunes and soul-wrenching gospel. Albert Finney played harmonica; Sarah Jane's husband picked banjo. Another man fired up a toe-tapping fiddle. Beside him, a young boy played spoons.

The foursome regaled the crowd with "My Old Kentucky Home," "Tenting on the Old Camp Ground," and "Oh! Susanna."

Faith's favorite was "Amazing Grace." No matter how often she heard the song, it was so beautiful, so heartrending, that it brought tears to her eyes. June had sung "Amazing Grace" a cappella as they lowered Papa into his grave.

Late in the afternoon Sissy played with a ball that had seen better days, its torn leather having been stitched for the last possible time.

Lilly demanded all of her father's attention. The baby was determined to inch her way off the blanket. Just as Dan blocked her path or took hold of her diaper to slow her down, she turned and crawled in the other direction. The rambunctious baby kept Faith and Dan busy.

Nicholas, Liza, Vera, and Reverend Hicks sat on a blanket nearby, watching the display of family unity. Faith was uncomfortable with their close perusal, but she vowed not to let it spoil her day.

"Afternoon, good people." Jeremiah wandered by and paused to tickle Lilly under her chin.

"Hello, Jeremiah," Faith replied. "Would you like to join us?"

"You're more than welcome, Jeremiah. We've got more food than we could eat in a week," Dan invited. "I do believe you'll find Faith's cookin' to be the best around."

Jeremiah nodded, smiling. "I'm most certain it is, and I do

thank you for the tempting invitation. But I was just about to pay my respects to Liza."

Dan winced. "Good luck."

Faith glanced over to see that Liza was now sitting alone. Reverend Hicks and Nicholas were setting up a table in the brush arbor. Vera hauled out watermelons.

"Thank you, my good man. I'm sure I'll be needing all the help I can get." Jeremiah smiled and continued toward the Shepherd blanket.

"Poor Jeremiah." Faith sighed, her gaze following him as he approached Liza, sitting under a tree. "If he isn't careful, Liza will serve him up for lunch."

"I have a feeling Jeremiah can hold his own with Liza." Dan leaned over and snagged Sissy by the hem of her dress. "Who wants to play ball with me?"

"I do!" Sissy screamed.

"Me too!" Adam shouted.

Dan tossed the ball to Adam. He threw it wildly to Sissy, who scurried to catch it.

Faith lay down on the blanket, cradling her head on folded arms, watching Jeremiah. She'd been taught not to eavesdrop, but the temptation was just too great.

Jeremiah removed his hat. "Afternoon, Liza."

Liza lifted her arm, shielding her eyes against the glare. Her eyes skimmed Jeremiah, and she grumbled, "What's so good about it?"

"Why, everything!"

"Too hot," Liza snapped. "What do you want?"

"Nothing more than the pleasure of your company."

Faith strained to hear the conversation. The idea of Jeremiah trying to win favor with Liza—she didn't know whether to laugh or cry.

"May I sit with you a spell?"

Liza brushed an imaginary fly away from a plate of chicken. "You most certainly cannot."

Jeremiah smiled, rubbing his chin. "I'd be no bother."

The poor man. He obviously didn't know Liza the way Faith did. Jeremiah would have better luck trying to lasso the moon than winning Liza Shepherd's favor.

"Well, then, would you do me the honor of sharing a cool glass of lemonade?" Jeremiah motioned toward his blanket spread generously with food, a pitcher of fresh lemonade, and a single yellow rose in a crystal vase.

"Are you out of your mind?" Liza busied herself with her handwork. "Go away—people are staring—go away, you old goat!"

Jeremiah politely bowed. "As you wish, madam. Please accept my apologies. My intentions are most honorable. You see, I thought I was inviting a lady to share an idle moment with me, but sadly I was mistaken. I didn't realize I was extending an invitation to an *old crab!*"

Liza's jaw dropped as Jeremiah turned and walked off.

Biting her lip, Faith lowered her head, her body shaking with mirth. *Old crab.* Jeremiah had called Liza an old crab!

Adam shouted for Faith to join them in the ball game. Collecting herself, she sprang to her feet, catching the ball Dan tossed to her. She threw it to Sissy, who missed. Sissy chased the ball and threw it back to Faith. Running backward, Faith stretched as tall as she could but missed the reckless throw. She heard a dull thwack and whirled to see Nicholas rubbing the back of his head. For a moment her steps faltered, and she wasn't sure what to do.

Nicholas calmly bent down and picked up the ball. Faith backed up as he walked toward her, cupping the ball in the palm of his hand.

"Does this belong to you?"

Faith nodded, for once speechless. Nicholas handed her the ball. Their hands brushed during the brief exchange, and Faith felt a current. For a moment she was certain Nicholas felt it too.

"Try to keep it in your court."

"I'll do that."

Oooohhhhhh, he was so *infuriating,* she thought as he walked away—so downright smug!

Faith's temper gave way and she reared back, hurled the ball, and hit him squarely in the back of the head, hard. Nicholas spun around and shot her a look of disbelief.

"Faith, I wouldn't do that," Dan cautioned. "Nicholas will only put up with so much."

Faith met Nicholas's stern look with one of her own. "I could have knocked him cold if I'd tried."

Dan looked mildly amused, then cleared his throat. "Get the ball, Sissy!"

"Anyone care for watermelon?" Reverend Hicks shouted.

Picnickers made a beeline to the brush arbor. Amos and Vera were busy slicing watermelon, serving adults first, then children. Sissy and Adam were anxious to get their piece of the juicy pink melon. Dan took them by the hand and asked Faith, "Want me to bring yours?"

"No, thanks." She brushed grass from the back of her dress, glancing at Liza still sitting alone on her blanket. On closer look, Faith saw the woman was crying. Liza, crying? She looked again, just to make sure. Liza was silently sobbing into her handkerchief.

Regardless of their differences, Liza's tears softened Faith's heart. God would not want her to ignore another's pain. She had no idea how her presence would be received, but she couldn't just stand here without offering help. If Liza sent her away, so be it. It certainly wouldn't be the first time she had been rebuffed by Nicholas's mother. It surely might be the last.

Edging toward the Shepherd blanket, Faith proceeded with caution until she was able to kneel beside the older woman. Liza quickly dried her eyes.

"Liza, may I get you a slice of watermelon?" Faith asked softly.

Liza refused to look at her. "I'm surprised you'd offer."

Faith sighed, gently touching her shoulder. "Well, I care about you, Liza. I wish we could be friends."

Liza's gruff demeanor evaporated, and vulnerability took its place. Tears spilled down her cheeks. "Oh, Faith, how *could* you care about me? After the way I've treated you—the way I've treated everyone. I'm so ashamed . . . so ashamed."

Papa always said Faith was blessed with a forgiving spirit. She knew she wasn't, but in this instance she found it easy to forgive. She knew Christians weren't perfect, just forgiven.

"Liza, I know I'm impetuous at times, and I'm not the easiest person to get along with. I have a stubborn streak a mile long," Faith admitted. "But I've never meant you or Nicholas any harm."

Liza reached out for Faith's hand, and held it. She trembled like a small child. "You've done nothing wrong. You stood up for something you believed in. I've been so impossible, so vile to you. And I'm sorry I came between you and Nicholas." She broke off, sobbing into her handkerchief. "It's just that I don't know what's wrong with me. I don't mean to be hurtful."

Faith put her arms around the broken woman and held her tightly. "Sometimes we just need a good long cry," she comforted. "Cry, Liza. I'll hold you."

And cry she did, until Faith felt there were no more tears left to fall. Liza must have had them stored for a powerfully long time.

When the storm passed, Liza sat up, wiping her swollen lids. "I'm sorry. I haven't always been like this." She drew a deep, shuddering breath, then gave a faint laugh. "Always a little headstrong, but never this mass of weeping emotions. The death of a loved one is devastating. I miss Abe so much! Sometimes the pain just takes my breath away."

Nodding, Faith tenderly brushed a lock of hair stuck to Liza's damp cheek. "It must be difficult to accept." Nicholas was a dutiful son, that Faith knew only too well; but Liza needed another woman, a daughter, to comfort her when she hurt, to understand the depth of her pain, to hold her hand during uncertain times.

Liza brought her hand to her mouth, whispering, "I know God is to be the center of our lives, but oh, how I long for my husband. When Abe died, a part of me died with him—my best part. Sometimes I feel so empty that I rail against God, wishing he had taken me, not Abe."

"I know it's not quite the same, but I felt empty and lost when Papa died."

Liza blew her nose, and her gaze centered on Jeremiah. "What must he think of me? I've treated him so badly."

Faith smiled, thinking how strange life was. Never in a million years would she have thought she'd be having this conversation. Not with Liza. Especially not with Liza. "Well, I can't speak for Jeremiah, but I suspect he doesn't think badly of you."

"The whole town thinks badly of me. They can't understand that it isn't the money. . . ." Liza paused, drained of emotion. "I can't recall when I wasn't on the front pew come Sunday mornings. I've been there for revivals, christenings, baptisms, never failed to give the Lord his 10 percent and thank him for his bountiful blessings. I've tried to raise Nicholas in a Christian home, but oh, I've fallen short so many times. I'll be the first to admit to that. For so long now, I've been in this awful deep valley. I'm not sure why, or how, to find the strength to climb out."

"Papa said sometimes God takes us through the darkest times because he's preparing us for a higher mountaintop." Faith reached for Liza's hand, squeezing it. "Something in my spirit tells me you're not in a hopeless valley; you're just getting ready to climb a new mountain."

"How can you say that, child?" Liza questioned softly. "My husband is gone. I've lost my youth; my body betrays me. Nicholas will be married—another woman will take my place in his life. I have nothing. I have no one."

"Yes, Abe is dead. But you'll always have his memories; nothing can take those away from you. And you know he's with the Lord now. Why, he's probably smiling down on you right now, saying, 'Hold on, Liza; we'll be together again soon.' And, Liza, you'll never lose Nicholas. You have raised him well. He's a good and godly man who will always honor his mother. And his family will be your family."

Faith drew the woman back to her breast and gave her a good hug, something she'd obviously not had in a long time. "As for youth, don't cry over lost youth, but glory in the knowledge that each year that passes brings you one step closer to going home to be with our heavenly Father, home to be with Abe."

Liza's shoulders heaved as tears fell anew. "Right now I just feel very old, old and tired, unloved, and horribly forgetful. I misplace everything, and I'd forget my name if I didn't write it down."

Liza's admission brought Faith a pang of guilt. "I'm afraid I have a confession to make. . . ."

Liza looked up. "A confession?"

"You're not as forgetful as you think. I've been hiding your snuff—not out of spite. I hid it because I thought if it wasn't there to tempt you, you might decide to give up the habit." Faith wrinkled her nose. "I hid it behind the mantel clock."

Liza patted Faith's hand. "I know, dear. I found it each time I rewound the clock. You're lucky, young lady, I didn't take a switch to you." Liza shyly grinned through a veil of tears. Faith was stunned to see she wasn't old at all. Quite pretty, actually.

"I hope you aren't upset with me."

"Quite the contrary. I haven't touched snuff for weeks now. And I have you to thank for making me think about what a bad habit I had developed."

Should she mention the brown vial? No, they were making progress on their friendship. She didn't want to spoil the effort by introducing more problems.

The women shared a good laugh. Then Faith grew serious. "See, you're not as forgetful as you think. And you're not old, either. You're still beautiful and—" she raised her eyebrows—"there's a certain gentleman who would very much like to know you better."

Liza blushed, her gaze fixed on Jeremiah sitting across the yard. "Well, I doubt that he likes me any longer. I've managed to run *him* off, too."

"Oh, I have a feeling he won't be gone long. Jeremiah knows a good thing when he sees it. I doubt he'd let you slip away without a good fight."

Liza blushed. "Faith, I—I don't know how to thank you. I realize now that I haven't turned my problem over to God, haven't let him heal my pain. I know better; I read

God's Word every day. It's odd how easy it is to forget his
promises in the midst of one's pain."

"God loves you, Liza, and he's waiting to give you peace."
My yoke is easy, and my burden is light, Faith remembered. She
hugged Liza again briefly. Her sister, Hope, always said she
hugged the life out of people, but she didn't care. She never
got enough hugging herself. "If you're feeling better, I had
better be getting back. The children will be looking for me."

"Run along . . . and thank you for listening to an old
woman's problems."

Faith pointed a stern finger at her. "You're *not* old."

Faith was about to walk away when Liza latched onto
the hem of her skirt. "All the apologies in the world aren't
going to correct what I've done. Nicholas is stubborn, so
like his father. It seems you've wounded his pride by turning to Dan—although I accept full responsibility. I'm so
sorry, Faith. As much as I would like, I doubt that I can
undo the wrong I've done. Pride destroys all it touches."

Faith nodded. "I know. It doesn't matter anymore. I've
decided to return to Cold Water. Perhaps when this is over,
Nicholas will find a woman here in Deliverance to marry."
She thought of Rachel, taking no joy in the thought. "A
grandchild is just what you need to take
away your loneliness."

Faith said good-bye and rejoined Dan and the children.
Now she knew the reasons Liza had erected so many barri-
ers—to protect herself from further loss. The woman she
thought she could never like, now appeared to be someone
she could truly love.

But it was too late. Too late for Liza, and too late for Nicholas and her.

Toward sunset, Nicholas wandered down to the pond. Faith and the children were sitting on the bank, fishing; Dan and the baby were napping at the church ground.

Watching Faith bait her hook, Nicholas felt a tightening in his throat. With stark clarity he realized God had not sent Faith to him; he'd sent her to Dan Walters. Dan's children loved her—Dan was in love with her himself; it didn't take a wise man to see that. And Faith was falling in love with him. Nicholas saw the blush in her cheeks, heard her bubbly laughter. What a blind fool he'd been. He'd sweated blood over their situation, wondered, prayed if he should ask her to come back. Ironically, today he realized the state of their relationship was no longer in his hands. Faith belonged to Dan.

"Looks like Adam and Sissy could use some help baiting those hooks."

Faith looked up, surprise crossing her sun-kissed features when she saw him. Like Lilly, he thought, Faith refused to wear her bonnet. "Oh, we'll manage." She jerked, missed a catch, and brought her line back in.

The moment felt awkward and strained. Where was her earlier laughter; the laughter she shared so easily with Dan?

"Tried your luck lately?" she asked.

It wasn't exactly an invitation, but Nicholas took it as one. Walking to the edge of the water, he stood for a moment, watching water skimmers on long, comical legs skitter across the pond. He'd never noticed how nice Faith looked in a dress. The blue-and-white gingham brought out the violet in her eyes. Had she worn the dress before?

Adam jerked, and his line snarled around a nearby stump. He pulled back, popping the hook. It shot by Sissy's ear like a bullet. She screamed and dropped her pole on the ground.

The boy whipped the rod in the opposite direction and caught the brim of Sissy's hat, yanking it into the water. Bending over, Sissy picked up a rock and hurled it at him.

Nicholas moved in. "Hold on now—no rock throwing." As he walked past Faith, he leaned down, his breath warm against her ear. "I'd like to call a truce."

Faith looked up. "A truce?"

"If you're agreeable."

He could see she must surely be tempted to remind him of the past month, a month when he had managed to torment, tease *and* ignore her; but she didn't. Would she be willing to call an end to their childishness? *Blessed are the peacemakers.*

"If that's what you want."

"I'd like that very much." He missed her, more than he thought he'd miss any woman. The thought left him unsettled. "Shake on it?" Nicholas extended his hand.

They shook, sharing forgiving smiles.

"Sorry I was so short with you."

"Sorry I've been such a twit."

Sissy and Adam reminded Nicholas that he needed to bait

their hooks. Nicholas reluctantly released Faith's hand. "I'm sorry our arrangement hasn't worked out."

"So am I."

Why hadn't they tried harder to make it work? Why hadn't *he* tried harder? Pride? Was pride blinding him the way it so often had Papa?

"No hard feelings?"

Faith deserved a husband closer to her age. As much as Nicholas hated to admit it, Dan would be good for her. Nicholas was older, more set in his ways. He couldn't imagine playing ball with young children, frolicking around the churchyard like frisky colts, running hand in hand with Faith through fields of bluebonnets. But for one irrational moment he wanted to. A thought hit him like a thunderbolt. What would their children have looked like—blond and fair like he was, or dark and olive-skinned like Faith? He had never pictured himself as a father, but he realized either would suit him just fine.

"No hard feelings," she granted.

"Mr. Shewperd, are yew gonna put this woorm on my hook or not?" Nicholas was jolted from his thoughts to find Sissy, cane pole in one hand, an ugly-looking night crawler dangling in the other.

He frowned. "Are you sure you want that hearty fella on your line?"

Sissy solemnly nodded.

Nicholas looked at Faith and wrinkled his nose. "That's what I was afraid of."

Time passed too quickly. Before Nicholas knew it, the sun had set in a purple-streaked sky.

"Faith, it's almost time for the fireworks!" Adam breathlessly announced after his fourth journey to the churchyard.

"Adam, you come on now," Dan yelled, holding Lilly in his arms and standing on a small rise at the back of the churchyard.

"Be there in a moment, Adam," Faith promised. The little boy allowed his sister to take his hand and lead him up the steep embankment.

Nicholas helped Faith gather poles and other tackle. "Kids love those fireworks."

"Adam's been looking forward to them all day."

As they started up the incline, Faith suddenly stopped, whirled, and reached up to give him a little peck on the cheek. Then she simply gazed at him. "I'm sorry, but I can't leave without doing that."

Surprised, Nicholas didn't know what to say. "I'm glad you didn't . . . leave," he clarified. "Without doing that."

She released a breath of what sounded like relief. "I hoped you'd see it that way." Playfully rubbing the goose-egg-sized knot on the back of his head, she confessed, "I need to say I'm sorry about hitting you with that ball. That was most impolite of me."

"If that's what it takes to get a kiss from you, you have my permission to fell me with a ball bat."

He heard her say softly, "Well, actually, my kiss was about more, but that's neither here nor there."

He frowned.

She stopped his next question by resting a fingertip on his lips. "The fireworks will be starting. I promised I'd watch them with Adam. I don't want to disappoint him."

As they started up the steep incline, Nicholas reached for her hand. Hand in hand, they climbed the hill. When they reached the top, he reluctantly released her hand and headed back to his mother.

Nicholas had thought that once he apologized to Faith and settled their dispute, he'd feel better.

Oddly enough, he felt worse.

Before the fireworks started, Faith shredded paper and bunched it into a loose ball. She told Adam to hold out his hand.

"Why?" Adam questioned.

"It's a firework," Faith answered. "Not a real one, but a pretend one. I want you to *see* what one looks like."

"Really?"

"Really. Are you ready to use your imagination?"

"Yes, ma'am!"

"OK, here we go." Faith stood over Adam. "Feel all the little bits of paper, rolled into a ball?"

Adam carefully examined the paper ball with his fingers. "Yes."

"Well, that's a firework before it's lit. But when its fuse is lit, the firework shoots far up in the sky, exploding into a hundred million brilliant colors and shapes as it falls back to earth."

"What are the colors?" Adam asked excitedly.

"Blue—"

"Cool," Adam squealed. "Like the ice!"

"Red—"

"Hot!"

"Like the stove," Faith said. "Now close your eyes, and we're going to shoot off our pretend firework. You'll feel the little pieces of paper when they fall on your face. Imagine the real ones falling from the sky, only they're hot and burn themselves out before they reach the ground."

"That's a good thing, huh, Faith?" Adam turned sober.

"A very good thing. If they didn't, we'd all have little blisters. . . ."

"'Cause they're red-hot!"

Faith laughed. "Are you ready? The fireworks are about to begin!"

"Yes!"

"Are you using your imagination?"

"A whole bunch!"

Faith made a sizzling, sputtering sound like a rocket about to take off. Loosening the paper ball, she clasped his hand to hers. They tossed the tiny pieces in the air, letting them burst free and cascade down on Adam's face as the first rocket went up. The crowd ooohhed and ahhhed as the missile soared into the heavens, exploded, then rained down in a myriad of spectacular colors.

"Fireworks! Red, blue—hot and cold—I can see them, Faith! I can see them in my 'magination!"

Tears sprang to Faith's eyes. Adam didn't need eyes to see

the beauty. God had given him a lively imagination, one where virtually nothing was out of his reach. "Aren't they beautiful!"

"They're *beautiful*," Adam repeated, jumping up and down. "So *beautiful!*"

Dan looked at Faith, his eyes filled with gratitude. "You're amazing."

Faith shook her head. "No. Your son is the amazing one. And I like to think that somewhere your wife, Carolyn, is looking down, so very proud of him right now."

Just then the sky lit up with another explosion. Faith sat beside Adam as the rockets burst in midair, their dazzling colors a stark contrast to the nighttime sky. Sissy squealed with delight, hopping on one foot, then the other. Lilly bawled, wanting her bottle. Hand in hand, Adam and Faith watched with a new appreciation for Deliverance's Founder's Day fireworks display.

The celebration came to an end. Weary mothers and fathers loaded sleepy children into wagons. While Dan packed the buckboard, Faith stepped over to talk to Jeremiah.

"Jeremiah, may I have a word with you?" she asked, not exactly sure how to broach the subject of his relationship with Liza.

"You most certainly may." Jeremiah smiled. "How can I help a pretty little thing like you?"

"I couldn't help overhearing you and Liza earlier today. . . ."

"Water under the bridge, I assure you."

"Jeremiah, maybe it isn't." Faith searched for the right words. She didn't want to make the situation worse. "I think perhaps Liza realizes she was a little . . . shall we say, brusque with you today?"

"Oh, I believe she made herself quite clear." He laughed, but his eyes exposed deep hurt.

"I don't think she meant to be so harsh. In fact, I think you should give Liza another chance."

Jeremiah eyed Faith. "Another chance to insult me and turn me down?"

"No. I have a feeling you'll be getting a different response from now on."

"And what makes you so sure?"

Faith had no intention of betraying Liza's confidence. But she believed that once Liza surrendered her hurt to God, he would be swift to lighten her burden. She winked at Jeremiah. "Just trust me on this one. Please?"

Jeremiah hesitated, absently stroking his beard. "Well . . . I'll take the matter under consideration."

"Thanks, Jeremiah." Faith stood on tiptoes and kissed him on the cheek.

"My," Jeremiah said. "What's brought this on?"

"Nothing." Although Faith wanted to tell him she was leaving, she feared she would get emotional. She gulped. Better to warn him now than to betray his friendship. "I must leave, and you must keep my secret."

He frowned.

"Nicholas has left me no other choice."

"Child, with time—"

"Please, as my friend, allow me this."

He nodded.

When they arrived back at the Walters home, Mary Ellen and Albert waited as Faith helped Dan get the children into the house.

Less than an hour later, exhausted but happy, the two women sat at the Finneys' kitchen table, each thinking about the strange day.

Faith had fallen in love with Nicholas Shepherd.

She had realized it this afternoon at the pond. Nicholas had tried to smooth things over, but it just made her want more of him. Somehow he had seemed more relaxed, at peace, and he was wonderful with the children. Her heart ached. She supposed worse things could happen than falling in love under these circumstances. But the thought somehow failed to cheer her.

Chapter Thirteen

LIZA?" Doc got up from his desk and motioned Liza into his office.

"Hi, Doc. I took a chance you weren't busy."

"Never too busy for you." Doc pulled up a chair and invited her to sit down. Perching on the edge of the desk, the portly, silver-haired gentleman smiled. "How's Nicholas?"

"Fine, just fine."

"Heard that he and Miss Kallahan are having quite a time gettin' the knot tied."

Liza didn't care to discuss Nicholas's personal problems. Molly Anderson and Etta Larkin were doing a fine job of that. "Seems that way."

Doc's features sobered. "Something I can do for you, Liza?"

It was the moment she'd dreaded, yet now she fully welcomed it. It was the first step to relinquishing all her hurts and disappointments to God. The thought no longer frightened her; she felt a peace for the first time since Abe's death. But she had to know how much time she had left. There were matters to be set in order.

"I . . . haven't been feeling myself lately."

"Oh?" Doc frowned. "How long?"

She shrugged. "A couple of years . . . since Abe . . . since Abe left. At first I thought it was grief. Now I know it's much more than that."

Doc's mouth fell. "Liza!"

"You know I don't hold with doctors," she snapped.

Getting to his feet, Doc eyed her sternly. "Tell me what you've observed about your health. Think this through. I need to know everything that has been going on with you and when each symptom began." He picked up his pencil and paper and settled in a chair close to her.

Liza burst into tears, ailments pouring out of her like lava: night sweats, hot flashes, loss of memory, bouts of depression, paranoia. When the flood subsided, she dried her eyes and braced herself for the worst. "I know I don't have long, but I need to know how long, so I can make plans."

Doc nodded, listened to her heart, looked down her throat, peered into her ears, thumped here and there as she talked.

"Hummmm."

When the examination was over, she gazed up at him. "How long, Doc?"

Doc shook his head and moved to the medicine cabinet.

"Hard to say, but listening to your heart, I'd guess no more than thirty, forty years."

Liza nodded. Thirty to forty years. That's what she'd thought. . . . She sat up straighter. "What?"

"How old are you now, Liza? Fifty? Fifty-one?"

"Fifty-two in November."

"Monthlies ceased?"

She blushed, then nodded.

"Cross as a settin' hen?"

She nodded, miserably wringing her hands. She hated to think how regularly she'd pinned Nicholas's ears back.

Doc took a bottle off the shelf, then closed the cabinet door. "You're going through the change of life, Liza. Nothing to be worried about. It falls to every woman. The symptoms are uncomfortable and annoying, but it won't kill you."

He put the bottle in her hand, squeezing her fingers shut. "Pinkham's Tonic. A lot of physicians think it's hogwash, but I don't. I have women who swear by it. Take a couple of teaspoons three times a day, and you'll be your old self in no time at all."

"Change of life? That's what *Grandma* went through."

Doc nodded. "And her mother, and her mother, and her mother. I suppose even old Eve gave Adam a fair run for his money when she hit the right age."

Liza stared at the brown vial of *Lydia E. Pinkham's Vegetable Compound*. "I'm not going to die?"

He chuckled. "Not any time soon—now, of course, you understand, I don't make those kinds of decisions. I leave that up to the Lord."

Liza rolled the bottle of medicine in her hands and took a deep breath. "I . . . I've been using . . . " She couldn't look Doc in the eyes.

"You've been using Pinkham's Tonic?"

"I had heard, uh, had heard it might help."

"What dosage did you use, Liza?" the doctor asked gently.

"I only took a swallow when I really needed it." She straightened, and her chin shot skyward. "I knew I could handle whatever trials the Lord sent to me. Until Abe . . . until Abe left . . . died." There, she'd finally admitted it. Abe was gone, residing now with his heavenly Father. "I thought perhaps it was grief that made me feel so awful."

"Liza, trust me. Take the medicine and follow my instructions. You'll be over this before long." He squeezed her shoulder. "Nature makes these changes in your body, and once you understand what is happening, it's much easier to accept. Now, I want to hear from you soon about how you're feeling."

Leaving the office a few minutes later, Liza closed the door and sagged against it. She wasn't going to die.

Clutching the full bottle of tonic to her chest, she lifted her face to the afternoon sun, letting the glorious assurance wash over her.

She *wasn't* going to die.

"Mama!" Nicholas burst through the back door and slammed it shut. The cat, sunning on the windowsill, jumped as if shot. "The chickens are in the garden again!"

Liza glanced up from the stove. "Well, put them back in the pen."

"You put them back in the pen." He threw his hat on the kitchen table, rattling a cup and saucer. "It's your job to keep them out of the garden."

Slicing a beef roast, Liza calmly motioned him toward the washstand. "Wash up. Dinner's almost ready."

Nicholas reached the washbowl in two angry strides. When Papa was alive, if a chicken went near the garden, it would have been swimming in a pot of dumplings that night!

Reaching for the bar of soap, he lathered his hands and elbows. The image of Faith swam before his eyes. Muttering under his breath, he forced her image aside. The woman was on his mind day and night. What was happening to him? It was almost as if she'd cast a spell over him, a spell he was powerless to escape.

She was a curse—had been from the moment she rode into town on the back of Jeremiah's mule. Stirring up the town with talk of a school for the blind, spending time with Dan Walters—she, and she alone, was responsible for all these hushed whispers and sympathetic stares coming his way.

How soon was Miss Kallahan going to make it worse?

Nicholas wondered how soon she was going to marry Dan and make Nicholas look like an even bigger fool. Paying her way here, putting her up all those weeks—he should never have gone on that cattle drive. That's when the problem had started. If he'd stayed home, he and Faith would be married.

He scrubbed harder. He'd bet Walters took his meals at his own table with Faith at noontime. His stomach spasmed with the thought as he scoured his arms so hard they hurt. The woman just plain made him mad. He couldn't eat, couldn't sleep. Toweling off, he stalked to the table.

Setting a bowl of greens on the table, Liza eyed him. "My, aren't we in a temper."

"Chickens don't belong in the garden." Nicholas reached for an ear of corn and slapped butter on it.

Taking her seat at the opposite end of the table, Liza bowed her head and quietly blessed the food.

"Seems to me," she continued as she shook out her napkin, "you've had a burr under your saddle lately."

"I don't know what you're talking about."

"I'm talking about Faith."

Nicholas froze at the sound of her name. The mention of Faith Kallahan had been banned in this house. Why Mama chose to bring it up now escaped him. "Well," Nicholas said as he reached for the platter of roast, "I'm *not* talking about her, Mama. So let's eat in peace."

Liza took a bite of meat with her eyes still fixed on her son. "Saw Faith today while I was in town."

Was she going to wear out that name right here at the dinner table? Nicholas grumbled, "What took you to town on a weekday morning?"

"A little this, a little that." Liza thought about the new brown bottle of Pinkham's Tonic hidden at the bottom of her bureau drawer and smiled. Picking up the bowl of greens, she spooned a helping onto her plate. "Faith's fixing the town steeple."

"She's what?"

"Fixing the town steeple. There she and Dan were, on the church rooftop, big as you please, Faith dressed in overalls and men's boots, hammering and painting to beat the band. I must say, the old steeple's going to look a sight better."

"Fixing steeples, sawing wood, delivering cows—what next?" Nicholas shoved a bite of meat into his mouth.

Liza casually speared a slice of tomato. "Seems she and Dan were meant for each other. They have the same interests; Faith takes to those kids like a moth to a flame—wouldn't surprise me if Dan didn't snap her right up."

"I thought he already had."

"Nicholas . . ."

"Mama, I'm trying to eat."

"I was wrong about Faith, Nicholas." Liza's humble admission rattled him. She had been *wrong?* Well, now was a fine time to admit it.

"No, you weren't wrong, Mama. Your instincts about Faith were right. I'm just glad I found out she was fickle before I married her."

"This whole misunderstanding between you and Faith is my fault. I'm sorry I was so unreasonable and that I didn't try to befriend her—perhaps if you were to start over—"

"Don't be foolish. You were right about the steeple, and

I'm right about Faith. No caring woman would have left the moment my back was turned."

"I could be right about the steeple, but not about Faith. And she didn't just up and leave. If you blame anyone, blame me. My irrational ultimatum left Faith little choice but to seek refuge at the Finneys'. I treated her unfairly, Nicholas—and I indicated she was feeling something for Dan that I don't think she's really feeling. I deliberately planted that seed in your head, and I was wrong, so wrong. I'm sorry . . . if I had it to do over—"

Nicholas cut her off. "What's done is done." He was tired of talking about Faith Kallahan. Six days out of seven they ate their meals in silence. Why, of all days, did Mama have to pick this particular meal to philosophize? He bit into an ear of corn and wiped juice off his chin.

Liza took a bite of roast, her eyes fixed on him. What was she looking at? Couldn't a man eat his dinner in peace?

"You feeling all right lately, Nicholas?"

"Fine."

She reached for a biscuit, breaking it open. "Good dose of Epsom salts now and then never hurt a body."

He lifted his head and eyed her sourly.

They lapsed into silence, their focus on their plates.

"Reverend Hicks stopped by earlier."

"What did he want?"

"Money for the holiday baskets. He's starting the drive early this year."

Nicholas forked a bite of greens into his mouth. "Give it to him. Make a generous donation this year. We've got more money than we can ever spend." Lord knew they'd been miserly enough the past couple of years.

Liza reached for her fan as color saturated her face. Nicholas watched the familiar red flush creeping up her neck.

"Are you hot again?"

"It's a little warm in here." She sheepishly avoided his stare. "Don't you think?"

Nicholas shook his head. "Feels comfortable to me."

The flush receded, and she snapped the fan shut. "Eat your dinner before it gets cold."

Late that afternoon Nicholas was loading an order of feed at the mercantile. Oren Stokes and Jeremiah were discussing the weather. Hot, could use a good rain, the two men decided.

Jeremiah was another person on Nicholas's short list. If he hadn't encouraged Faith, she wouldn't have gone off half-cocked to open a school for the blind. Jeremiah knew Nicholas hadn't endorsed the idea, yet he had continued to encourage Faith.

Nicholas had been at the store last week when two large crates arrived from Boston. Jeremiah had hurriedly loaded the bins onto a cart, and hauled them off. Nicholas suspected the boxes had something to do with the proposed school, but Jeremiah refused to say.

Just then Jeremiah came out of the store and down the steps. He smiled at Nicholas, nodding pleasantly.

Heaving another sack aboard the wagon, Nicholas grunted what passed for a civil greeting. He didn't feel very "civil" at the moment.

Jeremiah paused on the lower step to light his pipe. Giving a hearty puff, he gazed up at the flawless blue sky. "Hot, isn't it?"

Nicholas swung another sack onto the wagon, hoping Jeremiah wasn't going to start in on the weather again. How much more could be said about a hot June day? Oren had pretty much exhausted the subject.

"Yes, sir." Jeremiah patted his vest, drawing on the pipe. White smoke swirled above his head. "Fine time for traveling—though it could get a mite dusty."

Hefting the last grain sack onto the wagon, Nicholas took off his hat and wiped the sweat off his forehead. "Suppose it could—if anyone was going anywhere."

Jeremiah cocked a brow. "You haven't heard?"

"Heard what?" Nicholas reached for the dipper in the water barrel.

"Why, Miss Kallahan is leaving us soon."

The statement hit Nicholas like a cannonball. His hand paused, the dipper suspended in midair. His eyes darkened to a troubled hue. "You must be mistaken. She doesn't intend to leave; she intends to marry Dan."

Drawing on the stem of the pipe, Jeremiah shook his head. "No, don't believe she does. She's leaving on the stage in the morning. Saw her purchase the ticket myself, couldn't have been more than thirty minutes ago."

Nicholas tried to find his voice. Faith leaving? Lifting the dipper to his mouth, he took a long, thirsty drink. If Jeremiah expected a reaction, he wasn't going to get one. This whole mail-order bride mess left a bad taste in Nicholas's mouth. She had told him at the dance that she didn't intend to marry Dan Walters but to return to Michigan. But when he'd seen her at the Founder's Day celebration, with Dan and his children, he'd been sure that she was in love with Dan and had changed her mind. Apparently she had decided to keep her word to him.

The thought should have left him with a measure of satisfaction; instead, he felt empty, as if he'd lost something rare and irreplaceable because of pride and stupidity.

Jerking the brim of his hat low, he said quietly, "That's too bad. I'm surprised Dan would allow her to go."

Jeremiah struck a match and frowned at his cold pipe. "I'm sure if Dan had any say in the matter, he would insist that she stay." He touched the match to the rim, puffing, "Unfortunately, he doesn't. Faith came here to marry you. Since that no longer seems likely, she's decided to return to her aunt in Michigan."

Nicholas removed his gloves, stalling for time. "What about the school for the blind?"

"Pity," Jeremiah said. "Faith's a fine figure of a woman—smart, too. The town would have benefited greatly had she been allowed to open the school."

Nicholas slapped the gloves against his thighs, his features taut with frustration. "No one's running her out of town. She can stay if she wants."

"Oh, I think she'd find that entirely too awkward." The

pipe flared to life again. "True, Dan would marry her in a heartbeat, but she doesn't love Dan." He fanned the match out, smiling. "Love's a strange thing; never know where it's going to pop up, or with whom."

Jeremiah's tone implied she was in love with him, Nicholas. Nicholas inwardly ridiculed the idea. It was not only wrong, it was laughable. How could Faith love him? He'd given her every reason to feel the opposite.

Swinging aboard the wagon, Nicholas released the brake. "Tell her I wish her the best."

"Why don't you tell her?"

He couldn't. He didn't wish her to leave at all.

Nicholas rolled to his back and hurled a boot at the open window. Blasted crickets! They'd kept him awake half the night.

Settling back on the pillow, he closed his eyes, only to see Faith's face for the hundredth time. Why should he care if she left tomorrow . . . yet he did. How could he ever make up for all that had happened between them—and all that hadn't happened?

Shifting to his side, he wadded his pillow under his head, soundly thumping it. He heard the clock strike two; then, what seemed like hours later, it struck three, and he sighed.

Twisting to his back, he stared at the ceiling. He'd done the work of ten men today trying to put Faith and her fickle nature out of his mind. He should be sleeping like the dead, but instead he was staring at the ceiling, wondering what he'd done wrong.

He had been polite, respectful, careful to make Faith comfortable during the time she was under his roof. Their brief talks on the porch at night had made him think they were warming to each other. Their wedding was delayed twice—no, three times—well actually four, but she'd seemed to understand why. A man wasn't expected to lose a good herd of stock for a ten-minute wedding ceremony, was he? Faith hadn't expected him to let the town burn to the ground, had she? Babies had a way of coming at the most inconvenient time—he'd heard that himself. Miss Kallahan couldn't pin that one on him. And the herd, well, that was pure common sense in the cattle business.

He switched back to his side. It was Dan Walters's fault. From the moment she'd arrived, Dan had his eye on her, and Carolyn barely cold in her grave. He listened to the pesky cricket near the windowsill.

Walters needed help. Three small kids under the age of five—one blind. He guessed he'd be looking for help too if he were in Dan's shoes.

He rolled onto his back and frowned in the darkness. Faith certainly hadn't lost any time making herself useful to Dan. Naturally he'd take to her—no, he was being unfair. Dan didn't just *need* Faith; he was attracted to her. That was the hardest to admit, and it stuck in his throat. He'd seen the admiration in Dan's eyes, the expectant way he looked at Faith, the way the two of them shared a confidential smile when the children did something cute.

Why hadn't Faith looked at him that way? Or had she, and he'd been so busy trying to solve Mama's problems that he failed to notice? Questions nagged him. He thought he'd gotten Faith out of his system, but she was back, haunting his thoughts, making him feel as though *he* were at fault, not her. He professed to be a Christian, but where was his faith now? What had become of his initial trust—the belief that God had sent Faith for him, not for Dan?

Faith had brought sunshine back into his life. She brought laughter into the house. After Papa's death the house had become a tomb. Mama went about her work, he went about his, and two years passed by. One day he woke up and realized he was thirty-four years old. Thirty-four. Before long, life would pass him by.

If he'd had any idea that posting that blasted ad would bring this kind of grief, he would have cut the journal in a hundred pieces and fed it to the hogs. What had he been thinking? Just because he was thirty-four and single, did that give him license to order a bride? Send off for a wife like he would send for a new plow? Well, it hadn't worked. He'd only served to make a fool of himself.

If he had it to do over, he'd try harder with Faith. He would marry her before the problems ever got out of hand. Pride, ugly pride, had kept him from going to her. When was he going to turn that pride over to God?

It wasn't easy to welcome a stranger into his home, and it took time to build a union between a man and a woman; but they had struck a bargain. He'd given his promise; she'd given hers. If he'd married her the moment she got off Jeremiah's mule, he wouldn't be going through this! He punched his pillow. Pride be hanged. He should have seen this thing through. It wasn't the worst idea he'd ever had. The worst was when he'd decided not to go after her the moment he returned from San Antonio.

Sitting up in bed, he realized his mistake. He was obligated to keep his promise. The town would see his rationale and not hold it against him. He'd sent for Faith to be his bride, and a man wasn't much of a man who refused to honor a commitment.

Tossing the sheet aside, he got out of bed and reached for his trousers.

Faith lifted her head off the pillow, roused from a deep sleep. The sound of Nicholas's raised voice behind the closed bedroom door startled her.

"I want to talk to Faith!"

Albert's hushed voice tried to quiet him. "She's asleep, Nicholas, has been for hours—"

Faith cringed at the note of authority in Nicholas's voice. *"Now,* Albert."

Climbing out of bed, Faith dressed quickly, then twisted her braid on top her head. Pinching color into her cheeks, she slipped out the door.

"Nicholas?"

Nicholas's eyes burned with intensity. "I want to talk to you."

Faith glanced questioningly at Albert. "Certainly—Albert, would you mind—"

"Not here," Nicholas said. "Horses are waiting outside."

"Nicholas, that's highly improper," Albert reminded him. "Faith is without a chaperone—"

"Faith and I are both adults. I can assure you I have no intention of dishonoring Miss Kallahan."

"It's all right, Albert." She reached for a light shawl. "I'll only be gone a short while."

"Do you want me to come with you?"

"No, you stay with Mary Ellen and the children. I'll be fine, really." She brushed coolly past Nicholas on her way out of the door.

Her mind whirled. Where was he taking her? Was it wise for her to entrust her well-being to this man? A new, hopeful thought dawned on her. Had he discovered she was leaving and come to stop her? No, the only ones who knew she was leaving were Dan and Jeremiah. Dan had promised to keep quiet until she was safely gone, and Nicholas would never have talked to Jeremiah.

She paused when she saw the two Appaloosas standing by the rail. For a moment she wanted to cry. *Now* he was taking her for that promised ride.

"Pick the one you want. I promised you a ride when I got back."

Faith nuzzled a warm, black nose. "Do you keep promises, Nicholas?"

"I try, Faith. I try very hard."

Biting her lip, Faith picked the animal on the left. They

were both magnificent creatures. But she didn't want a
horse. She wanted Nicholas.

Nicholas lifted her onto the saddle, and their hands
brushed. She felt a thrill of anticipation and quickly smoth-
ered it. Tucking her dress between her knees, she flicked
the reins. The horses galloped out of the yard and into the
lane. A full moon hung overhead. Nicholas rode beside her,
his jaw set in determination. Whatever had prompted this
nocturnal visit, she guessed she'd soon know.

An hour, then two, the horses traveled back roads and
forded dry creek beds. Faith shivered, hunched beneath her
thin shawl. How dare he burst into the Finneys' house and
demand to see her at this time of night? He had no
right—no right at all to act as if he owned her!

The animals climbed steep inclines and picked their way
through valleys dotted with Shepherd cattle.

The moon sank lower and lower in the western sky as the
horses clopped along dirt roads. The silence was altered only
by the changing cadence of hooves, fast, then slower. And
still, Nicholas didn't speak. For what reason had he come
calling for her tonight? His stern features seemed at war
with himself. Did he want to say something? Tell her
something? Confess something?

Darkness gradually gave way to dawn. The sky lightened,
spreading tendrils of pastel pinks and golds across the distant
horizon. Faith dozed, her head bobbing with the horse's
easy gait.

The animals came to a stop, and Faith sat up, trying to
orient herself. They were back in the Finneys' yard. She

looked at Nicholas's tired features and knew that indeed a war raged within him, but he seemed determined not to permit her to know his enemy.

"Nicholas," she said softly, wanting to erase the pain she saw in his eyes. "What is it?"

Shaking his head, he refused to answer. She'd known all along he wasn't a man who easily expressed his feelings. But she was powerless to help until he exposed the demons that drove him.

Getting off the horse, he came to stand beside her mount. She waited, holding her breath.

"I'd like to kiss you," he stated quietly.

"All right," she agreed in a hushed whisper.

Lifting her off the saddle into his arms, he kissed her, his kiss even more bewildering than his actions. Tentative, yet possessive. Needy, yet reserved. What was going through his mind?

When their lips parted, he said softly, "Good night, Faith."

"Good night, Nicholas."

The rooster crowed the beginning of a new day as she let herself in the back door, still wondering what he'd wanted.

The sun was coming up as Nicholas closed the door to his bedroom. Sitting on the edge of the bed, he thought about the past few hours and realized that Faith must think him loco. No matter how hard he'd tried, words had failed him. How could he tell her what was in his heart? How could he explain blind pride and what it does to a man when he fails to turn it over to God? What kind of man takes a woman on a long ride in the middle of the night and doesn't say a word? Papa would have carried on a conversation, wooed the woman he loved . . . but he wasn't Papa. Had he caught the same strange affliction that plagued Liza? He wasn't good at expressing himself—with Faith, he was completely inadequate.

He sat staring at the floor. He hadn't treated Faith respectfully. He had been too proud, too quick to judge. Papa would never have treated Mama like he'd treated Faith. He'd acted like a blind fool, let envy, jealousy, and pride rule him. He should go to her, get down on his knees, and confess his love, and ask her and God to forgive him for the way he'd acted.

His mind churned. Why? Why couldn't he do that? *Please, Father, take away this horrible pride. Don't let me lose Faith.*

He'd fallen in love with Faith. And he prayed to God that she loved him back. That's what he'd wanted to tell her tonight. For the first time in his adult life, he was in love.

Heaving a deep sigh, he ran his hands through his hair and accepted the truth. He was deeply in love with Faith, and he prayed that God would allow him to correct his mistakes, that it wasn't too late to win her love, to give her the honor and respect she so justly deserved.

Springing off the bed, he threw open the door and yelled. "Mama! Get up! I'm going to ask Faith Kallahan to marry me!"

Slamming the door shut, he sat back down on the bed, drawing a shaky breath.

After a while, a smile started at the corners of his mouth and quickly spread to an ear-to-ear grin.

He amended his declaration silently. He was going to *get down on his knees* and ask Faith Kallahan to marry him.

Chapter Fourteen

WHAT had Nicholas tried to tell her? What words did he find so impossible to say?

Faith packed her bags dispiritedly. The Irish linen was the last item folded and tucked away in her satchel. The dress was ruined, and the thought of Aunt Thalia seeing what had happened to the once beautiful garment broke her heart. Tears misted her eyes. She wished she had listened to wise-and-wonderful Aunt Thalia. Perhaps she would have been spared the agony of the past two months.

Faith changed into the green paisley print and laced up the pointy shoes. Studying her image in the mirror, she shook her head. She would help at Dan's one last morning before Jeremiah took her to catch the stage.

But could she face Dan looking this way? Her face was blotched and swollen from crying and lack of sleep. Dipping a washcloth in the basin, she pressed the moist cloth against her eyes. By the time she had hugged all the Finneys and said her long good-bye to Mary Ellen, and Albert had delivered her to Dan's house, the red was almost gone.

Faith sat at Dan's kitchen table, fortifying herself with strong coffee.

One by one the children entered the kitchen. First Adam, who begged her to stay in Deliverance. It was difficult to explain the delicate situation to a boy so young and innocent of the world's heartaches.

Then Sissy climbed onto her lap, eyes filled with tears, and pleaded with her not to go. Faith tried to comfort the children, but it was impossible when her own heart cried out to stay. Lilly made her presence known from her crib. Faith went to get her, sitting back down at the kitchen table to cradle the infant to her breast. She looked at Adam and Sissy. "I'll write often. I promise."

"But I can't read," Adam said, shuffling his feet against the oak floor.

"Me can't wead needer," Sissy sobbed.

"Well, your papa can read." Faith struggled to keep a brave front. "He'll read my letters to you."

"It won't be the same as you being here," Adam said.

"No, not the same, but we can make a game of it. I'll write each letter like a story."

"Don't want no story. Can't play no games with yew. Yew be in Wishigan." Sissy sobbed harder.

Faith gathered the child in her arms. "Sissy, Michigan isn't

so far away, not when you're right here in my heart. Each
of you will always be in my thoughts and in my prayers."

"No, me *won't!*" Sissy wiped her nose on the sleeve of her
gown. "Papa says me can't go out of the yarrd."

Faith laughed. "And you must always listen to your papa,
young lady. He wants to keep you safe."

Adam's lower lip trembled as he fought back tears. "I love
you, Faith."

"Me loves you too!" Sissy cried.

"And I love both of you, so very, very much. More than
you could ever know," Faith whispered. Baby Lilly made
cooing sounds as Faith held the infant close to her heart.

She was going to desperately miss Dan and the children.
She prayed someday, somehow, Adam would have an
opportunity to attend a school for the blind. Adam was
capable of so much. She wished she could have opened the
world to his eyes.

Around noon Jeremiah arrived in a buckboard. Dan and
she agreed there would be no good-byes at the depot. No
sense in making it any harder than it already was. But Dan
seemed at ease about the arrangements.

She sat solemnly next to Jeremiah as he drove the wagon
into town. Faith bit her lower lip, resigned that marriage to
Nicholas Shepherd, and the school for the blind, were not
God's will after all. She'd prayed until her lips were blue,
knelt until her knees felt callused, and the answer was either
no, not now, or wait. She wasn't sure which, but she felt
certain it wasn't the "wait." Once she returned to Michigan, she would never be back to Deliverance.

The vast countryside blurred as tears gathered in her eyes. Everywhere she looked, there was something to remind her of Nicholas. She passed the field where they'd helped the mother cow birth her calf; charred grass, reminders of the fire; Reverend and Mrs. Hicks's house. She thought of the cattle drive; four failed attempts at marriage. She saw the pond embankment behind the church where she'd kissed Nicholas during the Founder's Day celebration. Each cross-roads reminded her of the previous night's strange ride. She wasn't sure which of the many forks they had taken, but she felt certain they'd encountered every last one of them.

The stagecoach was just pulling into town when Jeremiah and Faith arrived. Already there was a good number of people gathered at the station.

Faith still harbored the tiniest shred of hope that Nicholas would be there, like a knight in shining armor, ready to profess his unrequited love at the last possible moment. Her eyes scanned the crowd, and her heart sank when she saw his wasn't among the familiar faces.

"Faith, I wish you would give this more time," Jeremiah said. "Are you sure you won't change your mind?"

"Oh, Jeremiah. We both know there's nothing in Deliverance for me. I've prayed about the situation, and it's clear to me that if Nicholas doesn't want me, I need to go home. Other than Dan and the children, there's no purpose for me here." When Jeremiah opened his mouth to respond, she stopped him with a quiet reminder: "I know Dan would marry me today, but I don't love Dan."

"You didn't love Nicholas, but you came all the way here to marry him," Jeremiah gently rebuked.

"But I love him now," she whispered. "That's the difference." Fresh tears swam to her eyes.

Jeremiah handed her a handkerchief. "Now, now. God has a way of working things out in spite of his children's hindrance."

Faith nodded, wiping her eyes. But she didn't think he was going to work this one out to her satisfaction.

"Are you going to be all right?"

"Yes. Thank you. You've done so much for me. I'm sorry about the school for the blind."

"Well, you tried, child." Jeremiah patted her hand.

Tears rolled in rivulets down her cheeks.

"Good land," he said as he tried to stem the flood with the hanky. "Are we going to have to build an ark? If you love the man that much, why don't you tell him?"

"Why don't you . . ." she hiccuped, "tell Liza you love her?"

Jeremiah paled. "I value my life."

"See." Faith took the handkerchief and cleared her eyes. "I can't tell Nicholas I love him. He has to tell me."

"Is this a new rule I'm not aware of? The man must tell the woman?"

Faith nodded.

"Huh." Jeremiah scratched his head. "I'd like to know who makes these rules."

Jeremiah handed her bag to the stagecoach driver, then came back to the buckboard for Faith.

"Are you sure?" His gentle eyes pleaded for her to stay.

Faith knew he hoped she would have a last-minute change of heart. She wished she could. But if she stayed, knowing the way she felt about Nicholas and the way he didn't feel about her, she would only be hurting herself.

Helping her from the buckboard, Jeremiah walked her to the stage. She smiled at the gathered townsfolk: Vera, Lahoma, Oren Stokes, Molly, Etta, Reverend Hicks, Rollie Zimmer. She frowned. What was Rollie doing here?

Rollie gave her a toothless grin, waving at her.

Faith waved back, then awaited her turn to board as passengers started to descend from the stagecoach.

A heavyset mother rocked the stage as she stepped down with two rowdy children, calling out to her husband. Obediently a tiny, thin man scurried through the crowd to take her bags.

The second traveler to get out was a flamboyant-looking man with shifty dark eyes and a long, black handlebar mustache. For a long time he stood by the stagecoach door, scanning the crowd. He wouldn't be staying in Deliverance long, Faith predicted. Even to her naive eyes, *carpetbagger* was written all over him.

She looked closer when the last passenger departed. A petite young woman stepped gracefully out the door, her tiny foot daintily pausing on the step. Faith contrasted this comely vision with her own unorthodox descent upon Deliverance. She had been hot, disheveled, and riding with Jeremiah on the back of his mule.

The young woman wasn't the least bit in disarray,

although she must have been traveling for days. Her bustled emerald dress made a striking contrast against her long, copper-colored hair and almond-shaped eyes. Jade, Faith noted. Her eyes were the color of jade. The latest Paris hat fashion shaded her delicate complexion from the harsh Texas sun. Even the bonnet feathers were dyed to match her gown, as were her suede shoes, pointed, Faith noticed. She seemed to have no problem walking in them.

The beautiful stranger had "city girl" written all over her. What did she expect to find in Deliverance? Jeremiah helped Faith into the stagecoach and closed the door. "I'm not very good at good-byes," he told her through the open window.

"Neither am I." Faith's eyes welled. "Thank you for everything."

Jeremiah nodded. "You write when you can."

"I promise."

"I need to move the buckboard. There's getting to be a crowd." Jeremiah reached out and lightly brushed a knuckle over her cheek. "Nicholas doesn't know what he's losing." He nodded. "You take care of yourself."

Faith sniffled. "You too."

Jeremiah turned and walked away but not before Faith caught a glimpse of the moisture suddenly misting the old man's eyes.

She waited for the driver to climb aboard his seat. As she waited, she stared out the window. The fashionable young woman was anxiously searching the crowd, apparently looking for someone.

Faith sat up straighter when she heard a ruckus break out in the crowd. Peering to the far left, she saw Dan hurriedly threading his way through the onlookers, his gaze anxiously searching the area. Was he looking for her? They had already said their good-byes. . . .

Dan stepped into the clearing and even from her vantage point, Faith saw his eyes lock on the beauty. The woman broke into a radiant smile, and she ran to meet him.

As the implication of Dan's appearance hit Faith, her hand came to her mouth. Heavenly days! Dan had ordered a mail-order bride!

His inquiries had been so subtle, so minute, that she never once suspected what he'd had in mind. But there was no mistaking the look on the young couple's faces as they met for the first time. In a moment the children were climbing all over the woman. She didn't seem to mind, patiently smiling at them and Dan.

Dan Walters looked like a besotted suitor.

Scooting back in the seat, Faith fumed. *Liza's happy. Nicholas is relieved to see me go. Dan replaced me before I'd even left town.* If she thought her heart was broken before, she felt as if it might explode now.

As the driver and guard climbed atop the stagecoach, Faith blinked back tears.

An old woman entered the coach and took the seat opposite Faith. "There, there, dear. Don't cry," she comforted, bending forward to pat Faith's hand. "Why, you'll be back before you know it!"

Faith burst into tears.

"Oh, gracious me." The white-haired woman looked startled. "I hope I haven't said anything to upset you."

Shaking her head, Faith sobbed uncontrollably. "It's just—that—I'll *never* be coming back."

"Dear child, one mustn't ever say never." She smiled angelically, a sparkle in her warm brown eyes. "We never know what the Lord has in store for us. Why, our next miracle could be waiting just around the bend. Yes, just around the bend."

"The only thing waiting around the bend for me is Michigan," Faith sniffled. "And Edsellllll Martinnnnnnn!" She leaned over, sobbing harder as the stage lurched and wheels started to roll.

Suddenly a buckboard wheeled wildly down the road. A familiar voice shouted, "Stop that stage!" Faith jerked upright in her seat. What was that?

Jeremiah looked up, then whirled and shouted. "Driver! Hold that stage!"

The driver tightened back on the reins, bringing the four-horse team to a halt. "Somebody better have a mighty good reason! We got a schedule to keep!"

Jeremiah grinned, looking in Faith's direction. She could barely hear his words. "Well, thank you, Lord. I was beginning to wonder if you were listening."

Nicholas sprang from the buckboard, followed by Liza. Running toward the stage, his legs covered the ground with long, powerful strides.

The stagecoach jerked forward as the horses threatened to bolt. "Driver, wait!" Nicholas shouted.

"I ain't goin' nowhere. You're spookin' the team!"

Bounding aboard the stage, Nicholas jerked open the door. Faith was face-to-face with him. For a moment nobody spoke.

"Faith, you can't leave."

"Why not?" she sniffled.

"Because . . . I'm in love with you. I . . . I want us to start over."

She opened her mouth to speak, but he laid his hand across her mouth. "I'm a thickheaded, opinionated man. Sometimes I say too much; other times I don't say enough, and rarely do I get out what I actually mean. My pride has cost me something very rare and precious. I surrendered that pride to God this morning, Faith, asking him to free me of that burden. I love you, Faith. I thought I could marry you and Mama would have someone to keep her company, but instead I fell in love with you. I hope—no, I have prayed, all night, that you will someday feel the same about me."

Their eyes met and held for what seemed like an eternity.

"I take heart that you're leaving town," he admitted.

"Pardon me?"

"You're leaving town; that means you really can't be in love with Dan."

"No . . . I don't love Dan," she conceded, glancing at the Walters family happily gathered around the stylish young woman. "I've told you that before, Nicholas. Dan is not the issue."

"Then could you ever love *me?*" Nicholas inquired softly.

Pride, the same that had affected Nicholas, made her want to say no, but her eyes—and her heart—gave her away. Lowering her eyes, she whispered, "Yes, I just don't like you very much sometimes."

Nicholas's features turned as solemn as a hanging judge's. "I can safely promise that I will spend the rest of my life working on that."

The old woman leaned forward and whispered under her breath, "See, dear? Always a miracle waitin' just around the bend."

Faith's eyes steeled as she recalled the torturous weeks Nicholas had put her through. "How do I know you're not doing this out of obligation?" Nicholas was foremost an honorable man.

"You don't. You just have to trust me on this one." He looked so needy, so repentant. How could she do anything but trust him?

"Will you marry me?"

She nodded. "Yes."

"Right now?"

"Now?"

"The sooner the better! I love you! And I've already checked. Reverend Hicks is in town today, and he is standing by for a wedding tomorrow." He threw his head back and laughed. His mood was infectious. Faith found herself laughing with him. In the years to come, she planned to make him laugh more often. A lot more often.

His laughter gradually receded, and he reached for her hand. Love shone brightly in his eyes. "Tomorrow, we will be married, regardless of birthing cows, raging fires, needy mothers, cattle drives—this time in a church ceremony, dressed in our finest, with the whole town looking on."

Faith's eyes glowed with wonder. *Ceremony.* Now that was so much nicer than "recital of vows."

She rested her fingers lightly against his cheek and silently thanked the Lord for this hour. Her faith had seen her through. She had prayed for faith that she and Nicholas would be married, and sure enough, God was listening. It finally made sense now why she'd always felt that God meant her to marry Nicholas. She'd prayed for the faith to believe that, but as circumstances had changed, she'd lost that faith and had begun to believe she had been mistaken all along. But now, at the last hour, God was giving her her heart's desire after all.

"Yes, my darling. . . . Tomorrow I will marry you." It wouldn't be in her finest, and they'd have a lot of inviting to do if the whole town was to be there—but, yes! she most certainly would marry him.

"All in God's plan," the old woman sitting across from her observed.

Faith took a closer look at the old woman. Her silvery white hair framed her angelic face like a halo. Faith remembered passages from the Bible about how the Lord sometimes sends special messengers.

Faith asked softly, "Are you an angel?"

"An angel? Me? Mercy no, child. I sell eggs. I have a chicken ranch just outside San Antonio." She leaned forward, a merry twinkle in her eye. "I'm Bessie Lewis, Carl

Lewis's sister. Been visiting my brother, and we sure have been praying hard for you young people." She winked. "Where one or more are gathered to pray?"

"Oh, thank you—but please, you *can't* leave now."

"She's right. You have a wedding to attend," Nicholas said.

The old woman beamed. "Why, I reckon I can stay around a spell longer. It would do my heart proud to see you young'uns finally tie the knot."

Nicholas helped Bessie out of the coach. Carl Lewis and his wife were there with welcoming smiles. They expressed brief congratulations, then escorted Bessie back to their wagon.

Nicholas gently lifted Faith from the stage, momentarily holding her in midair as he kissed her.

"Why, Mr. Shepherd!" Faith accused breathlessly as their lips parted.

"Nick, to you, Miss Kallahan." He kissed her again.

"Oh, yes—Nick," she murmured against his mouth. "That sounds so much better." Faith's senses were reeling. So this was what love felt like. *Thank you, wonderful, merciful God!*

The roar of applause from the crowd quickly brought her back to earth. Her face flushed bright red. She'd been so in love with Nicholas, so swept away, knowing he loved her right back, that she'd forgotten they were standing in the middle of town. And kissing, of all things.

Nicholas turned to the waiting crowd. "My friends! I'm getting married! And you're all invited!"

"It's about time!" Dan shouted, hand in hand with his mail-order bride.

Dan's pleasant features sobered as he pulled Faith aside. For a long moment he just looked at her. "Nicholas has held your heart from the beginning. I knew that—everyone can see it." His unspoken words were clear to Faith. "I needed to move on, to find a woman I could love—one who could love me back."

Faith smiled. "I understand, Dan. I hope you will be wonderfully happy!" She hugged him tightly. Then she turned back to Nicholas and hooked her arm in his.

Everyone, young and old, shouted in ear-piercing unison, *"It's about time!"*

Faith gazed up at Nicholas. "Did you hear that, Mr. Shepherd?"

"I heard." His eyes openly adored her. "But they're mistaken."

"Mistaken?" She frowned.

"It's *past* time." He kissed her again, long and hard. It really mattered not that she would be married in her second-best dress.

The embrace ended, and Faith slipped her arm through his. She felt as if she were walking on clouds as they strolled to the buckboard. So love must be the secret to walking in pointy shoes, she mused, realizing her feet didn't hurt at all.

Liza sat in the wagon, smiling. As Nicholas helped Faith aboard, Liza quickly scooted to one end of the bench. She had been strangely quiet during all the activity, but Faith realized the sparkle in her eyes looked downright cagey.

Liza patted the bench beside her. "Hello, dear. I believe your place is here, beside Nicholas."

Faith smiled, waiting for the other shoe to drop. "Thank you, Liza."

"No." Liza's features softened. "Thank you, Faith. You've made my son very happy."

Everything was happening so quickly that Faith wasn't sure if she was dreaming. But if by chance she was, she hoped she'd never wake up.

"And, Nicholas, I want to thank you for bringing Faith into the Shepherd family. You've made me very happy. Your father would have been proud of your choice of a bride."

"Thank you, Mama. For the first time in years, I agree with you." Nicholas glanced at Liza, smiling. "And whatever's in that brown bottle you've been sipping out of, I think it's helping." He clicked to the horse, and it trotted off.

Faith gasped. "You knew all along about her drinking?" she tried to whisper to Nicholas.

A hearty laugh from Liza caused another gasp. Was the woman mad?

"Oh, my dear, dear girl. That was medicine in the bottle. Doc told me it would help my . . . my—" she turned bright red, then took a deep breath—"Doc explained that my actions were not only a result of my grief when I became a widow. My age had a lot to do with my emotions. It really is part of God's plan."

"But why did you hide it?"

"That was before I saw Doc. I wasn't taking enough of Pinkham's Tonic to help me . . . and I didn't believe medicine would help. I know now I was foolish. And I caused a great deal of grief by being so bullheaded. The Lord and I have had a good long talk, and I've turned all my hurts, all my sorrows over to him. Should have done that all along."

Faith's arms tightened through Nicholas's as the wagon rolled along. He refused to let her go now that they had found each other.

Liza reached over and patted Faith's hand. "I know I've said it before, but it bears repeating. From the moment you arrived in Deliverance, I have made life difficult for you. I've whined, complained, and been a downright—"

"Mama!" Nicholas cautioned.

"Pain," she finished. "I didn't consciously set out to be so difficult, and I'm not sure I've fully explained why I've acted this way. We'll save that for tea and cookies. I only know I'm sorry for all I've put you through. I pray you can find it in your heart to forgive me."

Liza's words touched Faith's heart even more deeply than those spoken in confidence at the Founder's Day picnic. Her heart swelled with love. She knew that from this day forward they would share a solid relationship, based on respect. After all, they loved the same man.

Who said mother and daughter-in-law couldn't be friends?

"Mother Shepherd, you are forgiven, and all is forgotten." Faith gently squeezed Liza's hand. "As long as you remember your place." She flashed an impish grin. "And that's right here, beside Nicholas and me."

Liza shook her head with wonderment. "Thank you, Faith. I'll try to be a good mother-in-law. When my grandbabies come along—"

Nicholas glanced over. "Whoa! Is there a conspiracy going on I should know about? Did you say grandbabies?"

Liza's eyes lit up. Faith could see that Mother Shepherd liked the thought of grandchildren as opposed to grand-child. "Yes. Grandchildren!"

Faith chimed in. "At least one boy and one girl. Or maybe two of each. And kittens, lots and lots of kittens!"

They all laughed. This time as Faith rattled on about cats and babies she could tell the Shepherds loved the sound of the warmth and laughter. Faith's eyes fell on a familiar wagon ahead.

Jeremiah, who was watching from his buckboard, waved as the Shepherds' wagon approached. His gaze focused on Liza, and Faith could have sworn she saw Mother Shepherd blush.

Liza quickly averted her head and pinched both of her cheeks, hard. "Ouch." She muttered under her breath, "Now I remember why I stopped doing that."

Faith grinned. "Mother Shepherd!"

Liza winked. "At my age, a woman needs all the help she can get."

Faith noticed that the usually taut braids strapped tightly across Liza's head were now styled into a loose French braid. A few wisps of hair softly framed her face.

"Mother Shepherd, you look absolutely—stunning!"

A natural blush colored Liza's face. "Thank you, dear. A certain wise young woman once told me, 'You're only as old as you feel!'" Liza grinned. "And right now, I feel about as young as a body can—for my age."

She turned and waved at Jeremiah as the wagon flew past. His hand shot up, returning the greeting.

Faith suddenly stood up in the wagon floor, shouting over her shoulder. "Hey, Jeremiah! I'm not leaving after all! Sorry to have troubled you! *I'm getting married!*" She made pointy jabs with the tip of her finger at Nicholas. "To Mr. Shepherd!" she silently mouthed, almost losing her footing as the buckboard whipped around a sharp bend in the road.

Chapter Fifteen

A SPLENDID sunrise ushered in Faith Kallahan's wedding day. The air smelled sweetly fragrant from rain that had fallen intermittently during the night.

Early morning sunlight filtered through the open window, spreading rays of warmth across the quilt Faith snuggled beneath. She lazily stirred, thinking how symbolic the rising sun was to her heart. Warm and wonderful. Not a single doubt to be found. She had never thought Nicholas Shepherd could produce such a fuzzy feeling inside her, but he did—oh, how he did! Smiling, she stretched, wiggling her toes. *Father, your goodness takes my breath away!*

To know Nicholas loved her in return made her heady with delight. Liza, willing and eager to accept her as her daughter—it was more happiness than one woman could expect in a lifetime.

Faith took ample time to count her blessings and the way God had intervened at the last possible moment. She was reminded that often that was his way. She smiled, knowing his way was divine and perfect. "Just around the bend," Bessie Lewis had predicted.

A gentle knock at the door broke into her musings.

"Faith?"

Nicholas. She'd warned him the night before that the groom was not to see the bride on their wedding day until she walked down the aisle. That tradition was strictly adhered to on Papa's Irish side of the family. As for her French heritage, those customs had never been explained to her.

"Are you awake?" Nicholas called.

Clutching the quilt to her neck she called back, "Yes, Nicholas. I'm awake. Is something wrong?" She would *not* permit anything to interfere with the day's festivities, no matter how dour. By nightfall she was going to be Mrs. Nicholas Shepherd.

"No, I just wanted you to know I'm leaving now."

Faith bolted upright in bed. "Leaving?"

"I'm going to the church."

She glanced at the sunrise. It couldn't be much past six. "Isn't it a little early? The wedding isn't until two o'clock."

"Are you getting cold feet?"

Tension drained, and she grinned sheepishly. "No, Mr. Shepherd, *I* don't have cold feet."

"Neither do I." His voice dropped to a low timbre.

"Make sure you're there on time. I'd hate to put on my Sunday best to be jilted at the altar," he teased.

Her breath caught and shivers raced down her arms. "I promise you won't be jilted. Why are you leaving so early?"

"There are a few things that need my attention. And you're the one who insisted I am forbidden to lay eyes on you until the ceremony."

"You can't." She grinned. "And don't you be forgetting it."

His tone sobered. "I love you—be at the church on time."

"I love you, too." Faith toyed with a strand of her long dark hair. "But it's going to cost you."

"Cost me? I've already spent a fortune on this wedding!"

Faith playfully tossed a pointy shoe at the door, hitting the target with a dull thud. "That was merely a down payment."

"Name your price, darling." His voice was soft and sincere. "Whatever the price, I'll pay."

"The rest of your life," she murmured. "For richer, for poorer. In sickness, in health. Until—"

"Death do us part."

"That long and more," she returned softly. "I'll meet you at the church, Nick." Her eyes welled as she slid back on the pillow, listening to the sounds of his footsteps receding down the hallway.

Throwing the covers back, she jumped out of bed, eager for the day to begin. No more talk of recitals of vows and parlor weddings. On this very day, Nicholas Shepherd and Faith Kallahan would be joined together in the sight of

God. As she pulled her bag from beneath the bed, she heard the sound of Nicholas's horse leave the yard. For a fleeting moment she was tempted to rush to the window to sneak a last peek at this wonderful, handsome man who would soon be her husband. How she wished Hope and June and Aunt Thalia could be here to share her happiness, to meet Nicholas and Liza.

Faith hefted the satchel onto the bed and opened it. Reality hit hard when she unwrapped the soiled Irish linen.

She forced a smile. As painful as the loss of that gown was, she wasn't about to let anything spoil the joy of this blessed day. Besides, it wasn't the dress that formed a happy union. God bound the soul.

Sorting through her limited wardrobe, she selected the blue-and-white gingham. She'd worn it the day she'd kissed Nicholas at the pond. Spreading the dress on the bed, she smiled, thinking, "married in blue you'll always be true." And that's exactly how she felt. She would always be true to Nicholas, in every way.

A second knock sounded at the door. "Faith, may I come in?"

"Of course, Mother Shepherd."

Liza entered the room and joined Faith at the bedside. "I always thought you looked so pretty in that dress, dear."

Faith was surprised by her candor. Liza'd never commented on Faith's appearance other than to scowl when she wore overalls.

"I should have told you before." Liza lightly traced a hand over the pretty material. "But as nice as you look in this one, you were stunning in the white linen. Did your aunt make it for you?"

"No, she had it specially made by a seamstress in Cold Water, Rose Nelson."

"Such a waste. . . . I wish there were some way of repairing the damage, but I'm afraid it's impossible." Liza picked up the dress, studying it. "I imagine you had your heart set on wearing it on your wedding day."

Faith sighed. "Rose worked very hard to finish it before I left."

"I can see she did. Rose is an excellent seamstress."

A companionable silence filled the room.

Finally Liza spoke. "Faith, my dear. You will be a most beautiful bride no matter what you wear."

Faith smiled. "Thank you, Mother Shepherd."

"Even should you decide to wear those disgraceful overalls!" Liza's eyes twinkled playfully.

Faith joined in the good-natured teasing. "I don't think Nicholas would be too happy about me showing up at the church wearing overalls."

"Nicholas would be proud to marry you, regardless."

"Well, I'll play it safe and go with the gingham," Faith promised. "I'd hate to be left standing at the altar!"

As their merriment faded, Faith looked at Liza. She hated to ask, but she had to know. "Mother Shepherd, do you think Rachel will be there?"

Liza looked puzzled. "At your wedding?"

Faith nodded, her face flaming.

"Oh, no dear." Liza took Faith's hand. "Haven't you heard?"

She shook her head. "Heard what?"

"Yesterday, after we left, Rachel boarded the stage."

"Why?" Faith was confused. "Has she gone to visit kin?"

"Oh, Faith. There's no easy way to say this. Rachel's husband was killed in a bar fight in San Antonio. Rachel has gone to bury Joe. Afterward she plans to return to the East to live with friends."

"I'm sorry . . . I didn't know." Faith felt very sad for Rachel. How tragic her marriage had been.

"I'm sorry no one told you. In all the confusion . . ."

Faith suddenly felt sick to her stomach. "What about Nicholas?"

Liza busied herself straightening the bed. "What about Nicholas?"

"Well, Joe being dead does change things."

Frowning, Liza plumped a pillow. "I can't see how."

"Joe is dead. Rachel is no longer married."

Faith waited for Liza to make the connection.

"Oh . . . oh, my goodness, Faith. Nicholas was over Rachel years ago." Liza took her by the shoulders and gently shook her. "Look at the poor man; he's a besotted fool! I heard him singing this morning as he shaved. *Singing,* Faith. He hasn't sung since Abe died. He's in love with you, darling. He doesn't know other women exist."

Faith hugged her. "Thank you."

Liza's features sobered. "Faith, I came to see you for a

reason. I'm not sure how to approach the subject, but I know I've beaten around the bush long enough."

Faith studied her, but there wasn't a clue in the woman's eyes as to what she was thinking. "Have I done something—"

"Heavens, no!" Liza patted her hand. "It's just that I . . . Well, I can show you much better than I can tell you. If you will come with me?"

"Of course. Just give me a minute to change."

"Oh, you needn't bother. We'll only be a minute."

"But, I'm still in my nightclothes, and someone—"

Liza smiled. "It's just us girls. And besides, you might want to change again." Taking Faith's hand, she pulled her toward the door.

"Shouldn't I at least put on shoes?"

"I don't think so, dear. You might be wanting—oh, never mind. You'll see. Besides, you look like a child on Christmas morning in your nightgown, barefoot and sleepy eyed." Her eyes softened. "Just like the daughter I always longed for."

Faith trailed Liza as she led her to the end of the hallway. Removing a brass key from her apron, she slipped it into the lock and jiggled the door open. Streaks of sunlight lit the narrow staircase.

"Don't fall," Liza cautioned as they climbed the creaking steps to the attic.

Ornate sunburst windows were cut into each gabled end of the house, bathing the rustic room with more light than Faith had ever seen in the Shepherd house. She thought it odd that such beauty was hidden away in a dusty attic. It was even stranger that she'd never noticed the lovely windows from outside.

Faith's eyes roved the huge attic. She glimpsed their reflections in an intricately carved cheval mirror abandoned in an alcove. The room was filled with crates, portraits, and discarded-but-beautiful pieces of furniture. Treasures tucked away for no telling how long.

Liza located a large steamer trunk and turned, motioning for Faith to join her.

"Now, before you say yes or no, just let me say, the choice is entirely yours. But, my dear, you would honor me greatly if you would accept my gift."

Liza opened the trunk, removing an exquisite ivory satin wedding gown, lavishly trimmed in the finest Belgian lace. As she held the dress for Faith to see, her eyes grew misted, and her voice fell to a whisper. "This is the gown I married Abe in."

"Oh, Mother Shepherd!" Faith cried, "I've never seen anything so beautiful!"

"Yes, it's quite lovely." Liza sighed, a faraway look in her eyes. Faith sensed Liza's thoughts were drifting back to her own wedding day.

"This is the gift?"

Liza nodded, handing the gown to Faith.

"May I wear it today?" Faith couldn't contain the excitement in her voice.

Liza's eyes lit with expectation. "You would do this?"

"Oh, it would be my honor!"

"Wonderful!" Liza clasped her hands together, then she reached back into the trunk.

Faith held the gown up to her and looked in the mirror. It was breathtaking.

"Faith," Liza called, carefully removing items and setting them aside. "Come see if you like this."

Faith hurried to see what other treasures Liza had pulled from the steamer trunk. Gently placing the gown on a rocking chair, she knelt beside Mother Shepherd.

"This is my veil," Liza said, unfolding the many yards of lacy material. "It's made from the same Belgian lace as the gown."

"Oh my!" Faith sighed.

"Let's see how it looks." Liza secured the lacy veil on Faith's head with two combs decorated by tiny gold leaves and pearls.

"My goodness!" Faith smiled beneath the floor-length veil. "I feel like a princess!"

"And you're every bit as beautiful as one," Liza said.

Faith gathered the folds of her nightgown and waltzed before the mirror. The sight of the bride-to-be, dancing barefoot in a dusty attic, hours away from her wedding, stirred laughter from both women.

"Do you like these?" Liza asked, holding up ivory-colored pointy shoes that laced up the side, with mother-of-pearl buttons on the front.

"Do I like them!" Faith exclaimed. "Those have got to be the most beautiful pointy shoes I've seen in my life! And you know how I feel about pointy shoes."

Liza laughed. "Yes, I've noticed! But they don't hurt half as much—"

"When you're in love!" Faith smiled.

"I remember well." Liza agreed. "There's also a pair of white silk stockings in here somewhere. Do you see them, dear? I wrapped them in paper. I know they're here. . . . Ah, here they are."

Faith hugged Liza close. "Liza, I don't know how to thank you for everything you've—"

"Child, you are marrying my son." Liza dabbed at Faith's tears. "And you are soon to be my daughter. I'm the thankful one. I only want to see Nicholas happy. Now, we best get busy!" Liza smiled. "We don't want to be late for the church!"

Faith, bathed and dressed in her new wedding attire, stood in her bedroom before the mirror, unable to believe the radiant image reflected back at her. Liza's gown was truly the most beautiful creation she'd ever seen.

"May I come in?" Liza asked, tapping at the door.

"Yes."

"Oh, my dear!" Liza said breathlessly. "You're every bit as beautiful as I knew you would be!"

"Thank you, Mother Shepherd!" Faith whirled. "And thank you, again, for the wedding dress. I can't believe I'm wearing something so elegant."

"It fits as if it were made for you!" Liza's eyes glowed with excitement. "Now, let me help you with the veil."

"Oh, I almost forgot!"

"It's those wedding-day jitters! They'll sneak up on you

every time." Liza laughed, slipping the combs into Faith's long, dark hair. "There. What do you think?"

Faith looked in the mirror, tracing a nervous hand down the length of the lace sleeve, scalloped at the wrist. Suddenly she turned to Liza. "I think you look beautiful, Mother Shepherd."

And she did, dressed in a fashionable powder blue dress, accentuated with a blue-and-white cameo pin. Her hair was loosely secured with matching combs.

Liza blushed. "Oh, as good as an old woman can look."

"Liza, have you been pinching your cheeks?" Faith teased.

"No, but I suppose we should."

Liza and Faith turned to face the mirror in unison and gave themselves a quick pinch.

"Ouch!" They laughed simultaneously.

The sound of a wagon pulling to a stop outside Faith's window broke the moment.

"There's yet another surprise awaiting you!" Liza took Faith by the hand.

Faith followed Mother Shepherd to the front porch. The driver stepped down from the buggy, tipping his Stetson at the ladies.

"Oh, my goodness!" Faith cried.

"Do you like it?"

"Like it?" She stammered like a schoolgirl, looking at the elegant buggy with its fixed roof and curtains. "I love it!"

"I thought you might, so I had Nicholas send for Rusty to fetch it from the barn. It's been stored there since Abe—"

"Liza, it's lovely. But are you sure? We could always take the buckboard."

"No buckboard for my daughter-in-law!" Liza's eyes glowed. "It's too special a day not to bring out the Jenny Lind. Abe wouldn't have it any other way. And neither would I."

Hand in hand the women walked to their waiting buggy. Rusty opened the door. Liza introduced Faith to Rusty as he helped them onto the fine leather-upholstered seats.

Drawing back the curtains, Liza leaned her head out the window. "Thank you, Rusty."

"My pleasure, ma'am."

"Are the rest of the boys coming?"

"Wouldn't miss it for the world!"

As the buggy pulled up in front of the church, Liza reached for Faith's hand and held it tightly. "I know how fond you are of Jeremiah. I've taken the liberty of asking him to walk you down the aisle today."

Faith had been silently wishing her father were here to give her away. Mother Shepherd's last gift was truly the nicest of all.

Tears glistened as she tried to speak.

Liza nodded knowingly. "The next time we meet, we will officially be family. But in my heart, we already are."

Moments later Jeremiah came for Faith. His kindly face glowed with pride. "Hello, my dearest. Are you ready?"

"Oh yes, Jeremiah."

Jeremiah helped Faith from the buggy. Sissy was standing beside him with a basketful of yellow rose petals.

"Hi, Faith! Were gettin' marrwid!"

"Yeah," Adam said. "And I get to *see* you get married!"

Faith hugged the two children. She looked over to see Dan and his mail-order bride smiling. Forming an *O* with thumb and forefinger, Dan winked.

Vera, Molly, and Etta were waiting for Faith on the church steps.

"You look beautiful, dear." Vera beamed.

"Yes, you do," Etta added, handing Faith a flowing bouquet of yellow roses and ivy. "These are from my garden, for you."

Faith was speechless at the generosity.

"Thank you," she murmured, overcome with emotion. God had truly given her a new home.

The church doors swung open, and heavenly music poured from the foyer. Sissy walked ahead of Faith, sprinkling rose petals. Jeremiah placed Faith's arm through his, and they started down the aisle. The church was packed. Some folks had to stand. But the only thing Faith saw was her handsome groom, waiting for her at the altar.

Twenty minutes later Mr. and Mrs. Nicholas Shepherd sealed their union with a kiss, lingering perhaps just a little too long as guests began to giggle. The next thing Faith knew, they were headed out the door, rice being thrown from every direction.

Rusty had the Jenny Lind waiting. The bride and groom

were escorted to their reception in grand style as children ran alongside the buggy.

Nicholas had made the arrangements for their reception to be held on the church grounds. The brush arbor was elegantly decorated; every kind of food imaginable filled the long tables, in addition to a four-tiered wedding cake and bowls of bright red sparkling punch.

"How did you do all this so quickly?" Faith exclaimed.

Nicholas winked. "You'd be surprised what money can buy."

As the townsfolk and Shepherd hired hands gathered around the reception table, Nicholas turned to thank them for coming.

When the crowd quieted, he spoke. "I want to thank each of you for coming to help me share the happiest day of my life." He gazed at Faith, and she blushed.

The guests applauded the newlyweds.

"Faith and I thank God for his presence in our lives and for the miracle of bringing us together." Grinning, he handed Faith a gaily wrapped box.

"For me?" she asked.

"For you. Open it."

Faith glowed as she slipped the ribbon off the package and opened the deep blue velvet box to find a key.

"Oh, by the way," Nicholas handed her an important-looking piece of paper. "This goes with it."

She looked up. "I don't understand. . . ."

"Read the piece of paper; it will explain."

Faith unfolded the document. It was a deed, and as she quickly scanned the legal writings, she realized it was to the

Smith place. She squealed with joy, hugging her husband around the neck. "Does this mean what I think it means?"

Nicholas held her tightly. "If you're talking about a school for the blind, it does."

Faith was speechless for a moment. "Oh, Nick."

"But," Jeremiah stepped forward. "What good is a blind school without Braille slates?"

"Oh, yes." Faith's face fell.

"But then, I just happen to have a few crates on hand."

"Jeremiah! However on earth did you get Braille slates?"

"Young lady, I used to be a schoolteacher at an exclusive boarding school for boys. But I got real tired of seeing parents dump their kids off and go on to pursue their own pleasures. It hurt to see bright young boys neglected while their parents stockpiled earthly treasures and neglected their most important treasure—their children. I tried to make a difference, but nothing I did seemed to do any good. So I came here, asking for nothing more than to be left alone.

"You, however, have helped restore my faith in humanity. I think you'll do real well with Adam Walters, and with others God will bring your way.

"Now, about those Braille slates. . . . I suppose I could donate them if a certain woman in the crowd would agree to let me court her."

Liza's head shot up.

Jeremiah grinned, stepping over to take Liza's hand. "How about it, young lady? Want to squire around with me?"

A smile spread over Nicholas's face. "Professor Montgomery is a good catch, Mother. The two of you could spend the rest of your lives helping Faith teach the blind to read at the Faith Shepherd School for the Blind."

"Oh, Jeremiah." Liza blushed, squeezing his hand. "You old . . . sweet-talker, you."

Nicholas leaned over and stole another kiss from Faith.

Jeremiah frowned at Liza. "I take that as a yes?"

"It's an 'I'll give it some thought.'"

"Well, don't hem and haw too long. At our age—"

"At our age, Jeremiah, you're only as old as you feel!" Liza winked at her new daughter-in-law.

"I think 'The Liza Shepherd School for the Blind' sounds better." Faith smiled at Nicholas.

"No, Faith." Liza said. "The school should bear your name. After all, you are the one who envisioned it—"

"I insist, Mother Shepherd. It's my gift to you."

"I don't know what to say."

"That's a first." Jeremiah playfully yanked a lock of her hair.

"Say yes!" Little Adam shouted from the crowd.

Liza turned to look at the precocious boy. "Yes!"

"Does that go for my proposal, too?" Jeremiah teased.

"I'd be right proud to 'squire around' with you, Jeremiah Montgomery," Liza said.

Nicholas cleared his throat. "I think Mother has some-thing she wants to say."

"Oh, yes. I almost forgot." Liza faced the guests. "With this day being such a joyous occasion, and one with many gifts, I feel the Lord should share in our offerings. I would like to announce that the Shepherds will pay the full amount to have a new steeple erected."

For a moment, a stunned hush fell over the crowd.

"Faith and Dan repaired the steeple," someone in the crowd reminded.

"Repaired, yes, but the steeple's not good enough for Deliverance." She looked at Reverend Hicks. "It's going to fall on somebody's head one of these days. A new steeple, the finest money can buy, will be in place for Thanksgiving services." Liza glanced at Faith. "If there's one thing I've learned, money can't buy happiness."

Suddenly everyone was cheering and applauding.

Cake was cut and punch served. Children played on the church grounds, and laughter filled the air.

It was late afternoon when the guests began departing. Night would be upon them soon. It was a long drive home for most, and many of the guests still had chores to do.

Best wishes and hugs were exchanged. Faith and Nicholas met Dan's mail-order bride. Her name was Ruth. Faith decided they were meant for each other. When she saw the way Dan looked at Ruth, she was reminded of one of Papa's favorite sayings: "If you want to make God laugh, tell him *your* plans."

Most important, Dan's children adored Ruth as much as she did them. Faith had a very good feeling about Dan and Ruth. And Liza and Jeremiah as well.

But most especially about Nicholas and Faith.

The moon was rising as the newlyweds were driven home. Soon a full "Shepherd's Moon" hung suspended in the sky. Faith glanced out the carriage window.

"Look at that moon. It has to be the brightest moon I've ever seen."

Nicholas's head touched hers as he bent to look out. "It's a beauty."

"Yes, tonight it seems extra special. The way it lights up the road reminds me of the light that the school for the blind will bring to so many children."

Drawing her back in his arms, Nicholas said softly, "God has brought us together to be more than just man and wife. This light you talk about, it's as though God has turned a light on in all of us, especially me. I thought I was walking close with the Lord, but I realize now that my light was dim until you came along." Nicholas gently kissed her.

Snuggling closer, she sighed. "Do they really call it Shepherd's Moon?"

"Most do," Nicholas said. "But I plan to change that."

"Why is that?"

"Well, before, I guess I never quite understood the full meaning behind it."

"You mean being known as the richest man around?"

"Exactly."

Faith remained silent.

"I think I would like to be known for something more important than money."

Faith grinned, wiggling closer to her husband. "And how would you most like to be remembered, my darling?"

Nicholas answered softly and without a moment's hesitation. "For a Shepherd's faith."

About the Author

Lori Copeland, Christian novelist, lives in the beautiful Ozarks with her husband and family. After writing in the secular romance market for fifteen years, Lori now spends her time penning books that edify readers and glorify God. She publishes titles with Tyndale House, WestBow, and Steeple Hill. In 2000, Lori was inducted into the Springfield, Missouri, Writers Hall of Fame.

Lori's readers know her for Lifting Spirits with Laughter! She is the author of the popular, best-selling Brides of the West series, and she coauthored the Heavenly Daze series with Christy Award-winning author Angela Elwell Hunt. *Stranded in Paradise* marked Lori's debut as a Women of Faith author.

Lori welcomes letters written to her in care of Tyndale House Author Relations, 351 Executive Drive, Carol Stream, IL 60188.